The Henchmen's Book Club

Danny King

The Henchmen's Book Club

Copyright © 2020 Danny King

ALL RIGHTS RESERVED

No part of this book may be reproduced in any form, by photocopying or by any electronic or mechanical means, including information storage or retrieval systems, without permission in writing from the copyright owner.

All characters and events in this book are fictitious. Any similarity to real persons, living or dead, is coincidental and not intended by the author.

Cover art by the author.

Sixth edition

First published as an ebook in 2011 by the author.

ISBN: 978-146794479-3

For Katie
Our beautiful daughter
with all of our love X

ACKNOWLEDGEMENTS

My thanks to John Williams, David Matalon, Nate Pedersen, Clive Andrews, Michael King and Andrew Crockett, not to mention, of course, Jeannie, for getting behind this book and giving me the belief to put it out. Lastly, a special mention for my grammar henchmen & women: Jon Evans, Burt Arkin, John Harding, Stephen Blackwell, Julie 'Joo' Stacey, Andy Ford and Dr Tina Ambury – my thanks and humble apologies in equal measure *(updated 29 October 2020)*.

1. TO READ OR DIE

"WELL, I THOUGHT it was bollocks," said Mr Cooper, stunning no one. This was Mr Cooper's assessment of everything: films, music, museums, exhibitions or roller coasters. In fact, if you'd thought of it, spent five years developing it, registered patents to protect it, trademarks and copyrights, then employed a team of highly skilled and dedicated professionals to put it all together, Mr Cooper would take one look at it and dismiss it as bollocks without breaking his train of thought.

In this case, we were talking about a book.

"It didn't make sense. I mean one minute he's walking around being an adult, the next he's a kid again. I didn't know what was going on. And what was all that stuff with his missus? She was all over the place an' all. One chapter she's a girl, the next she's a woman. And he's married to her? I couldn't follow a bleeding word of it."

"Yeah well, there was something of a clue in the title, Mr Cooper," Mr Chang pointed out.

Mr Cooper looked at the cover of the book and rolled his face.

"*The Time Traveler's Wife*. Bit obvious isn't it?" he reckoned.

There was no reasoning with Mr Cooper when he was in this sort of mood; his mind was made up and there was nothing I, nor anyone else, could do about it. Some people were just like this. Some people felt uncomfortable about leaving themselves open to new experiences so they slammed the door shut at the first sign of the unfamiliar and wedged a chair under the handle in case they inadvertently found themselves liking *Sense and Sensibility* or *Who Framed Roger Rabbit*.

"Well, what about everybody else? Did anyone like it?" I asked the assembled lads.

"Yeah, I liked it a lot," said Mr Smith. "It was a really clever and romantic story. And I liked how it came full circle and how all the strands connected to other strands. I mean, Henry and Clare's story wasn't like a traditional story that unfolded bit by bit, but more a foggy whole that gradually came into sharp focus as the book went on. I thought it was beautiful. Really really lovely."

"Yeah, and I liked the stuff where he was a kid," Mr Chang agreed. "When he goes back in time and shows himself the ropes and tutors himself about his life to come. That was good."

"I thought there could've been more of that stuff, to be honest," Mr Petrov said. "I liked the time travelling chapters the best but they got less and less as the book went on. It became more about his relationship with Clare rather than about him going back in time, which I thought was the most interesting stuff."

"No, his relationship with Clare was the whole story," Mr Chang disagreed. "The time travel aspect merely set what is basically an old fashioned love story against a… a… a… supernatural backdrop."

"Well, I just liked the time travel stuff," Mr Petrov maintained. "I thought there could've been more of it. He talked about other trips he'd been on and said he sometimes went back and forwards fifty years into the past and the future so I would've liked to have seen more of those chapters and less of the ones with him and Clare washing the dishes."

"Man, you've got no soul," Mr Smith told him.

"Hey, I didn't say I didn't like it. I thought it was great, but who watches *Jurassic Park* for the kids?" Mr Petrov said.

"Who doesn't?" Mr Schultz chuckled, rubbing his hands together and beaming broadly to remind me of the company I was keeping.

"Bottom line, it was a page-turner..." Mr Chang started before his beeper interrupted him. "Oh damn, I've got to go," he frowned, looking around for his stuff.

"Okay, well before we all dash off, let's take a vote on it. What marks are we giving it?" I asked.

"Out of five?" Mr Smith asked. "Five," he shrugged.

"What's the highest, five or nothing?" Mr Chang double-checked before committing.

"Five of course. Who's going to base a series of scoring on nothing being the highest?" I pointed out, imagining Mr Chang in Blockbusters with half a dozen 0/5 turkeys under his arm.

"I'll give it four and a half then."

"No halves. They make it harder to tot up the final scores."

"Alright then five."

"Mr Schultz?"

"Four, but mostly for the gay wanking stuff," he winked, making sure we all knew what page his copy would flop open to if dropped.

"Mr Petrov?"

"Four. But it would've got a five if there'd been more about the time travelling, like if he'd gone back to the stone age and had a look around then."

"It wasn't meant to be *Doctor Who*," I reminded him. "Mr Cooper?"

"Nothing. It was bollocks," he grunted.

"Hey you can't give it nothing, that's just stupid," Mr Chang objected.

"I can give it what I want, it's my score, if I wanna give it nothing, I'll give it nothing," Mr Cooper insisted, standing up to meet Mr Chang's challenge.

"But you're going to drag all our scores down with your protest zero," Mr Petrov fumed.

"Then you should've picked a better book, shouldn't you!" Mr Cooper glared, giving us a glimpse into what this was really all about, namely our collective and unanimous veto against his suggestion, *Vinnie: My Life* by Vinnie Jones.

"He is entitled," it pained me to confirm, although I mentally put aside a big fat zero for Mr Cooper's next nomination, even if it was my own autobiography.

The room settled down and all eyes turned to me.

"Five," I shrugged, upping my own score by a point to redress the injustice.

"Oh, you fucker!" Mr Cooper spat.

"Which gives *The Time Traveler's Wife* and a provisional total of… about three-point-eight out of five," I declared doing the maths on a scrap of paper. "Well done Mr Chang, good suggestion."

Mr Chang looked suitably pleased with himself, then slipped his mag belt over his arm and reached for his Beretta Model 12.

All at once, my own beeper burst into song, quickly followed by the beepers of Mr Cooper, Mr Smith, Mr Petrov and Mr Schultz.

"Hang on a minute, what is this?" I baulked, looking around at the equally anxious faces of my fellow readers.

"Let's go!" Mr Cooper said, grabbing his webbing and SPAS 12 as the rest of us tore into our equipment, pulling on our Kevlar and lock & loading our weapons. My own choice of weapon was the Austrian-made AUG 9 Para. It was converted from the Steyr AUG assault rifle, so it's a lot more accurate than most other 9-mm sub-machine guns. And this job had been good because we'd been allowed to pick our own weapons. I hated those jobs where they forced you to carry whatever guns they wanted you to carry just for the aesthetic beauty of seeing fifty blokes all lined up in matching orange boiler suits with crappy M16s.

"Come on!" Mr Chang said, kicking open the door of the Pump House and charging out into the jungle.

"Wait," I shouted after him. "Hold up!"

Me and the others followed hard on Mr Chang's heels, out of our unofficial book club HQ and up the hill towards the main bunker network. As soon as we were outside we heard the explosions: great big booming blasts and accompanying cracks that were coming from the direction of the command structure and Doctor Thalassocrat's Tidal Generator.

Through the blasts, I could also make out the crackle of gunfire and agonised screams, so I tried to reach the Command Centre on my radio, but there was no response.

"What are you doing? Come on!" Mr Cooper barked at me when he saw me slowing up.

"Wait!" I insisted. "We don't even know what we're running into."

"Trouble," growled Mr Schultz, snapping back the shoulder stock on his M203 theatrically, like a big idiot. "And it's going to get its ass kicked."

He, Mr Cooper and Mr Petrov ran on after Mr Chang, leaving me to urge caution to Mr Smith.

"Just be careful mate. If this place has been overrun already then there ain't no point sprinting into a hail of bullets."

"I agree," Mr Smith nodded, "but we'd better make a show of it if we don't want to get chiselled for our dough." And with that Mr Smith ran off up the hill and towards the sounds of disaster.

I made sure my Kevlar was firmly done up before following, reaching the crest of the rise after five minutes of huffing and puffing through the vegetation. There I found Mr Smith, Mr Schultz, Mr Petrov and Mr Cooper, but there was no sign of Mr Chang, though I didn't notice this at first in light of the sight that greeted us. From the crest of the hill we could see the whole of the island and down towards the eastern coastline I spotted the command structure – or at least what was left of it. The shiny steel and glass tower that had previously dominated the tree line was now a twisted smoking heap on the jungle floor. Enormous balls of flames billowed into the air as each of the tower's twenty-two condenser units blasted into the next. And way down on the coastline itself, the once dominating Tidal Generator was completely gone, lost to the deep forever.

"Oh dear," Mr Smith clucked. "Looks like we're out of work again guys."

"But how?" Mr Schultz asked, apoplectic.

The answer jetted over our heads a second later; Jack Tempest, agent XO-11 of the British Secret Service, ripped away in Doctor Thalassocrat's escape rocket with that old bike he'd come ashore with the previous day. To add insult to injury, as he was passing overhead, Tempest clocked us and gave us his best shit-eating salute before disappearing out into the big wide blue of the Pacific Ocean.

"What a twat!" Mr Cooper said, voicing all our thoughts for us.

"Come on, let's at least see if there's anything we can salvage."

Jack Tempest was Britain's most decorated Executive Officer and a right royal pain in the arse to boot. He was forever landing in other people's ointment and ruining everything for everyone. And some of these jobs had taken a lot of time and effort to set up. I'd been on two outings he'd scuppered in the past, though my friend Mr Rodríguez had been on four. Imagine that? Four jobs? I mean it wasn't like we didn't have mortgages to pay but no one worried about that, did they? At least the British government didn't. I'd already borrowed twenty grand off Linda's folks just to stay afloat and I'd promised them I'd be able to pay it back by the end of the year – with interest. Now that had gone for a Burton too.

Fucking XO-11.

I couldn't even understand how it had come to this. We'd had him. We'd had him banged to rights. Mr Chang and I had personally caught him on the Tidal Generator, found the explosives he'd been planting and taken him to see Doctor Thalassocrat.

"Well done men, excellent work," we'd been congratulated at the time. "Sweep the entire island and make sure Tempest didn't have company," which we'd done, finding that little blonde sidekick of his with the tiny arse and distracting cleavage hiding down by the docks. We couldn't have done any more.

By the time we'd gone off duty, Jack Tempest and his squeeze had been sealed inside Thalassocrat's main water pipe, bracing themselves for a quick swim through the turbines, which is what Thalassocrat had been dying to do to someone for ages, the horrible bastard. Yet here we were a few hours later, with our base in bits and our boss nowhere to be seen – just an ominous red cloud of chum floating in the bay five hundred yards away, driving the seagulls potty.

Worse than that we then found Mr Chang. He was lying a hundred yards away from the rocket launch pad with his head torn open and a look of total surprise frozen onto his face. But then what had he expected tearing off like that in the direction of gunfire without a clue as to what he was running into? It was so pointless. Such a waste.

"Are we still counting his score?" Mr Cooper asked.

"Yes, we are, you nasty git."

"Just a thought."

I went through Mr Chang's pockets and found his Agency ID card before cautiously pressing on.

We couldn't get anywhere near the command structure, it was too much of an inferno, so me, Mr Petrov and Mr Smith rounded up what was left of the men while Mr Cooper and Mr Schultz checked out the boats. The first one blew up the moment Mr Cooper started the engine, erasing him and his zero from the face of the Earth, while Mr Schultz was a bit more cautious, locating the pack of C4 connected to the second boat's ignition, only to take out the entire dock when he rested his rifle against the wrong rubber ring.

"Christ almighty!" I cried as the shock wave knocked us onto our faces. Bits of boat and berth rained back down as me and Mr Petrov dived into a nearby cave for cover.

"Tempest has booby-trapped this whole fucking island," Mr Petrov said and this was further confirmed when one of our fellow survivors, Mr Fedorov, picked up a watch he'd spotted in the wash and paid for the lapse dearly. I raced down to the beach when I'd heard his screams and could barely bring myself to look at what I found there.

"Oh God, help!" he was choking as blood poured into the sands from a broken stump that used to be his arm. "Help, please help. Please. I want to go home. I want to go home," he said over and over again in Russian.

I did everything I could to try and stem the

bleeding, tying a tourniquet around his elbow and giving him morphine to ease his pain but Mr Fedorov soon lost consciousness and drifted off into a sleep from which he'd never awake. Poor old Fedorov, I'd really liked that guy. He used to tell brilliant jokes, even in English, though I could never remember them afterwards to tell anyone else. Mr Fedorov stored them up like a computer though and often had the whole mess in stitches. The only joke of his I could remember was this one: What has eight legs, four wings and gives ugly Americans heart attacks? KFC's Bargain Bucket.

I thought about this joke as I tucked Mr Fedorov's ID card into my pocket but now it just made me sad, so I took my jacket off, laid it across Mr Fedorov's face and headed down the southern shoreline where Mr Smith and the others were waiting.

"Did you send the signal?" I asked Captain Campbell, the highest-ranking surviving officer, when I got there.

"Yeah," Captain Campbell confirmed with a glower, and so that was that. The Agency would come and pick us up – hopefully before the UN, or worse still, the US got here – and we'd live to fight another day. We wouldn't get paid because The Agency would keep our entire signing on fees to pay for the service but at least we'd be spared a prolonged vacation water-boarding in Guantanamo Bay, or wherever it was they did that from these days. Not that this brought much comfort to many, not after spending six months in this Godforsaken dot in the ocean, putting up with Mosquitoes, lice, crabs, jellyfish,

Thalassocrat's tantrums and bloody Vinnie Jones's highs and lows courtesy of Mr Cooper. Some things could never compensate a man enough for that.

"Where were you guys?" Captain Campbell asked, almost accusingly.

"Off duty. Where were you?" I asked right back in case he felt like pointing the finger.

"You weren't in the barracks," Captain Campbell worked out for himself, seeing as the barracks were no longer standing. "What were you doing? Drinking or something?"

"No actually, we were reading," Mr Smith answered for me when he saw I was getting ready to stick one on Thalassocrat's chief tea boy.

"Reading? Jesus!" Captain Campbell sneered, pulling a face but saying no more on the subject.

We sat on the sands under the baking hot sun for a few more minutes, checking our weapons and the horizon for the rescue plane before Mr Ali broke the silence just behind me.

"What were you reading?" he asked. "Anything good?"

2. FROM THE PACIFIC
WITH EMPTY POCKETS

THE EXTRACTION TEAM arrived three hours later. A big Beriev Be-200 swooped low over the island dropping dinghies and life jackets into the water and landing a quarter of a mile out to sea. Most of us swam out to the dinghies, but Captain Campbell had to take charge of one of them and go back for the guys who were either too wounded to make it on their own or bleeding too heavily to swim in these infested waters.

Captain Takahashi was at the door to help us onboard, meaning it was station Japan that had been dispatched to pick us up.

"Hey boys, no joy?" he guessed as he helped each of us onboard. "Never mind, we got hot drinks and cold beer for you on the plane. Just make yourselves comfortable and leave everything to my crew."

Captain Takahashi had picked me up before and he remembered me when he ran my Agency ID card through the scanner.

"Ah, I get you before, in Siberia wasn't it?"

"Yes, I remember. Thank you for picking us up Captain," I replied, as it never hurt to kiss the arse of someone who had the power to kick you out over the middle of the Pacific.

"You not having a good run, no?" Captain Takahashi deduced.

"It seems not Captain," I sighed, accepting his hand and climbing aboard.

"Well, we take good care of you today, you hear? Captain Takahashi number one friend to boys in trouble," Captain Takahashi reassured me, handing me back my card and pointing me in the direction of one of his saucy oriental attendants. "You go with her and just take it easy my friend, okay?"

"Okay," I agreed, receiving a little bow from the beautiful porcelain girl in front of me. I made to head back to the seats but the girl stood her ground in front of me.

"Excuse me, but I will take that now please," she said, dropping her eyes to the AUG 9 slung over my back to remind me this job was over.

"Oh yes, sorry," I said, slipping the gun off my shoulder and handing it to her. She removed the clip, ejected the chambered round and stowed the rifle in a locker at the front with the rest of the boys' weapons. I handed over my Glock 21, Taser, Mace, field knife and brass knuckles too before I was passed back to another equally beautiful attendant and shown to my seat.

"We hope you enjoy your flight. If there is anything you require today, please let us know," she said, handing me a complimentary packet of peanuts and a miniature bottle of Japanese whisky, before returning to the front of the aircraft.

Oh yes, Captain Takahashi and his famously sexy flight attendants. He was well known for them the business over, which is probably why he got so many jobs now that I come to think of it. But I wouldn't have dared try it on with any of his girls, not without a parachute. Takahashi's attendants were strictly for show only.

Well, not quite.

You see, not all of the people who'd been employed by Doctor Thalassocrat were on The Agency's books. Some of them came from other outfits, some were long time associates known to Thalassocrat personally, while others worked freelance – like the lab technicians for example.

These were the guys who really came a cropper on this job.

Three lab technicians survived the inferno and swam out to the plane with the rest of us. One of them was stupid enough to try using a dead Agency guy's ID to get onboard the plane and the same pretty girl who'd taken and stored my weapon a moment earlier now drew her own and shot him straight between the eyes without so much as a bow. There was always one, wasn't there? On every pick-up, there was always one.

The attendant slipped her weapon out of sight again and carried on disarming the boys as they came aboard with a smile and a bow as if she'd done no more than have a quiet word with an unruly passenger, but no one was left in any doubt as to the perils of trying it on with Captain Takahashi. The other technicians were wise enough to identify themselves upfront as not being on The Agency's books and had to agree to recompense The Agency for their passage home. They are expensive tickets at two million dollars a seat but preferable to option B.

As for the boys with rival outfits, they were in a slightly more fortunate position in that their bills got sent directly to their own agencies. If their outfits had standing agreements with The Agency, that was. If not, then they too were advised to have a few million air miles going spare or a rubber dinghy and arms like Popeye.

Captain Takahashi's co-pilot popped his head out of the cockpit and barked something at the Captain in Japanese. I couldn't understand the words but body language is the same the world over, particularly the body language of someone who'd just seen the Old Bill closing fast on the radar. Captain Takahashi barked something back at him and the co-pilot disappeared to start the engines as Captain Takahashi finished dragging the rest of the survivors onboard.

Captain Campbell and the worst of the injured men were last to be pulled onboard. One of them, another Russian I just about recognised as Mr Andreev, was in a terrible state. I really couldn't see him lasting the journey, but Captain Takahashi took the time to get him aboard all the same because he held an Agency card. A few of the more unscrupulous blokes I've worked for would've just put two in his head and left him for the sharks, but Captain Takahashi didn't even contemplate it despite his co-pilot's running commentary over the intercom. He eased him through the door, then slammed it shut the moment Mr Andreev's ankles were over the threshold and shouted at his co-pilot to step on it.

Two of Captain Takahashi's girls laid on top of Mr Andreev to stop him from plummeting down the aisles, while the rest of us were slammed back into our seats as the plane accelerated across the water.

Captain Takahashi wasn't the sort of bloke to let a take-off stop him from wandering around his own plane though and he fought his way forward until he was behind his seat and flipping buttons alongside his co-pilot.

The first of these pinged a seatbelt sign on over all of our heads advising us that we were in for a bumpy take-off – as if we didn't know – while rest started deploying flares and smoke from the rear of the plane.

"Looks like it's going to be a close one," Mr Petrov said in the seat alongside of me and a moment later we left the water and banked hard right.

All sorts of alarms started screaming in the cockpit up front and Captain Takahashi responded by pumping chaff and flares out of the back to tell us Mr Petrov was more right than he knew. Above the din of the engines, I heard a whoosh as the first missile ploughed through the chaff and missed our tail by a whisker, and suddenly we were banking hard left. The plane was at a virtual right angle as Captain Takahashi dodged and weaved all over the sky and from the port side window I could suddenly see our pursuers; three warships stretched out across ten miles of open ocean and closing in to mop up Tempest's mess. While we'd been in the water we'd been sheltered by the island, but as soon as we'd taken off we'd announced ourselves to their radar.

Captain Takahashi now dove toward the sea hard and levelled off barely fifty feet from the waves, only to then sweep north. All around me faces and knuckles were almost opaque with fear, all except those of Captain Takahashi's girls, who looked like they were having another mundane day at the office.

A stream of white-hot tracer fire suddenly lit up the skies around us as our pursuers realised they were getting nowhere with their Sea Sparrows but a little more dodging and weaving and we were across the horizon and out of range. More Sparrows were launched after us, but Captain Takahashi's bird was jam-packed with the latest radar deflecting technology and after two more minutes of aerial dodge ball, he flicked off the seat-belt sign and announced that this afternoon's in-flight movie would be *The Time Bandits*.

*

Eighteen of us survived Thalassocrat's job. Nineteen if you want to count the lab technician who'd got himself shot trying to sneak onboard, but only eighteen of us made it onto the plane, lived through the take-off and managed to last an hour of *The Time Bandits* before it was turned off by popular demand. It isn't a bad film, I've seen it before, but no one was in the mood to watch Snow White's mates running around history after we'd lost our wages – particularly the two surviving lab technicians who were near inconsolable at the thought of having to sell their houses, belongings and spare kidneys to pay for their flights home.

But you know what, eighteen wasn't bad.

I've been on jobs where hardly anyone made it through to the other side. That Siberian job that Captain Takahashi had picked me up from being a case in point. Only four of us had survived that one, which was probably why Captain Takahashi remembered me. He came back to my seat during the flight and talked to me some more about that day.

"You worked with that fella with the funny name, didn't you? In Siberia? What was his name again?"

"Polonius Crump."

"Yes, that it, *Polonipus Crumb*," the Captain laughed, shaking his head and urging his girls to laugh along too. Some smiled politely, though the others just regarded me with cautious indifference. "Funny name him. Funny."

And a funny end he met too, old Polonius. He'd had some potty notion about knocking the Earth off its axis by a dozen degrees to melt the polar ice caps and bring the Equator further north to transform the frozen tundras into rich fertile land – while sinking every other square inch of rich fertile land under a few billion gallons of freshly unfrozen seawater, you understand. Of course, he didn't have a clue, he didn't. Even the lads on the job didn't think he could do it, but he was a nice enough bloke and paid well – in Russian gold no less. And if by some miracle he did manage to pull it off… well, I'd rather be sunning myself with old Polonius on the new Arctic Riviera than standing on my roof in Sussex wondering where all this bloody water had come from.

But no, I don't need to tell you that he didn't manage it. Russian agents backed by Spetsnaz commandos brought the whole place crashing down around our ears while we were testing his stupid defridgerator (*patent pending). Polonius himself took a tumble into a temporarily defrosted lake trying to flee on his snowmobile, so that when the ice set again he was frozen inside a big block of it like something out of a *Tom & Jerry* cartoon. Apparently (I didn't see it myself) the Russians cut him out and carted him off as a souvenir.

"Funny," Captain Takahashi smiled again, squeezing my shoulder and heading back to the front check if Mr Andreev wanted *The Time Bandits* back on.

Yeah, hilarious. I'd ended up with moths fluttering out of my pockets on that job too.

A little while later Mr Smith came over and sat with me.

"So Jones, what are you going to do when you get back?" he asked.

I rubbed my face and opened another little bottle of Japanese whisky. "I don't know," I shrugged. I hadn't met Mr Smith before this job but we'd got on well and become firm friends. He was an American while I'm British so it's natural for people who shared a common language to eat their sandwiches on the same table of any international canteen, though it wasn't just a language thing. Mr Chang for example, had been a lovely bloke, as had been Mr Fedorov, while I could've happily watched Mr Cooper getting blown up, and then revived, and blown up again all day long, so it was more than just a language I shared with Mr Smith. We shared a sense of humanity too. And in a profession predominated by killers and psychopaths that was a rare old thing.

"Are you going to re-register with The Agency?" he asked, cracking open a half bottle of Okinawan Merlot.

"I don't know," I said, and I didn't. I didn't want to. Tempest might've had nine lives but I only had the one and I was rather attached to it. But then again what choice did I have? This job was supposed to have paid off my mortgage, settled my debts, gold-plated the farm and left me enough so that I never had to look at another price tag again.

If things had worked out.

Damn Tempest.

Damn Thalassocrat.

"I'm going to," Mr Smith said. "I've got to go and see my kids first, but as soon as I'm done I'm heading over to Cody to put my name on the list again. Even if it's a long-termer, I don't care, I'll do it."

Long term contracts, middle term contracts and short term contracts. These were what we signed up for, with scant few other details available. Due to the generally secretive nature of the work we did, the employers cherry-picked their workforce, not the other way around, which makes sense if you think about it. No point tipping off MI6 or the CIA about what you're up to with a card in the front window advertising for dinner ladies with space station experience. All we got to know was the length of the contracts and how much they paid. Short term contracts were usually anything between a month to a year, middle term contracts between a year to five years, while long term contracts could conceivably last the rest of your life. But then again, so could any of these contracts, so suck the bullets out of that if you please. Personally, I only ever signed up for short to middle term contracts. I had plans, namely finishing off my farmhouse and filling its wardrobes with Italian suits, so I didn't want to see out my days tunnelling towards the Earth's core in a silicone plastic bubble twenty thousand feet beneath the Azores (unless the perks were exceptional).

"You're not serious are you?" I asked. "Long term?"

Mr Smith just shrugged. "Gotta do something, I guess."

"Signing your life away isn't doing something, it's doing nothing for the rest of your life, for no good reason. You can't be that desperate," which he couldn't. Only refugees, unemployed Taliban and condemned men ever signed on for long term contracts. Guys from Philadelphia with nothing in the bank and debtors at the door may have been desperate, but they couldn't have been that desperate surely.

"How we've changed," Mr Smith pondered. "A hundred years ago a job for life was what we all aspired to; safety and security, knowing what we were going to be doing and how we were going to be eating when we were fifty-five. That was all we wanted. Now it's seen as a curse. Interesting don't you think?"

"Yeah, fascinating. Why not get a job at the Post Office then?" I suggested.

"I don't like lines."

"And your kids? What about them?"

Mr Smith didn't answer. He merely contemplated his cup of wine and glossed over that one with a frown. He didn't say more and I didn't press him.

Well, you just don't, do you? The fact that Mr Smith was on The Agency's books at all meant that his past was a no-go area, just as it was with mine and every other Affiliate on this plane. The basic rule was, don't ask and we won't kill you. I knew Mr Smith had kids and returned home to the East Coast after each job because he'd felt comfortable enough to confide this much personal information to me. Just as I'd been comfortable enough to confide in him that I lived in the south of England, had been married once before and hated sweet corn on my pizzas. This was actually quite a lot for Affiliates to tell one another. There were some fellas on this plane, like Mr Petrov for example, who I'd worked with several times before that didn't even know this much about me. And vice versa by the way. Which was why we often looked for other things to talk about. Safe things. Neutral things. Unrevealing things.

As if to demonstrate, Mr Smith stroked his stubble and finally said:

"I'll tell you what, if we end up on the same job again, we should start another book club, you and me. That was good, that was. I enjoyed that."

"Yeah, sure," I agreed, suddenly remembering the late but unlamented Mr Cooper. "And if it turns out to be a long contract, we can even read Vinnie Jones's book if you like."

Mr Smith chuckled. "Man, you really do have me down as desperate, don't you?"

3. TIME ON TIME AGAIN

WE LANDED IN Sendai and spent the next two weeks debriefing to an infinite number of Agency monkeys. Some Affiliates didn't like the whole debriefing palaver, the sheer utter mind-numbing repetitiveness of the process, but it's a necessary evil if The Agency are to continue to offer the service they do and we're all to stay out of prison.

Besides, the accommodation's not bad and there's all the music, movies and exercise equipment you could wish to distract yourself with during your stay. And in return, all you had to do was repeat the same story over and over and over again until you didn't even know what the words meant any more.

And then, just when you'd reached the point at which the words "I see, and what happened then?" caused you actual physical pain, you were asked to repeat it all again some more.

It's boring and it's frustrating, annoying and exhausting, but no worse than visiting your Nan in hospital. And as long as you stuck to the facts and your account tallied with everyone else's, you had nothing to worry about, not even if you'd dropped the clanger that had sunk the whole sorry operation. The Agency was good like that. They understood. I mean everyone makes mistakes, don't they? We're not robots, in spite of what some of our employers like to think, so The Agency didn't get nasty if you'd made a mistake, because what would be the point? It wouldn't bring anyone back or resurrect whatever hare-brained scheme you accidentally thwarted when you left the front gates open and let all them Ninjas in, so they just made a note of what happened, what went wrong and who's fault it was, then dropped you from their books to end your career. But that would be the worst of it. You wouldn't get a bullet in the brain. Not if you'd been honest with them. As long as you'd been honest with them, you'd usually be okay.

If, however, you tried lying or passing the buck that was generally when your head started developing new and unnecessary holes. The Agency has no time for anyone with anything to hide, hence the repetitive debriefing. It's the best way to catch someone out. Deceptions lie flat when a story's told in chronological order, as that's the way a liar learns his lies. But if you were to turn the story around and ask it from a different angle, or from Mr Smith's perspective or from Mr Cooper's, suddenly that's when the lies stand out, like boot polish on a bald spot or reading glasses on a footballer, and the façade begins to slip.

"And so who else was in this reading group of yours?"

"Mr Petrov, Mr Smith, Mr Chang, Mr Cooper, Mr Schultz and Mr Clinton."

"So there were seven of you in the Pump House?"

"No, six of us; Mr Clinton was on duty."

"But you were not?"

"No, we were all off-duty. Me and Mr Chang had just come off, while Mr Smith, Mr Petrov and Mr Cooper were just about to go on."

"And Mr Schultz?"

"It was his free day, so he wasn't due on until the next morning."

"I see. And the book you'd all read was *The Time Machine*?"

"No, *The Time Traveler's Wife*."

"Which scored three-point-six out of five?"

"No, three-point-eight out of five."

"And who gave it the lowest score?"

"Mr Cooper, he gave it a zero."

"Really? I thought it was rather good myself. Better than the film."

"I haven't seen it."

"It had Eric Bana in it as the guy."

"Who's he?"

"He was in the *Hulk*."

"Really? I thought that was Edward Norton."

"No, they did a Hulk film before the Edward Norton one."

"I don't think I saw either of them."

"He was also Henry the Eighth in that Anne Boleyn film with Scarlett Johansson."

"Edward Norton?"

"No, Erica Bana, the guy in *The Time Traveler's Wife*."

"Oh, I think I know who you mean now. Who was Clare?"

"I can't remember."

"I'll have to look out for it."

"I'd probably give it a three and a half."

"The film?"

"No, the book."

"That's a bit harsh."

"You think?"

"Yeah, I thought you said you thought it was rather good?"

"I did, but it wasn't brilliant. It had some good bits in it, but I wouldn't say it was the best book I'd ever read. I was just saying it didn't deserve a zero, that's all."

"Oh."

"So when did you last see Mr Clinton?"

"We don't do halves."

"What?"

"In the book club, we don't do halves. It has to be a whole number."

"But you said *The Time Traveler's Wife* scored three-point-eight out of five."

"It did. But we all gave it a whole number score. It just came out as three-point-eight as a mean average."

"I see."

"So what do you want to do, give it a three or a four?"

The interviewer thought on this for a moment before answering.

"Four," he eventually concluded, another triumph for the gay wanking stuff no doubt.

After twelve days of debriefing, one of The Agency drivers drove me back to Sendai and I caught a commercial flight back to London via Tokyo. I didn't see Mr Smith when I left, but The Agency never releases its men at the same time at the end of a debriefing so I didn't think anything of it, although I did wonder if I'd ever see him again. I hoped so, because we'd got on well and had enjoyed a few nice chats during our time on the island. And in this testosterone-charged business of ours, that's a dividend that's not to be taken for granted.

I arrived back in Britain in the early hours of Sunday morning. I didn't know it was Sunday as I'd lost all track of the days over the last couple of weeks, but I saw that it was when I saw the Sunday papers on a newspaper stand.

I bought a copy of *The Observer* and read it from cover to cover on the train down to Sussex but there was no mention of Thalassocrat, Nanawambai Atoll or Hawaii's recent pickle with the Pacific. But then again I didn't think there would be. Very few of our jobs ever made the headlines, not least of all because very few of them ever came off. But more because few governments felt the need to panic their people into rioting or taking to the hills on a daily basis, so most of these jobs went unreported. After all, if the masses in the major metropolitan centres knew just how many plots, plans and schemes there were to blow them up, sink them, freeze them, bury, blind or bugger them on any given week, property prices would plunge through the mantle. And as most of the world's governments were little more than glorified landlords, this was not a situation that would win anyone a stay in office.

This was also why most of the boys lived in the sticks and all of The Agency's branches were in piss-pot little backwaters like Cody, Lincoln, Furukawa and Limoges instead of New York, London, Tokyo or Paris. Well, what self-respecting megalomaniac would go to the trouble of destroying Limoges when they could be remembered for toppling the Eiffel Tower?

So most of us bought places far enough away from the seas to dodge tsunamis, high enough in the hills to escape floodwaters and remote enough from the neighbours to avoid questions.

My own little bolthole was a nineteenth-century farmhouse just outside of the town of Petworth in West Sussex. It had original oak beams, adjoining stables, two acres of land and a mortgage you wouldn't wish upon your worst enemy.

A cab dropped me off outside my gate just before lunchtime and the driver accepted the fact he wasn't going to get a tip with all the grace of a dog being pushed away from a plate of chips. But my Agency allowance had to see me home, get my phone put back on, fill my larder with rice and tinned soups and get my hair cut, so I was buggered if I was giving him an extra quid just for demonstrating he could do twenty minutes on Tottenham Hotspurs without stopping to breathe. Especially after I'd foregone the luxury of a First Class seat on the way back from Tokyo just to bank a little extra.

I watched the cab vroom off up the winding country lane, checked my mailbox to see if I had any post and headed on through the gate and up my drive.

After six months in the Pacific, almost two thousand hours on patrol, three firefights, a hostile extraction, twelve days of debriefing and twenty-four hours in transit, I was finally home.

4. IN-LAWS AND OUT-LAWS

THE FIRST THING I had to do was see Linda's mum and dad in Arundel. Bill beamed when he opened the door, but his beam dipped a shade when he saw the apologetic look I shone back at him.

"No luck?"

"Not much Bill," I shrugged, gutted to find myself in such an embarrassing position. "Sorry."

Bill frowned, looked at the ground, nodded a couple of times then revived his smile.

"Well, it's good to see you anyway. Glad you're in one piece. Let's go and get a drink."

Bill almost had his stick out of the brolly stand when Marjorie gave up calling from the back room and came to see who'd just knocked on her door for herself.

"Mark!" she cried, wrapping her fingers around my neck and planting a big ruby kiss on my face.

"Hello Marjorie."

"Oh, it's lovely to see you. Did you strike it rich?"

Bill and me exchanged withering looks.

"Not quite, Marjorie, no."

"Well, how much did you get?" she asked, refusing to read between the lines.

"Nothing I'm afraid. We struck out," I shrugged.

"You struck out?" Marjorie glowered, letting go of me and stepping back into the hallway. "What do you mean you struck out? What about our money?"

"Marjorie..." Bill started but Marjorie just cut him short.

"Shut up Bill. Now you listen here Mark, we lent you that money in good faith because you were in a hole, but we have no intention of subsidising you as well as our daughter so we'd like that money back if you don't mind. With interest as promised, if you remember."

"Marjorie…"

"I said shut up Bill, I'm dealing with this."

"Marjorie please, I'm so sorry but I don't have it. Things didn't work out…" I tried to explain but Marjorie wasn't overly interested in what did or didn't work out. All she was interested in was the thirty grand's worth of interest I'd promised her in April in order to convince her to let Bill lend me the money (that's one hundred and fifty per cent in case you're interested).

"You owe us that money!" she demanded. "You owe us that money and you said you'd have it by now."

"I know. And I thought I would but I promise I'll pay you back. Money and interest. Fifty grand, you'll have it all."

Marjorie baulked in shock.

"Fifty grand?"

"Yeah," I confirmed, "Fifty. What?"

"How much did we lend you?" she asked.

I looked to Bill but Marjorie was absolutely adamant I didn't have any "phone a friends" left so I told her the truth. "Twenty grand."

"Twenty!" she croaked, and suddenly she opened up a second front on Bill. "You told me you were only lending him ten. You lied to me."

Me too as it happens, which meant Marjorie had actually been expecting three hundred per cent in interest back. Jesus!

"Marjorie please..." Bill tried once more, but Marjorie wasn't for appeasing. She held twenty grand's worth of IOUs on us and that bought her a lot of airtime.

Where was Takahashi when we really needed him?

*

Bill finally managed to grab his walking stick and we beat a stuttering retreat to his local, determined not to darken his and Marjorie's door again until we were in no fit state to be argued with.

"Women hey?" Bill tried to apologise, but there was no need. I was, or at least had once been, married to his daughter and Linda was nothing if not her mother's child.

"I'll pay you back, Bill, honest I will. Interest and all."

"I know. When you can Mark. When you can," he said, patting me on the back with his free hand.

We found a quiet corner of the pub by the fire and settled down to catch up properly.

"So what was the job?" Bill asked; his eyes not just illuminated by the flicker of wood flames but by the promise of adventures yet to be relayed. Duly, I told him everything that had happened over the last six months; Doctor Thalassocrat, the Tidal Generator, the plans, the payoff and the conditions and Bill listened intently. I'd not seen him since I'd first accepted the contract so this was all new to him – every little detail. He sipped his beer and asked the odd clarifying question here and there, but for the best part of half an hour he just listened.

Bill was a good listener. He didn't hold up the story with a dozen unrelated anecdotes of his own and he didn't feel the need to tell me what he would've done in my shoes, like so many people did. Linda had been terrible for this. I don't think I'd ever been able to finish a story in her company because she liked to take issue with every aspect of my anecdotes. Something like this:

"Red boats? What did they want to use red boats for? I would've used blue boats."

"Yeah, well anyway, that's not important, the point is…"

"No, it is important Mark, because you can see red boats from a long way off, whereas if they'd been blue they would've been invisible against the sea."

"Linda, we weren't trying to be invisible so it really doesn't really matter. What did matter was that the ferry was suddenly…"

"Look, just because they didn't need to be invisible for this particular part of the operation, you should always plan for the unplannable because you never know what's going to happen once an operation starts and if you're suddenly trying to get out of there, you've got a much better chance in a boat that doesn't stand out against the sea than one that's red."

"For fuck's sake."

"Now I remember this girl in the shop who used to use brown lipstick. Brown, can you believe that? Anyway, I said to her…"

That had been Linda. Not that she'd ever been on

an operation in her life or even in a boat as far as I knew, but that wasn't the sort of thing that would stop her from knowing all there was to know about boats, blue or otherwise. No, in fact, Linda had been a hairdresser, which is how she'd known everything there was to know about everything and counted as her specialist chosen subject whatever anyone else cared to talk about. Yep, there'd been nothing my ex-wife hadn't known, except perhaps how to shut the fuck up.

Bill wasn't like that though. Bill was a good listener and brought two things to the conversation that his daughter never did – ears and a brain. More than that though, Bill positively enjoyed hearing about the jobs I'd been on because it took him back to his own operational days when he'd been in the game.

Oh yes, Bill had been an Affiliate too.

Madagascar, Bermuda, the North Sea, Switzerland, South America; he'd worked on jobs that had threatened pretty much every corner of the globe but he'd hung up his guns more than a dozen years ago when an injury had eventually got the better of him and he missed the life greatly. Not so much the death and danger aspects of the job – no one liked these, except perhaps the main players – more the camaraderie and sense of purpose that came with each operation. After all, there were few better feelings in life than being part of something, particularly something monumental, such as taking off across White Sands in a fleet of moon buggies to steal the Space Shuttle. What overgrown schoolboy didn't dream of such adventures? Only Bill didn't have to, because he'd been there, done that and lived to tell the tale, which was no mean feat considering the number of jobs he'd been on. There weren't many old-timers on The Agency's books. Not too many veterans. But Bill had always been a cautious old stick and with each job came experience. "Just use your common sense. It'll save you nine out of ten times better than any bullet-proof vest," he would always say, so I respected and valued his opinion. And because I generally took his advice, he respected and valued mine. It was a nice relationship. In fact, if we'd been able to keep his daughter out of it, it might have been even better.

"Tempest again?" Bill frowned. "That little sod's got more jam than Robertsons."

"Didn't you run across him back in the eighties?"

"Yeah, eighty-nine it was. Up in Canada. He was only a whipper-snapper back then of course, but he beat the crap out of me and killed my mucker."

"How did he get the better of you?" I asked.

"Oh, it was stupid really. He had something hidden in his tie-pin which he dropped on the floor. I bent over to pick it up and it blew up in my face, choking me."

"Tear gas?"

"Yeah, bloody stuff. Anyway, I couldn't see a thing and got a smack over the head in the fight. When I woke up Tempest was gone and poor old Jack Cotton was dead, strangled with these fairy lights Tempest grabbed off our Christmas tree," he lamented.

"Christmas tree?"

"It was the boss's idea, meant to brighten up the

base would you believe. I think he was trying to be ironic."

"Oh, one of them," I understood.

"Yeah." Bill looks at me with hate in his eyes. "Anyway, get this, when I came round, guess what that arsehole had done."

"Who?"

"Tempest."

"What?"

"He'd only gone and put a Santa hat on old Jack's head, the evil bastard."

"What, after he was dead?" I recoiled.

"Yeah, like he was having some sort of joke or something," Bill fumed, bile clawing at his throat.

"That's just sick," I agreed.

"Yeah, too right it is. You don't do that to someone, no matter what. That was a man's life that was."

I could see Bill was genuinely upset about this. Even more than twenty years on it still gnawed at him. Losing a friend was bad enough, but having his memory so dishonoured to boot was an unforgivable act of desecration. How did he live with himself after doing something like that?

"You should've just shot him as soon as you found him, shot him in the head and taken no chances," Bill told me.

"I would've if it had been up to me, but Thalassocrat had ordered us to bring him any prisoners," I explained, which was an understatement to say the least. Thalassocrat had been most insistent on this point. He'd bullshitted us that he wanted to interrogate any and all prisoners personally but we all knew he really just wanted to feed them through the turbines, the big sadist.

"Couldn't you have shot him anyway, you know, sneaky like? Sorry about that boss, it was an accident," Bill suggested.

"You know what these maniacs like Thalassocrat are like. If I'd tried that, I might as well have taken my shoes and socks off and climbed in the turbines myself," which was always a danger whenever you worked for a megalomaniac with disappointment issues.

"So how did Tempest get away?"

"I don't know," I said. "But we all missed out on a big payday because of him."

"You reckon Thalassocrat let him out?"

"He's bound to have. I mean, there was no other way out of that pipe, short of swimming in a screw-like fashion at a hundred-and-eighty knots," I asserted. No, it was obvious, Tempest had probably teased Thalassocrat about Operation *Blowfish*'s chances of success or his own lack of physical prowess and Thalassocrat had fallen for it, pulled him out of the pipe to go *mano-a-mano* and blown it for everyone else whose Christmas bonuses depended upon wiping Midway off the *Pacific A-Z*.

"Someone should put a contract on him and be done with it," I suggested.

"It's been done before, in my time. You ever hear of Carlton Franks, XO-13?" Bill said. I hadn't. "He was around in the sixties and seventies. Spoiled a lot of jobs. Killed a lot of nice blokes. In the end, a contract was taken out on him before a particularly big job and he was shot in Monaco on his way home from the shops. Broad daylight. Dozens of witnesses. No attempt at subtlety or subterfuge, just bang bang bang right through the eggs and goodnight Vienna."

Bill took a sip of his pint as he recalled the reaction.

"Didn't make any difference though," he shrugged. "French Secret Service just followed the assassination squad's trail right back to the guy who'd hired them and sent him to the bottom of the Aegean with a pair of handcuffs and an anchor. The irony was that no one would've probably even heard of this guy or what he was up to if he hadn't bumped off Franks, so it just goes to show that you can never pre-empt these things. Just worry about yourself and keep your eyes on the prize."

He was right of course. Besides MI6 and the CIA, there were a whole alphabet of intelligence organisations out there; French, Russian, Hutu and Basque, practically every nation and every creed on Earth had their own secret service. Only the Maoris didn't bother any more, but that was only because their agents stood out in casinos no matter what colour hats they wore.

"I try, but what's the point when nobody else can?" I said bitterly.

"Mark…"

"Bill seriously, it's getting me down. I do everything right. I do everything you showed me and thanks largely to you I'm still here, alive and healthy and in one piece, but I'm skint."

"Not every operation goes wrong," Bill said.

"Most do," I pointed out.

"Yeah, well maybe, but you always get some up-front money."

"A few grand."

"Enough to keep the wolf from the door."

"But for how long?"

Bill thought about this and chewed on a smile. "Until the next job," he conceded.

"Exactly. It's no way to earn a living," I told him.

"Yeah, but Mark, all you need is for one of these jobs to pay out. Just one and you'll be sitting pretty, you'll see," Bill said before knocking back the last of his pint, grabbing his stick and hobbling up to the bar for two more bitters.

I thought about this while he was being served and came to a few conclusions. First off, it was dangerous doing what I did for a living. The stakes were high, but accordingly so were the rewards. The trouble was, the whole thing was a catch-22 situation. With The Agency contracts the way they were, we never knew what sort of jobs we were signing on for until we were on the boat or the plane or the submarine or rocket ship. And what's more, we never knew what sorts of guys we were signing on to work alongside until it was too late too. And as any given operation was only as foolproof as the most foolish member of the company, each job was like playing a hand of poker blind.

But then, I guess this was why blind hands paid out the best.

And were played by the players who had the most

to lose.

"Thanks young man, very kind of you?" Bill told some young boy-scout bar-teen who'd brought our pints over a few minutes later. He gave the lad a wizened old smile, just to underline his 'kindly granddad' credentials, then waited for him to leave before pressing me on my plans. "So what are you going to do? Are you going to try something else or are you going to sign up again?"

I rolled this over in my mind as I drained the first couple of inches. Mr Smith had asked me the same question on the plane back from the island. I hadn't known then and I didn't know now, though I doubt if either he or Bill believed me.

Come to that, I'm not sure I believed myself.

Some times, there simply were no choices.

No matter what we liked to think.

5. CAPRICORN IN ASCENT

THE FIRST THING I noticed was the pain in my neck. Something had hit me from behind and it had hit me *hard*.

The second thing I noticed was the headache that was splitting my skull in two. Right between the eyes, it was. Jesus, I could hardly see straight. I blinked a few times and rubbed my face before noticing the third thing.

My gun.

Someone had incapacitated me with a blow from behind.

But they'd left me with my gun?

What sort of brain surgeon did that?

I looked around the corridor and saw Mr Grey, who I'd been on duty with tonight, also spread out across the deck. I pulled myself to my feet and checked him over and found he too was alive but unconscious, and had similarly been left to sleep it off next to his rifle.

Christ, my head!

I somehow managed not to honk over the sleeping Mr Grey and hauled myself to my feet. I felt pretty wobbly on my pins, like Bambi on ice after too many alcopops, but eventually, I managed to steady myself against the wall until I had my balance. My head wouldn't stop throbbing and I scratched my face and rubbed my neck until I realised the violent throbbing was actually the bunker alarm. And it was then, only at this moment, that it finally dawned on me not all was as it should've been with Operation *Solaris*.

Oh God, not again.

I looked up and down the corridor for signs of intruders and saw that the steel door at the far end was open. I approached cautiously and peered around the corner. Four more guards littered this corridor, though these guys hadn't been as lucky as us judging by all the scarlet that had been splashed all up the walls.

What the hell had happened here?

I wracked my brains and tried to think. The last thing I remembered was talking to Mr Grey about *The Miracle of Castel di Sangro* by Joe McGuinniss, which half a dozen of us had just finished. We had been due to discuss it at our next dinner break but Mr Grey had chosen to disregard book club protocol to tell me that he thought Joe had overstepped his brief as a writer and had gotten too close to the Castel di Sangro team, which I thought was a valid point, if a little fucking obvious.

The next thing I knew, I was waking up with a splitting headache and a P45 in my pocket.

I followed a trail of death through the winding labyrinth of corridors, past the Communications Centre, in which everyone was also dead, and eventually, came to the main operations room. And it was here that I found Victor Soliman, our esteemed benefactor. At least, I think it was Victor Soliman. It was a bit difficult to tell without his name badge or skin. He'd somehow been cooked to a crisp between his enormous crystal refractors so that only his bones and glass eye survived – which is how I recognised him in case you're wondering.

Scattered all around were piles of scientists, technicians and guards, all of whom had been either shot, blown-up or crushed under fallen beams. I checked the ceiling to make sure the roof wasn't about to come in and reasoned I'd missed the worst of the fun and games, although judging by the plastique plastered everywhere, the party wasn't entirely over yet.

I sprinted on through, past the destruction, past the death and past caring, following the emergency lighting towards the surface when all of a sudden a voice stopped me in my tracks near the thermal guidance hard-drive.

"Look out Rip, he's got a gun!" it yelled, and I looked up to see two guys spinning around from planting charges around the mammoth computer system to glare at me.

"Oh nuts," I froze.

I recognised one of the men immediately. It was Rip Dunbar, formerly of the SEO (Special Executive Operations), a clandestine branch of the CIA, which was odd as I'd heard he'd hung up his guns to flog Bonsai trees somewhere. I guess he'd come out of retirement *again*. Anyway, he was the furthest away from me and about twenty feet from his own gun, while between us was some skinny looking Nguni, who'd obviously led Dunbar to us.

Like me, the Nguni was also holding his rifle, and while his wasn't actually trained on me, I was smart enough to realise my former colleagues hadn't all shot themselves, so slowly and very carefully I slipped the rifle off my shoulder and set it down on the grilled floor to show them I wasn't interested in disturbing them at work.

The Nguni broke into an evil smile and slipped the rifle strap from his own shoulder.

"Okay then, let's make this more interesting shall we?" he chuckled.

"What?"

Before I could say anything more, the Nguni had set his rifle down and was posing in front of me like an action figure.

"Jabulani, no!" Dunbar cried and I was in full agreement, but the Nguni wasn't listening and grabbed a couple of six-foot sticks from a nearby pile, hanging one over his head and holding the other out just in front of himself.

"Let's do this the Nguni way," he laughed, fully sold on the idea.

"You're can't be serious?" was all I could say.

The Nguni's eyes darted toward the pile of sticks and he urged me to pick up a couple and try my luck.

"Get bent!" I almost choked, damned if I was about to fight someone with sticks, particular someone who'd been fighting with sticks since before he could walk, but he was suddenly in show off mode and intent on proving himself to his Yank friend.

"Watch yourself Jabulani, Soliman's mercenaries are killers," Dunbar warned him, laughably overlooking the fact that none of his mates were dead while some forty of mine most certainly were.

"Argghhh arggghhh!" the Nguni screamed, coming at me in a blur and making me stumble backwards over my gun. I landed painfully on my butt and at the Nguni's mercy, but the Nguni stopped just short of me and instead, simply glowered with amusement and threw one of his sticks into my chest. "Fight!" the mentalist demanded.

Before he could molest me further, I hurled the stick back with all of my might, straight into the bridge of the nose and the Nguni screamed with pain. This bought me a precious few seconds and I used them well, snatching up my rifle and machine-gunning the bastard off to see his forefathers.

"Jabulani, noooo!!!" Dunbar cried in horror.

I swung my rifle his way and offered him the rest of the clip, but Dunbar whirled like a Dervish and dived behind a stack of wobbly crates. I sent another clip his way, splintering his surroundings to matchwood and Dunbar dashed out from behind them and found safety behind a huge reel of steel cables.

I continued to pepper his position with my AK, dropping empty clips onto the floor and slamming home new ones, but this was purely to keep Dunbar's head down while I desperately wracked my brains for ideas.

The position he'd taken up was in a direct firing line with the exit, so I couldn't make a dash for the surface, while behind me only death and detonation awaited.

Worst still, Dunbar had decided to take my recent stick fighting success to heart and called back from his shelter: "Okay, you *mother*, you just made this personal," which was simply astonishing. Like it was okay for him and his stick fighting little mate to wipe out everyone I knew but the moment Team Soliman got on the scoreboard suddenly it was personal. Unbelievable.

Once out of ammo I retreated back to the ops room to escape Dunbar's wrath, only to remember all the new plastique fixtures and fittings that now decorated the place. I was caught between a rock and a hard-head, but a burst of automatic gunfire told me Dunbar was intent on seeing the whites of my eyes when he avenged his termite-eating buddy. This worked in my favour.

I grabbed a fresh clip of ammo from a dismembered torso and ran back to the corridor I'd been guarding with Mr Grey, lock & loading as I went. Mr Grey was still flat out, oblivious to all our worries as I leapt him in a single bound and found a loose maintenance panel in the wall just behind where we'd been standing. This was obviously where Dunbar and stick boy had entered and how they'd got the drop on us.

I thought about hiding inside, then thought better of it and hid in the concealed broom cupboard a little further on. A few seconds later Dunbar appeared at the far end and scanned the space. He looked around, kicked the body of Mr Grey and told him to get up. Mr Grey didn't move, not even when Dunbar put a shot in his thigh and I realised then that Mr Grey's brains were probably porridge. Dunbar must've given him one hell of a whack when he'd first come in. And suddenly there he was, with his back to me, just begging to be shot.

I clicked the safety off my AK and began to take aim when I heard Bill's words again.

"Common sense. That's what you've got to use, your common sense," they said and knew he was right. What was done was done. And I'd almost fallen for the same distractions that had dazzled Dunbar and got him hunting for me in person when he could've just locked the door on the way out and triggered the plastique.

I lowered my gun, shook these daft notions of 'pay-back' from my head and focussed on staying alive.

"I know you're in here somewhere," Dunbar told the corridor. "Come out and show yourself you *sonovabitch!*"

In an instant, he swung and blasted what remained of Mr Grey in half, even though he hadn't moved so much as an eyebrow in the last half an hour, then he swept his smoking barrel back across the pipe-lined corridor. He moved slowly, taking his time, studying every nook, cranny and access panel, of which there were plenty. That's the thing about these bases I've found. There are no end of access panels, service ducts and maintenance hatches, all of which are usually just large enough for a heavily armed raiding party to crawl through. One day someone's going to ask themselves if all these ducts are absolutely necessary, because this is usually how the enemy gets in. Or out. Or away. Or manages to eavesdrop on our plans on their way to the poorly defended arsenal. One day, someone's going to realise this and the architect responsible is going to get fired – possibly through an electro-turbine – which'll be no bad thing.

For the moment though I was grateful because Dunbar didn't know which of the myriad of doors, ducts and grates I was behind, but he knew I was close because he kept talking to me as if I were a skulking child.

"I know you want me, so come and get me. Here I am. Just you and me. So let's get it on."

As tempting, if somewhat homo-erotic, as this sounded, I was damned if I was going anywhere near him while he was in this sort of mood and stayed quiet and let him pass without trying anything heroic.

"So, you like to play hide and seek, do you? Well, okay then, let's play, you cowardly motherfucker!" he snarled, lacing his invitation with a few strategic insults but still to no avail. Then, as if to underline the point, he started counting backwards from thirty as he pulled the corridor apart. "Twenty-nine... twenty-eight... twenty-seven... twenty-six..." panels were ripped open "... twenty-one... nineteen... eighteen..." tunnels were scanned "... fourteen... thirteen... twelve..." crannies were poked.

Dunbar swept the corridor methodically from side-to-side, pulling off and looking inside each service panel as he passed, though I noticed he didn't look inside the panel just along from my position.

The one that was *already* half-open. The one he and stick boy had entered through.

Hello, I thought. Got some booby prizes up there already have you?

No, Dunbar walked right past it as if it didn't exist, and instead, finished his countdown just outside my coat cupboard.

"... three... two... one."

Dunbar braced the rifle stock into his shoulder.

"Coming..."

His finger tightened around the trigger.

"... ready..."

His eyes narrowed.

"... or NOT!"

In that instant, he turned on a sixpence and machine-gunned the Coke machine opposite to bits.

The machine disintegrated in a ball of glass and sparks as he emptied his clip into its shiny neon belly until the only noises to be heard were the crackle of circuitry and the tinkle of shell casings as they tumbled through the steel grating walkway.

I was crouching just about as low as I could, right at the bottom of the cupboard, and curled into a little ball, though I still heard him tell the wreckage, "That was for Jabulani!" which suited me just fine; no Doctor Pepper and crisps for a week in exchange for that annoying little honey thief. That was a trade I could live with.

Unfortunately, Dunbar hadn't settled the score he thought he'd settled and his tearful manly rhetoric soon turned to whiney cursing when he found that I wasn't behind the lads' snack dispenser either.

"You fucking *mother*!" he spat, "where are you?"

I didn't say, so he stepped up his search.

The door handle of my cupboard was given a good hard rattle, but I'd locked and jammed it from the inside the moment I'd climbed in, pissing over his plans somewhat. Not to be deterred, Dunbar turned the door into Swiss cheese with his AK, but I'd seen this coming and was now cowering with a mop bucket over my head behind a load of Kevlar vests as the brooms around me bit the dust.

Another clip done, Dunbar spent five more minutes trying to bluff a confrontation out of me before chucking in the towel and killing a couple of bins on his way out. The SEO would come to view this as one of their greatest triumphs, but on a personal note, Dunbar ended his day on a bit of a downer. Which was good.

When he was finally gone, I kicked open the door and tumbled out into the corridor. I knew he wouldn't be waiting for me as big men like Dunbar didn't do sneaky things like that, so I shook the bucket from my head and considered my position.

I was the last man standing, with life and limbs intact. Which was good. But I was a mile beneath several million tons of African volcanic rock and the wrong side of an unnecessary amount of plastique explosives. Which was less so.

I had to get out of here.

And I had to get out fast.

Dunbar would've no doubt hit the countdown on his way out, which gave me just five minutes to get clear. SEO and CIA detonators always counted down from five minutes for some reason. I wasn't sure why. Perhaps they'd got them as a job lot on the cheap or perhaps they always set them to five minutes because this gave them just enough time to get clear of a standard blast radius, high-five a buddy, eat a Hershey Bar and salute a flag. Either way, I was at least fifteen minutes from the nearest exit and all out of hard hats.

I ran around in ever-decreasing circles, pondering my fate and considered risking Dunbar's less-than-inviting point of entry, before accepting that my best days were behind me. See, while the base had no end of tunnels and access ways, only a couple of them lead to the surface. The rest just circumvented the volcano and criss-crossed back and forth because that's what base tunnels did. My chances of picking the right tunnel without consulting a blueprint were less than impressive and my prospects were rapidly going down the pan.

The pan!

That was it.

I tore down two corridors and thundered into the men's latrines. The place was empty. No one dead with their heads down any of the toilets and no signs of any explosives, just a beaten up old copy of *The Miracle of Castel di Sangro* in the last cubicle.

I pulled the trigger on my AK and splintered the porcelain pan into a thousand pieces, then lobbed a frag grenade into the hole.

The frag widened the hole with a deafening thump and splattered the walls with second-hand stew. Victor Soliman would've been distraught at the sight of his brilliant white walls in such a state. I'd worked for a lot of fusspots in my time before but never one who'd been so anal about the brilliance of his latrines. Perhaps if he'd spent a little more money on the base's security measures and a little less on Vim we might've even got away with this one, but no, once again we all paid the price for signing on with a man who'd once tried to patent disposable toilet door handles.

I dived into the jagged hole the frag had just made and slid down a tube, landing in six inches of last night's supper. For almost thirty seconds, I lay on my belly gagging, retching and choking until I had nothing to add to the soup. Had I known I was leaving this way I might've grabbed a gas breather from one of the emergency stations, but I'd been in such a hurry to get out of here that the details simply hadn't occurred to me. In the event, I pressed on as best I could and tried to overlook the décor. It might've been cramped, it might've been slippery, it might've been toxic to the point of suffocating but at least it led to the outside world.

The pipe sloped down at an angle of about thirty degrees, so that once I had a bit of momentum behind me I was able to half drag, half slide my way to freedom, which might've been fun at WaterWorld, but was less so the morning after Tex-Mex night. Sewage splashed in my face, sweet corn collected under my nails and other people's piss filled my trousers, but at least I was making process, which was good considering I had only… two seconds left!

The first in a series of deep thunderous booms resounded behind me and I gave up caring about trying to keep my mouth closed as I flung myself down the sloping pipe. I scrambled and scampered, but it was too little too late – the blast caught up with me in a heartbeat.

It takes a lot to blow up a volcano. Volcanoes, by their very nature, can withstand mind-boggling amounts of pressure, so building an impenetrable base in one is a smart move if you're setting out to annoy countries with enormous air forces. However, you encounter a whole different set of problems when you attach a dozen blocks of plastique to pretty much everything that's combustible inside and light the blue touch paper. Because once you've filled your impenetrable underground bunker with a colossal store of energy, that same energy has to find a way out. And if it can't escape through the walls, because they've been forged out of Mother Nature's hottest furnaces, it will look elsewhere to escape.

Any nook.

Any cranny.

Any pipe.

These are places you don't want to be lingering when your impenetrable underground base blows up.

The sheer force of waste welled up on me from behind and shot me along the pipe like a bullet. The walls scraped my shoulders, the joints ripped my knees and the chilli almost drowned me, but nothing could slow my plunge into the onrushing blackness.

For twenty terrifying seconds, I lost all control of my senses as I was propelled towards the unknown. I think I even peed myself with fear – I'm not certain, I think some of it was mine – but providence took pity on me and together with a thousand recycled dinners I burst into daylight and flew fifty feet into a great septic lake of waste at the bottom of the eastern slopes.

The cool waters were dark and cloudy, but I managed to thrash in them enough until I popped to the surface and sucked in a lungful of pungent air. This did little to help the situation and I continued to gasp, splutter and drown until I noticed my presence had shaken the local inhabitants to action.

On the far banks of the lakes, watching me with raised eyebrows were a dozen freshwater crocs. If I'd been one of them, I would've sued and possibly eaten the estate agent, because their home waters were anything but fresh, but the crocs didn't seem to mind. In fact, they seemed to have grown fat on whatever Soliman had ejected from his pipes and judging from the looks on their craggy faces, they weren't quite full yet.

I struck out for the nearest bank as the waters across the lake churned against the force of eager swimmers.

"Come on, give me a break!" I implored, kicking and clawing for the rocks just twenty feet beyond the brown geyser.

I fought the urge to suck in my limbs and instead, beat them with all of my might until my fingers struck mud. I glanced over my shoulder just in time to see a rake of jaws flash by the back of my neck and tumbled clear to snatch my Colt from its holster. A blur of pink exploded into red as I punched two bullets into its epicentre and then emptied the clip into the rest of his colleagues. By the time I was done, there was more than enough fresh meat to go around and only two crocodiles left to squabble over it, so I scrambled away to leave them to their bounty and sought a vantage point from which to get my bearings.

The summit of the volcano was billowing smoke and a dozen vents and pipes along the eastern ridge were spewing flames. Dunbar hadn't been messing about when he'd set the charges. Nothing could've survived that inferno. Nothing. Not a computer chip, a lens refractor, not even a man hiding near a Coke machine. At least, with any luck, this was what Dunbar thought, though I'd probably used up my quota of luck for the day, if not the decade, so I took nothing for granted.

Instead, I emptied my shoes, threw away my handkerchief and started walking for home.

Whichever way that was.

6. LUCK IS NOT ENOUGH

AFTER ONLY A MILE or two of parched scrubland, the remorseless African sun had baked me – and whatever had left the pipe with me – to a golden crust. I couldn't decide if this was better or worse, but either way, I wasn't getting in the Ritz any time soon.

I trundled on for a couple of miles choking on the dust of my former colleagues' dinners until I found what passed for a road in these parts. It was wide, dusty and rutted with gaping potholes, but a road nonetheless. But a road to where? I didn't know. That was the thing about this job. It took me to far-flung and exotic locations, but I never actually got to see them. Most bases were self-contained: bed, board, recreation time and work, but as far as the surrounding countryside was concerned, I could have been anywhere.

One of the guys had told me that the local people around this way were Nguni, like my friend stick boy, but I didn't know where the Nguni were from. Nguniland would've been my best guess so I flipped a coin, ignored how it came down and headed south whatever.

At first, I ducked off the road and hid whenever a car came along but after four hours of murdering my feet, I decided to risk it and see if I could hitch a ride. After a few more minutes a shimmer of dust appeared on the horizon so I tucked my Colt into the back of my trousers and stuck out my thumb.

The shimmer neared.

My thirst was my most pressing concern. If I didn't manage to negotiate a lift, or at least wangle a bottle of water, I'd be dead by nightfall. Of course, I could always hijack whoever was coming along. A quick shot to the temple and thanks very much, but that sort of Karma always caught a man up in the end. No good ever came of no-good deeds. If a lifetime of Affiliating had taught me anything, it had taught me that.

Within the shimmer, a windscreen caught the sun and glinted with solastic brilliance. Victor would've been very happy.

The glinting flickered and grew until I realised the windscreen was too large for a simple car. It was a truck that was coming my way. This changed things for the stickier but it was too late to slide off the road. Whoever was driving had already seen me and was hooting his horn with excitement. I clenched my teeth, clicked off my Colt's safety and waved back.

A surprisingly spruce Zil131 roared up and threw a cloud of red dust in my face as it juddered to a halt in front of me. I barely had time to clear my eyes before the driver, his passenger and about fifteen militia all started pouring out of various exit points and swarming around me in an excited scrum. I could tell at first glance they weren't regular military. The togs were Russian Army and Navy surplus, Spetsnaz cast-offs that had been given to Oxfam when their new strip had come in circa 1978, so I figured someone local had their own little private army.

Some Johnny in a second-hand Admiral's uniform

seemed to be in charge of these boys, judging from the surplus of stars and paraphernalia across his shoulders, so I came to attention and gave him my best Private Benjamin salute. This took the Admiral back a step or two but then he broke into a broad toothy smile and rebounded a couple of fingers off his eyebrows in response.

"You a soldier?" he asked when he'd stopped grinning.

"Yes sir," I confirmed, pandering to his ego to save us wasting ammunition.

"And whose army are you in?" he asked.

"I'm currently between armies, sir," I told him.

"You are between armies?" he laughed. His men looked at each other and shrugged before a tall ebony lad off to the left translated for them and suddenly they were all doubling up theatrically as if I'd just told the best Knock-Knock joke in the world.

The Admiral continued to cackle too, milking it for all he was worth, while the ebony translator just stared at me with ice in his eyes. He would be the first one I'd put down when the laughing stopped, but the Admiral was enjoying himself way too much at the moment to let things descend to that.

"So tell me," he continued, his English good, but African-taught, "how are you here? And what is that on your clothes?"

"It's shit, sir," I told him.

No translation necessary this time, the boys all took to their sides once more.

"Shit?" the Admiral chortled. "And why are you covered in shit?"

It was a good question. I just wished I had a good answer. In the event, I told him; "I've had a bad day, sir."

This did the trick and it made him boom like kiddies' entertainer until his ebony C3PO reminded him that this wasn't the Comedy Store and business was pressing, calling time on the day's entertainment. The Admiral wound down to a thoughtful smirk, then asked me where I was going.

"I don't rightly know," I told him then played my Joker. "Perhaps you're looking for soldiers at the moment, sir?"

"Looking for soldiers?" he blinked.

"To serve in your army, sir," I elaborated.

"To serve in my army?" he repeated, giving me some insight into how he'd learn English in the first place.

"Yes sir. A very good soldier I am sir," I told him, saluting once more to demonstrate my pedigree. "I can help train your men, sir."

"Train my men? Train them to do what? Get covered in shit?" he asked, not unreasonably under the circumstances.

"Yes sir, when necessary."

"Ness-sess-sary? And when is it ness-sess-sary to get covered in shit?" he grinned.

"When all else fails," I told him. "Sir."

The Admiral's expression changed from amusement to one of genuine bewilderment and he obviously came to the conclusion that I was far too interesting to shoot for the moment because he had a quick word with his number two then invited me to join them in the truck.

"Er, no. In the back, if you please," he clarified when the man covered in shit started towards the passenger side door.

Now, there was one of two ways this day could unfold for me. Actually, there were dozens, but if we lumped most of them under the umbrella of "nastily" then we were left with just two. But when you're in the company of a 23-year-old African Russian Naval Admiral, there's simply no way of telling which it'll be. See, I was a soldier. At least I was from the moment I'd stood to attention and saluted Teen Amin, though between you and me I've never served so much as a day in any army the UN would recognise. I'd tried of course, when I was younger. I'd had a go at joining up. I'd caught a bus to Aldershot, stood around in my pants with a load of other spotty Herbert's waiting to be sexually assaulted by whichever Sergeant fancied wearing a white coat that day and passed with flying colours, only to get sent packing when they found out about my conviction for aggravated burglary. Seriously. It seemed a bit like double-standards to me, but I was denied the chance to burst in and out of Paddy's house and push him around simply because I'd taken the initiative and got in a bit of practise before I'd reached the age. The Foreign Legion weren't much friendlier. I had always thought they'd take anyone but they wouldn't touch me either. I don't think it helped my cause when I'd turned up at their recruitment centre in a stolen Renault, but then how else was I meant to get down to Aubagne with empty pockets?

I wondered if the Admiral was as pernickety about his troops as the Legion. From the looks of the evil-looking thug with one eye, seven fingers and the PK bi-pod machine-gun slung across his shoulders it was a possibility.

Of course, the best possible outcome from today's meeting would be an invitation to throw my lot in with theirs and join their crusade. I wasn't sure who or what they were crusading against. Anyone who didn't have a gun usually qualified in traditional African warfare but these chaps looked a cut above the box-standard bush militia. They were older, better dressed, better equipped and better disciplined, in that they hadn't tried to shoot me into little pieces or burn me alive the moment they'd seen me, so presumably, they had a few proper objectives. Then, when I was fed, watered and knew where I was in the world, I could nick one of their jeeps and an A-Z and make for the nearest airport. It wasn't a perfect plan by any means but it seemed to tick all the right boxes.

There was however one problem. Playing the lowly soldier card as I had was a risky strategy because on the one hand, I was saying, "look, you've no reason to kill me, I'm not a threat to you" but this often translated as "look, you've no reason NOT to kill me, I'm not a threat to you".

My only hope was the Admiral's ego. Because if there was one thing African bush Admirals liked better than mindlessly killing lost westerners it was being saluted by white soldiers – particularly white soldiers from proper armies. Nothing authenticated their rank quite like it.

7. ON HIS MOST EXCELLENT MAJESTY'S MOST SPECIAL SECRET SERVICE

AFTER A COUPLE OF hours touring the nation's potholes we pulled up outside a large, freshly painted former colonial farm. The order was given to dismount so we all piled out of the back of the truck and stood around in an informal line jangling our change. I for one couldn't have been happier that we'd finally arrived at our destination. The big ebony translator had made a point of sitting directly opposite me for the whole journey and despite the road doing its best to get us all ready for space, his eyes hadn't left mine for a second.

The Admiral breezed by to send the boys to dinner then ordered me to follow him up to the house. His translator came too, despite the fact that we didn't need a translator, walking in my shadow and burning his eyes into the back of my neck as we passed through a set of double doors and into a dizzyingly cool hallway. The Admiral glanced my way to see if I was impressed with the air conditioning and I duly shivered my appreciation.

An adjutant in crisp white duds rushed up with a pitcher on a tray and poured the Admiral a glass of iced water. The Admiral quenched his thirst with a smack of his lips then replaced the glass on the tray and sent the adjutant away. Once again, he glanced my way, though this time my appreciation was somewhat less than forthcoming.

"Commander Dembo, how was your reconnaissance mission?" a new crisp white adjutant asked as he waltzed by to greet us.

"Excellent," the Admiral confirmed, checking his breast apparel to make sure he had enough room for a few new medals. "Is His Most Excellent Majesty in? I wish to see him at once."

The adjutant eyed me as if I'd just dropped out of Commander Dembo's nose and deduced I was the reason for the urgency. The adjutant frowned.

"I'm afraid His Most Excellent Majesty is attending to some very important business at the moment, he cannot be disturbed."

It was now my turn to glance the Admiral's way and he liked this about as much as I'd liked passively drinking a glass of ice water, but His Most Excellent Majesty had better things to do and there was nothing to be done. Rank had spoken.

"Very well, we'll wait," the Admiral conceded. "But would you tell His Most Excellent Majesty that I'd like to see him at his earliest opportunity? I have something to give him."

"Is it this?" the adjutant guessed, pointing at me.

"Well, yes but…" the Admiral started, but the adjutant cut him off.

"Then might I suggest you wash it while you wait. His Most Excellent Majesty prefers not to receive gifts that make the eyes water so." And with that he swept away, leaving the Admiral and I to get better acquainted over a bar of soap.

*

A couple of the Admiral's men showed me to a water

barrel out back and I was dunked and scrubbed until I was as clean as the water would allow, then pulled out and stuck in some Russian infantry desert fatigues, with boots and cap to match – only minus the insignia. His Most Excellent Majesty's designers were no doubt still working on their own motifs, but I suspected they'd probably plump for a scorpion crawling over a dagger or something like that. Private insignia, if nothing else, served to reflect just what sort of dangerous bad-asses the men who'd ironed these patches on were.

The downside of my bath was the fact that I lost my gun. With an armed escort on hand, there was simply no way of hiding it. The moment it dropped from my belt the big ebony translator went spare at me for carrying a concealed weapon and ordered me to be frisked for further concealments to within an inch of my dignity. Happy I was finally harmless, both to life and nose, the Admiral took me back to the house and presented me to His Most Excellent Majesty, who pushed the peak of his oversized cap out of his eyes and looked up at me with suspicion from behind an enormous mahogany desk.

It was a kid. It was a ten-year-old kid!

The whole room awaited my reaction but I'd worked for screwier outfits than this in the past and would've happily saluted the coat stand had they'd introduced me to it, so I quickly snapped to attention and gave His Majesty a bit of the old King's Own.

The kid's eyes narrowed further.

"Your Most Excellent Majesty," the Admiral lip-smacked, "I bring you this man. A soldier. I captured him for you personally."

A few eyebrows went up around the room but on the whole, we let him have that one. The kid, or His Most Excellent Majesty, as he preferred to be called, nodded thoughtfully then congratulated the Admiral on a job well done and told him to consider himself promoted to the new rank of Colonel-General. I was tempted to ask if all the Admiral's promotions had been this hard-won and if so, suggest they either reset him back to Private once a year or sew a few more arms onto his jacket before the base's Spring clean. In the event, I just carried on saluting until my arm turned numb and my knees started to knock. The adjutant behind His Most Excellent Majesty's left shoulder whispered something into his ear and His Most Excellent Majesty suddenly remembered what was expected of him and returned my salute with a flick of the wrist.

I snapped this way and that and then stood at ease.
The kid began to grin.

He saluted me again, so I went through the whole pantomime once more, although not having ever having practised close order drill, I couldn't help but spot a few inconsistencies in my own routine. Nobody else seemed to notice though, which was surprising seeing as they had every opportunity when the kid started saluting me again and again and again for fun, forcing me through my ill-rehearsed moves until the adjutant asked His Most Excellent Majesty if he'd like to question the prisoner any yet.

"What?"

"The prisoner, Your Most Excellent Majesty.

Would you like to ask him any questions before we er…" the adjutant tailed off with a look at his shoes before leaving me to fill in the blanks for myself.

"Oh yes, very much," His Most Excellent Majesty confirmed, then looked at me. "What is your favourite football team?"

The adjutant spared me having to ask His Most Excellent Majesty what *his* favourite football team was when he steered him back to the script.

"What?"

"The questions we agreed, Your Most Excellent Majesty," the adjutant said. "You remember?"

"Of course I remember, Sissiki. What are you saying about me, that I am a fool?"

"Oh no, of course not Your Most Excellent Majesty. I am most humbly sorry."

"I should think so too because you are the fool, not me," His Most Excellent Majesty bristled and for one or two seconds a window of opportunity opened when any one of us could have suggested whipping down this kid's pants and belting the living daylights out of him to concord all around.

"You," His Most Excellent Majesty pointed at me, "what is your name?"

"Mark Jones, Your Most Excellent Majesty."

"And what do you do?"

"I am a soldier, Your Most Excellent Majesty."

"And where is your army?"

"Destroyed, Your Most Excellent Majesty. All dead."

"All dead?" he blinked.

"Yes sir," I confirmed. "All. I was the only one

who survived."

The newly-promoted Admiral-Colonel-General, His Most Excellent Majesty and the adjutant looked at me with mixed expressions. Only the translator continued to glare with as much mistrust as before.

"And how did you survive?" the adjutant asked. "Did you run away? Are you a coward?"

This hadn't occurred to His Most Excellent Majesty, who suddenly looked crestfallen at the thought, but I was able to quickly restore his confidence with some boy's own tales of dare-doing and heroism. When I was done, His Most Excellent Majesty stared at me agog.

"You killed fifteen men single-handedly?" he gasped.

I totted up my fantasy body count and confirmed that I had indeed killed fifteen men. Single-handedly.

"Oh, a hero, huh?" the adjutant cooed.

His Most Excellent Majesty picked up the baton and ran with it.

"A hero?"

"Yes," the adjutant sneered. "But not so much of a hero that he was able to save the lives of his comrades."

"Very true," I confirmed, "because we were attacked by over a thousand men, and I was only able to save my commander."

Now, this did catch His Most Excellent Majesty's attention.

"You saved your commander?"

"Yes, Your Most Excellent Majesty."

His Most Excellent Majesty mulled this over.

There was something about it that he didn't believe, but he couldn't quite put his finger on it. He suddenly got it. "If you saved your commander, where is he?"

"He escaped in the helicopter."

"The helicopter?"

"Yes, Your Most Excellent Majesty, I managed to get him to the helicopter and he escaped."

"And why didn't you escape with him?" the adjutant was dashed to know.

"I did, but the helicopter was too heavy. We were going to crash, so I jumped out to make the helicopter lighter and got left behind."

This finally broke the silence behind me.

"Preposterous!" the big ebony translator roared. "You jumped out of a helicopter and lived?"

"I landed in mud, a very dirty muddy lake, to be sure," I explained. "And that is why, when the…" I forgot what rank the Admiral was momentarily before remembering, "… the Colonel-General captured me I was covered in mud. Was that not so Colonel-General?"

The Admiral (which I think I'll keep calling him because he was still in his Russian naval uniform despite whatever rank His Most Excellent Majesty had just invented for him) was on shaky ground himself, what with the details of my capture, so he chipped in and corroborated my version of events in order to shore up his own pile of nonsense.

That did it for His Most Excellent Majesty and he confirmed that I was indeed a most excellent soldier, ending all concurrent thinking on the subject.

"But Your Most Excellent Majesty, what army did

he belong to? Why were they in our territory? What were they doing here? And who were they fighting? These are the things we need to know. Not jumping out of helicopters and single-handed fighting," the adjutant objected, but he'd lost his audience and the ten-year-old kid in a wobbly hat and over-sized uniform disagreed.

"Get away from me Sissiki. Do not tell me what we need to know. I am His Most Excellent Majesty, the Supreme Ruler and Commander-in-Chief of the First Lumbala Special Army and I know what we need to know, so do not keep telling me what to do. Unless of course, you think you would like to be the Commander of the Special Army?"

The adjutant thought about this longer than was prudent before apologising once more and expressing his undying loyalty to all things Excellent.

"You see Colonel Jones, my advisors are very stupid," His Most Excellent Majesty told me.

"I'm afraid I'm not a Colonel, Your Most Excellent Majesty," I told him.

"No?" he looked confused.

"No," I shrugged. "I'm just a…" a thought occurred, "… Brigadier."

"A Brigadier?" His Most Excellent Majesty repeated.

"Yes sir."

"What is a Brigadier?" he asked.

"It's like a Colonel-General, only more senior."

"Ha!" His Most Excellent Majesty clapped, pointing to the Admiral. "He outranks you!"

The Admiral chewed on this one and noted that I

did indeed seem to suddenly outrank him.

"So, would you like to be in the Special Army?" His Most Excellent Majesty asked me outright.

"It would be an honour Your Most Excellent Majesty," I saluted.

"Then that is settled," he declared, returning my salute three or four times. "You will be my chief of the guards and you will be in charge of saving my life if ever the enemy attacks."

I told him it was a job he'd never know me to fail at.

"Excellent!" he said. "I now need to speak with my Colonel-General alone but Captain Bolaji will show you to your quarters," he told me, giving our big ebony translator a name at last. "Good day to you, Brigadier Mark Jones."

"Good day to you too, Your Most Excellent Majesty," I saluted, then turned on a sixpence and marched out after Captain Bolaji.

The door closed behind us and the Captain turned to me and growled. "The Colonel-General is a fool. We should have left you by the side of the road where we found you."

"You're not really a people person, are you?" I deduced.

"Just know this," he jabbed, "I will be watching you closely at all times, and if you endanger our mission I will not hesitate to kill you."

"Brigadier," I reminded him.

Captain Bolaji's expression tightened up around his eyes. "Brigadier," he reluctantly concurred.

He turned and headed out through the double

doors and into the African heat. I kept pace with him step for step but Bolaji didn't look at me. He just rattled off the usual list of dos and don'ts that always gets rattled off whenever you join an organisation such as this one. ie. eight-hour guard shifts, alternate night duties, no shooting the local wildlife, my shampoo's the one with the A on it, that sort of thing until I had a general idea of what the daily grind was all about. The only thing that was still a mystery was the mission itself, but I didn't worry about that. I never do. That was the adjutant's department as despite the higgledy saluting order he looked like the brains of the operation. All I had to worry about was guarding my bit of the fence and watching my back until the first opportunity came to slip away. I had no intention of being here for the long haul.

Still, there was no reason to fritter away the time twiddling my thumbs so after Captain Bolaji allocated me a bunk in the main barracks block, I decided to ask about recreation time.

"Recreation time?" he stared.

"Yes, what do you do when you're not on duty around here?"

The Captain mulled this question over from all angles before asking me why I wanted to know.

"No reason. Just wondered, that's all."

"You just wondered?" he glared.

"Yes, if you read at all."

"If I what?"

"You know, read. As in books?"

Now the Captain was truly confused.

"Read?"

8. SHOULD OLD ACQUAINTANCE BE FORGOT

"I DO NOT UNDERSTAND how he made the perfume out of dead people. Dead people do not smell good," Savimbi said.

"Yes, they smell bad," Beye agreed. "Especially the women," which was a curious statement and one worthy of Grenouille himself.

"He wasn't making the perfume out of the dead women, he was just extracting one ingredient from their bodies," I argued, but the overall consensus was that nothing about dead people smelt nice so how could anyone make perfume out of them, least of all the most powerful perfume in the world.

"I think it is a metaphor," Captain Bolaji said.

"A metaphor?"

"Yes, all the women he killed were beautiful, the most beautiful women Grenouille could find."

"I would not have killed them, I would have fucked them," Mbandi grinned, slicing open a big papaya with his bayonet and sinking his pink-yellow teeth into the pink-yellow flesh.

"Then you would have had to kill them first, Mbandi," Savimbi quipped, prompting chairs and papaya to go flying in all directions as the third meeting of the Special book club descended into yet another punch-up.

Captain Bolaji knocked the bayonet out of Mbandi's hand while Savimbi's mates pinned him to the ground until he'd calmed down, then once order was restored we retook our seats and continued discussing Patrick Süskind's *Perfume*.

I don't know what it was with African men, particularly your typical African bucks. They loved – and I mean absolutely lived for – ripping the piss out of each other's virile inabilities but had a paper-thin sense of humour when it came to jibes about their own lack of sexual prowess. Perhaps it was a tribal thing; an ancient marker of accord, that their ability to pull virgins, impregnate them with a single thrust and leave the countryside dotted about with single mums reflected their position in society. So bigging themselves up as God's gift while dissing their mates as seedless grapes was all part and parcel of this primeval tradition. Locking antlers across the Serengeti, that's all they were doing. Locking antlers.

Of course, blokes in Britain did this too, only with Turtle Wax and Ford Mondeos.

Still, as quaintly ritualistic as this was, it did somewhat hack into the cut and thrust of our debate and turn our Friday morning meetings into African Gladiators. But on the plus side, they'd all read the book.

"Sorry Captain, you were saying?" I invited.

"Yes, I was saying it was a metaphor."

"A metaphor? For what?" Beye asked.

"For God's finger; that this mysterious ingredient, which was distilled from the most beautiful women in all of France, was not a smell at all, but an alchemic. Grenouille's perfume, as beautiful, hysterical and intoxicating as it was, was life itself."

Captain Bolaji attended every book club meeting.

At first, I figured it was just to keep an eye on me to ensure I didn't try to insurrect the men, but over the weeks he'd really gotten into the spirit of things and always made a key contribution, be it picking holes in Dan Brown's *Angels & Demons* or wrestling the pin back into Mbandi's grenade. Accordingly, I thought he made a good point here but Jaga wanted to know if life was so beautiful, why did Kasanje's feet smell so much?

Chairs went flying again.

Captain Bolaji looked to the rafters and rolled his eyes.

This time the fracas was interrupted by Vice-President General-Brigadier Admiral-Colonel Dembo, who'd been making out like a bandit in the promotions stakes in recent weeks.

"What is this? What is this" Africa's highest-ranking soldier cried as he waded into a twisted knot of arms and legs. "Captain Bolaji, call your men out immediately! We have visitors."

This caught the Captain's attention so he pulled a whistle from his top pocket and gave it two blasts, ending book talk for another day. The troops rushed to their bunks and collected their hats and rifles (which had been banned from book club after the first meeting) and we all filed outside into a scorching hot dust storm. Across the compound, a large Soviet helicopter was blowing His Most Excellent Majesty's daisies around and settling just in front of the main building.

The Admiral quickly arranged us into some sort of welcoming committee and found a suitably convincing smile for his face. A moment later the door on the side of the helicopter slid back and sixteen pairs of the very latest Russian issued army boots hit the ground and formed an honour guard of their own.

His Most Excellent Majesty, the Commander-in-Chief of the First Lumbala Special Army even made a rare excursion away from the air conditioner, making me realise that the money men must've flown into town. Sure enough, a couple of high-ranking Europeans in incognito khakis leapt from the bird and strode towards their host for a handshake. Naturally, His Most Excellent Majesty bemused and amused them by trumping their handshake with one of his newly learned salutes (these Commander-in-Chiefs, they grow up so fast don't they?), but they were good sports and played along to His Most Excellent Majesty's delight.

Words were exchanged and lost in the roar of the engines, then the money men played Santa and ordered a couple of their pink and sweaty troopers to drag a crate off the helicopter and plonk it down in front of His Most Excellent Majesty's smile. A crowbar knocked the lid off and a shiny black M16 was handed to His Majesty. Bullets were quickly found and a nearby bin dispatched, all to His Most Excellent Majesty's immense satisfaction, before the leading lights decided they'd had enough fun in the sun for one day and headed into the house for shadowier discussions.

The Admiral ordered those of us not invited to help offload of the rest of the crates so half a dozen of us mule-trained the remainder of cargo to the weapons bunker.

Being the only white soldier in a black African army was always likely to earn me a few looks, though one particularly tough-looking trooper eyed me with deep-set misgiving. His eyes narrowed further when a chrome lock-box came off the troop carrier and made its way to our bunker, followed closely at heel by a couple of white-coated boffins.

When all was unloaded, the Admiral ordered most of his men back under the carpet, but the most photogenic of us were posted outside the bunker to guard His Most Excellent Majesty's newest toys.

My tough-looking friend and a couple of his Russian comrades were given equivalent orders and a dozen of us formed up facing each other under the murderous African sun while the brass sloped off to change shirts.

My tough-looking friend's face cracked into a warm smile.

"Mr Jones!" he said.

I returned his smile with interest and stuck out a hand.

"Mr Smith!" I declared, beaming to see my old American friend again.

Mr Smith shook my hand warmly and we slung our rifles over our shoulders and jawed for a couple of minutes on old times.

"What are you doing here?" Mr Smith finally asked.

"Just trying to scrape a few pennies together to pay the bills," I explained.

Mr Smith wasn't convinced though. "You didn't get this job through The Agency."

"No, work on spec – 'situations vacant' sign hanging on the gate post."

Mr Smith decided against scrutinising that one too closely and asked me if I was being well treated.

"Well enough, I can't complain," I said, complaining as much as I could with my eyes out of view of my Special brethren. Mr Smith noted it and frowned in acknowledgement. Troopers on either side of us were staring with suspicion so we explained to our respective comrades that we'd served together before.

Captain Bolaji decided we'd caught up enough and reminded us of our orders. After a token glare of protest, I unslung my rifle and resumed my post, but Mr Smith stayed right where he was. I thought for one moment they were going to get into it with each other but in the event, Mr Smith just asked me what I was reading.

"We've just finished Patrick Süskind's *Perfume*," I told him, rolling up the sleeves of my tunic to show him the bruises.

"You've got a book club going?" he delighted.

"Of sorts. Just something to pass the nights."

"*Perfume*?"

"You'd be surprised what we've been able to get delivered from Durban," I told him.

"What did it score?"

"We haven't scored it yet. But *End of The Affair* got two-point-nine last week, while Alan Bennett's *Untold Stories* did very well with four-point-two."

"Really? That surprises me," Mr Smith said.

"Well, it was a bigger book, wasn't it? And in hardback. Better for fighting with," I explained.

Mr Smith understood. He thought for a moment, looking like he wanted to say something but didn't know how to put it, before asking me if I'd read *Papillon*.

"Henri Charrière yeah?" I said. "No, I haven't read that one yet."

"We just read it a few weeks back."

"We?"

"Yeah, we've got a little book club of our own going, like before," Mr Smith told me.

"Hey, that's great. Are you scoring and nominating and everything?"

"Yeah, same as we did back on the island. It's working out really well," he said, and several of his comrades nodded in agreement behind him.

"What did you give for *Papillon*?"

"I gave it four and it scored four-point-four overall. Went down very well with the chaps," Mr Smith beamed, letting me know whose nomination that had been. "Easily our best scorer. And you know what, that's for a book that's almost forty years old," he added.

"Perhaps we'll do that one next because my choices don't seem to be going down at all well," I said, as the door of the bunker swung open and the white-coated scientists emerged, rubbing their necks with handkerchiefs and checking their watches.

We whipped our hands out of our pockets and snapped to attention but the scientists were too preoccupied with their own cleverness to notice. The lead scientist, who I recognised as having also been on Thalassocrat's island with us, radioed in that they were all done and a minute later the Euro players were stepping out of the house and walking back to the bird, matching His Most Excellent Majesty salute-for-salute.

Mr Smith looked at me and gave me a formal nod. I returned his nod and said I'd catch him in the bookshop some time. Mr Smith held his retreat for just one moment and fixed me in the eye.

"Don't bother with *Papillon*. Try *The Fourth Protocol* instead. You'll like it, particularly the ending," he said, ladling on as much emphasis as he dared.

"But…" I started, but Mr Smith repeated his recommendation before sprinting away to catch up with the others as they climbed into the helicopter.

The whipping blades kicked up His Most Excellent Majesty's yard all over again and most of the guards ducked into doorways and behind buildings to shelter from the stinging hot dust.

But not me.

I stayed right where I was, staring up at the ascending helicopter in silent alarm.

Because I'd already read *The Fourth Protocol*.

And so had Mr Smith.

It had been one of the first books we'd all read together on the island.

It had scored four-point-one.

And I remembered only too well what had happened to Valeri Petrofsky at the end of it.

9. DIAMOND CUTTERS

THE COMPOUND VIBRATED against the roar of engines. Hum-Vees, Armoured Personnel Carriers, jeeps, light armour and even a couple of big guns – mobile artillery. American, Russian, French, South African. The Special Army was kitted out from all four corners of the continent with whatever our benevolent European backers could lay their hands on. Most of the vehicles were in good working order, while others were just about serviceable for one last suicide mission. My own Land Rover had clearly seen more action than me, but my MG 3 machine-gun that was fixed to a swivel just above the driver's head was as clean as a whistle, if slightly noisier.

Savimbi looked up at me from the driver's seat and asked me if I could hear what His Most Excellent Majesty was saying. I glanced forward to the little podium out front and saw His Most Excellent Majesty gesticulating and saluting away like the Duracell Bunny. I shrugged. I could've guessed the theme but I couldn't make out any of the small print. This was probably no bad thing though. Last-minute instructions to carefully laid plans by ten-year-old megalomaniacs rarely led to victory parades for anyone other than the other side.

Of course, before this day had come along, I'd finally found out why the Special Army had structured itself along the same lines as Musical Youth. Apparently, the European backers, dripping with money and eager to back a side (any side) had found themselves a Howdy Doody in the form of a local prophet boy who'd won friends and influenced people by tossing chicken bones about. He'd been quite revered in his local scrub but only to the extent that he was never short of pineapples. But then, all of a sudden, some chaps with heavy pockets and questionable judgement descended from the heavens to herald him as a living deity who'd been sent to bring order to his people and unite the tribes. They'd even backed up this rather ambitious declaration with money, guns, armour and men. Now, as odd as this seemed to many of the locals, they figured there must've been something to it. After all, rich Westerners didn't stay rich for long throwing their money around for giggles and despite being asked several times if they were sure there wasn't someone more qualified or taller they'd rather have lead their army, the Westerners were adamant. His Most Excellent Majesty was their man – or rather, their boy.

Any further doubts were assuaged with a consignment of the latest shoulder-fired Czech rocket launchers.

It seemed to work as well at first because a number of warring tribes soon put their differences aside to take His Most Excellent Majesty's shilling. Local skirmishes fell off and the Special Army's ranks swelled. The prophecy, it seemed, was true. God had surely sent this boy. And guided by the voices of their ancestors and advised by his loyal adjutant, his people would come again. Hallelujah!

And of course, let's not forget those benevolent Westerners who'd made it all possible and who'd never asked for a single thing in return...

What?

They wanted what?

Actually, it wasn't so much something they wanted, more something they suggested. A target; a target that would galvanise His Most Excellent Majesty's position and free his people from the bondage of economics.

Diamonds.

More specifically, the diamond mines around the Zambezi basin.

And more specifically still, the new excavation just outside Caia.

Belgian prospectors had sent ripples around the world with a series of stunning finds at Caia and were now pulling diamonds out of the ground the size of grapes with conveyor belt frequency; diamonds that would be fought for and argued over for years to come; diamonds that would lead to the rape and ruin of his people; diamonds that would corrupt the very fabric of his culture.

Diamonds that should be His Most Excellent Majesty's.

The plan didn't take much selling.

And so this became the Special Army's most secret mission. This was what we'd all been trained for.

And this was what we'd be doing today.

I was still a little sketchy on some of the finer points, like what were we meant to do once we'd seized the mine and how we were meant to hold out against the inevitable government assault when the Special Army numbered only three hundred men and a few Cold War APCs, but the Admiral assured us during our individual unit briefings that His Most Excellent Majesty had a bargaining chip up his sleeve that would dissuade any retaliation.

The chrome lock-box, I hedged.

The one we'd loaded onto the eight-wheeler at the rear of our raiding party. A cluster of APCs and mobile guns protected it on all sides and the Admiral took personal charge of the vehicle.

I had a really horrible inkling about what was inside it.

His Most Excellent Majesty emptied an M16's clip into the air to decorate the end of his speech with a few fireworks then signalled his forces to move out with a regal swirl of the wrist. The roar of the cavalcade increased and several of the gunners theatrically locked & loaded their fixed machine-guns, despite the fact that we were a good fifty miles from anyone to shoot. The scouts at the front of the column moved off and the rest of us duly followed.

Me and Savimbi were somewhere towards the middle of the fray and it was our job to protect the right flank of the convoy on our way to our objective, then break off and take out the foot traffic once we'd got there. The big guns would see to the fixed targets.

I pulled my goggles over my eyes and tied a bandana around my face. My gun was also covered, protected from the dust by a cotton sheet, but as we veered away from the main force to take up our position on the flank, I whipped it back to at least look operational.

Look operational?

Yes well, to be perfectly honest, my heart wasn't in

this job at all. I'd bided my time while I'd been on the base because I'd found myself earning surprisingly good money, but Mr Smith's covert warning had just reminded me of my desire to desert. The Special Army could stick its secret mission up its collective arse. And the urgency with which I wished to abscond was cranked up even further when I saw that His Most Excellent Majesty wasn't coming with us. Something that always got my alarm bells ringing for me. Very inspiring.

No one else seemed to question his absence from the convoy but then I guess most of them were tribal guys; locals who'd been in on this deity stunt from the ground floor. They were all going to the promised land, but it's different for mercenaries like myself. I couldn't give two figs about His Most Excellent Majesty, his people or his prophecies. The only land I was interested in was the couple of acres around my house in Petworth. Any and all other dirt I was happy to let the rest of the world fight over.

Time to leave.

I think Captain Bolaji suspected I'd try to make my exit during the mission because he took up a mobile position right on my tail, his MG 3 locked & loaded and just looking for an excuse to chew me and Savimbi to bits. Not that Savimbi had done anything to upset the good Captain, or earn his suspicion, but that was just too bad. You can't make an omelette without killing Savimbi, as they say around these parts.

I glanced to my rear. Captain Bolaji had his dust cover off too. I was going nowhere for the moment.

Well, nowhere except the diamond fields of Caia with a three hundred strong rolling battle group of the chosen few.

Hail hail! And watch your crossfire.

Overhead two Alouette attack helicopters buzzed us, spraying the convoy with even more red dust. They were our air cover, and our first weapon of assault. They'd hit the mine's defences five minutes before us with rockets and 20mm cannons, then circle and hold back any reinforcements while we filled the place with bodies.

No prisoners. That was the standing order. No one was to be spared.

I wondered if that included us.

The Fourth Protocol by Frederick Forsyth. The plot revolves around an undercover KGB agent called Valeri Petrofsky. He's selected by his General to travel to England to collect various packages smuggled in by KGB mules. The pieces look innocuous enough in themselves (metal discs, odd-looking pipes, etc) but once fitted together they make a nuclear bomb. This bomb is assembled in a little suburban house in Ipswich next to a USAF base and prepared for detonation. The idea is that the public would think the explosion was one of the USAF's unpopular cruise missiles blowing up, prompting a wave of anti-Americanism that would sweep the Yanks and their nukes from the UK and the socialist-infiltrated Labour Party into government. On the other side is an M15 officer called John Preston, who's investigating the infiltration of the Labour Party by the hard (and evil) left and who follows events to a little cul-de-sac in Ipswich. It's a good and exciting book, like all of Forsyth's, and believable and thought-provoking. But the bit that always stood out for me, and the point we discussed at length in book club, was when Petrofsky went to start the timer he found it had been reset to zero by nuclear boffin, Irina Vassilievna robbing him of his getaway in order to erase his (and the KGB's) involvement. I won't say any more in case you want to read it for yourself, but me, Smith, Cooper and Chang all spent hours going to town on this particular point because we all sympathised with Petrofsky. The foot soldier's lot is not a happy one. And we're so often in danger from our own side as much as from the enemy.

Expendable. That's how me, Mr Smith, Savimbi and Petrofsky were seen more often than not. Mere assets, to be rolled out and used like so much toilet paper. And when we'd done what we'd been asked to do, and our chiefs had the moon on a stick, our rewards were invariably the flushing of the chain.

Well, that wasn't going to happen to me.

Not again.

Not today.

I had no intention of being anywhere near that chrome lockbox when His Most Excellent Majesty phoned up the Admiral from the safety of a concrete bunker some fifty miles away and told him to look inside it now.

Smoke rose on the horizon after an hour on the road. Smoke and rolling balls of fire.

As we got closer, I saw our helicopters dancing backwards and forwards over the target like mating bluebottles, firing their rockets and emptying their cannons into whatever ran, walked or crawled below.

Radio silence was finally broken and the Admiral told us to break convoy and assume our attack formation. Savimbi immediately swung off the road and took to a dirt track that swept towards the mine's right flank. I shouldered the MG 3 and locked home the first round of a very long and heavy belt.

By now, we were travelling through populated areas: townships and makeshift dwellings that had sprung up around the mine to house its workers and their families. Dozens of confused faces looked out as we rolled through their camps. The cleverer ones ran. The silly ones lingered to watch what was going on. It was on a crossroads of one of these settlements that me and Savimbi encountered our first target – a police car. Not national police but the mine's own private security.

I swung the heavy machine-gun around and opened up on it, blasting it with a fifty round burst and reducing it to twisted scrap in a matter of seconds. The occupant inside fared little better, losing his life before he even knew he was in danger.

We rolled on by.

It's a terrible thing to take a life. I've killed quite a few people in my time (and a couple of crocodiles) and I'm sure if I were able to turn back the clock and meet them in different circumstances I'd find very few who'd deserved it. But I couldn't. And for that I was grateful. But let's not fool ourselves here. This was what I did. This was what the job entailed. It wasn't nice, it wasn't justifiable and it wasn't right.

It was crime.

Crime on an enormous scale.

A lot of people were going to die today.

I just had to make sure I wasn't one of them.

A small police station approached on the left. I swung my gun and peppered the doors and windows as we sped by but we didn't slow to finish the job. There was no need. The long line of vehicles behind us all chipped in and did their bit as they ploughed on past, ripping the station apart and blasting it with 7.62mm and RPGs until a burning shell was all that remained.

More and more security ran out in front of us as we got closer to the mine. Some took potshots but most were caught with their pants down and overwhelmed by the sudden appearance of such a heavily armed force. They had no chance. We attacked over a half-mile front with a hundred armoured vehicles. And as much as I wasn't silly enough to assume it was going to be a cakewalk, I did recognise a one-sided victory when I was gunning down fleeing security guards in the back.

The big guns opened up behind us, lobbing 152mm shells over our heads so that death and destruction awaited us around every corner. We hosed down the wreckage with machine-gun fire and continued on to our objective:

The mine itself.

It rolled into view over the next rise. A long wire fence peeled off in both directions, straddled by gun turrets and security stations. All hell was breaking loose at one end of the line. Elements of our column had reached the front and were smashing their way through the defences around the main gate. The front office was bright with flames and I saw several figures struggling to escape the windows. Gunfire picked them off as they tumbled out and the Caia mine sécurité burned where they fell.

One of the gun turrets started firing on our part of the column as we emerged from the rat-run of shanty streets. Me and Captain Bolaji returned fire, spraying the position until we were past it and out of range before turning into the mine's works through holes in the wire.

Captain Bolaji stayed right on my tail, his sights fixed on me as much as the enemy. We pushed on through, firing left and right alternately, mowing down green uniforms where we found them.

Before we made much headway though, bullets started pinging off our Land Rover's armour. I couldn't tell where the fire was coming from and neither could Savimbi but we'd turned straight into a cluster of small arms. I tried bringing the gun to bear, but their force of fire was too much and I had to drop out of sight behind the armour while Savimbi tried to extricate us from the ambush.

A grinding of gears and a desperate screeching of the tyres did little to put any distance between us and our persecutors and after a few more seconds a thump of blood from the driver's side told me Savimbi had left the building. The Land Rover was left to careen into the back of a beast of a mining truck before beat bopping about on the spot as its tyres and hydraulics were shot to pieces.

It was at that moment, after a sustained ten or twelve seconds under fire that I realised no one was coming to my aid – most notably Captain Bolaji. That son of a bitch! He'd been with us all the way, right through the settlement and past the mine's defences, blasting what we'd blasted and shadowing us slug-for-slug. Now suddenly we – or rather I – actually needed him and the bastard had his feet up, obviously hoping I'd cop one to save himself the trouble.

I opened the steel ammo case against the rear of the cab and started bowling grenades in the direction of the enemy. I wasn't close enough to take any of their sunglasses off, but if I could just get their heads down for a few seconds I had a plan.

Explosions started splintering between us, one after the other as a dozen grenades patiently waited their turn to rip the air apart.

I grabbed the M4 Carbine off the brackets just behind the passenger seat and scrambled across what was left of Savimbi and the windscreen, leaping over the bonnet and landing on the runner boards of the giant Earth Mover we'd crashed into.

As more explosions echoed behind me, I pulled myself up into the driver's seat and hit the ignition button. The diesel engine roared to life first time and belched a huge black cloud of smoke over the cab.

I threw the gears into reverse and floored the accelerator, launching the titan back to smash through the enemy's makeshift defences and fill its enormous treads with security guards. Several men attempted to board me but a couple of bursts from the Carbine soon put paid to them and moments later I was rumbling through the middle of a war zone, oblivious to fence posts, gate posts and guard posts. I also flattened several portacabins and a couple of vehicles (which may or may not have been ours) with my immense twenty-foot high tyres before I got the monster motoring in the right direction. And that was when I saw it – the Admiral's eight-wheeler, rolling through the gates and towards the mine with an unstoppable inevitability.

That's it, I figured, I'm out of here.

The upside of losing Savimbi and the Land Rover was that I also seemed to have lost Captain Bolaji. Taking this as my cue, I pointed the Earth Mover in the direction of the distant hills and flattened the accelerator.

Suddenly I was swimming against the tide. Jeeps, APCs and armour were pouring into the works while I was intent on leaving via the same holes. Luckily my Earth Mover could cart over three hundred and fifty tonnes when fully loaded, so brushing aside a few old Russian trucks hardly scratched the bumpers. The armour I pushed to one side, but the jeeps I just went straight over without jigging the windscreen wipers.

Sparks started to explode all around the cab as my former comrades voiced their objections, but I ducked beneath the steering wheel and carried on over the top of them until I was outside.

Once clear of the main perimeter, I found less people to run over. Most of the Special Army were now inside and attacking the mine's installations, while the population at large had taken to the hills. I'd momentarily lost the main road from having to duck under the dashboard so I made one of my own through a row of corrugated houses until I found the official road again.

For a few precious minutes I rolled away from the mine stupidly thinking I'd made it, but only too quickly bullets began strafing the cab again.

I glanced into my wing mirror and saw Captain Bolaji making free with his ammo moments before the glass disappeared in an explosion of shards. I swung the steering wheel into the Captain's direction, but he just popped up in the opposite wing mirror and carried on rattling bullets off my doors.

What was left of my windows disappeared in the next hail, but Captain Bolaji couldn't bring his arc of fire to bear on me. The driver's seat was a good twenty-five feet above the ground and protected from the rear by six-inches of solid steel. The only way to get anywhere near me was to shoot through the driver's doors but in order to do that, he had to make it past a trio of twenty-foot high wheels, which didn't appeal to his driver in the slightest.

I checked the clip on my carbine and resorted to my Colt when I found it was empty.

The road ahead was relatively straight, so I stuck the Carbine through the steering wheel and checked my rear. Captain Bolaji had disappeared from the driver's side, so I clambered over the seats and checked behind the right rear wheel. Sure enough there he was, bouncing bullets off the rubber in an attempt to burst my tyres, but having about as much luck as the residents of Caia were. Well, like I said, this truck carried over three hundred and fifty tonnes of dirt and rocks fully laden so they didn't muck around when it came to the tyres.

I took a bead on my target and pulled the trigger three or four times until I saw his driver's hat come off. Captain Bolaji's jeep immediately veered into my rear wheel and disappeared under the axles with a satisfying bump. Captain Bolaji himself leapt for his life but I didn't see what became of him as a crunch from the front suddenly grabbed my attention.

I turned just in time to see the side of a steel bridge vanishing under the front wheels of the Earth Mover and a river looming large in the windscreen. I gasped through sheer terror, but just about managed to hold onto the breath as I plunged thirty feet and crashed face-first into the mighty Zambezi.

10. DILEMMAS WITH HYDROGEN AND OXYGEN

EVERYTHING IMMEDIATELY went black and I tumbled and turned inside the cab until the Earth Mover hit the bottom with a thump.

My head hit the ceiling and I lost the breath I'd been saving for later, but when I spluttered and choked, I found to my surprise, that I could still breathe. A small pocket of air had accompanied me to the bottom of the river so I sucked in as much as I could and studied my latest share price.

Not brilliant, but things could've been worse.

And suddenly they were. The rear of the Earth Mover started tumbling after the front and the air began draining away as the machine twisted in the murk and came to a rest on its back. Fortunately, by the time I was submerged, I'd managed to pump my lungs full of air and was confident I had a couple of minutes before I had to find any more.

I'm pretty good at holding my breath these days. Most Agency Affiliates have to be. Besides marksmanship, flying kicks and unbreakable skulls, a good pair of lungs is all part of the kit. Very few jobs won't dunk you in the drink at some point, whether it be oceans, seas, lake or rivers, shark pits, moats, alligator enclosures or piranha tanks. And if you want to get out of them again and pick up your wages at the end of the job, you'd better know how to hold your breath. The Agency actually runs courses for surviving water. And pretty vigorous they are too.

More than a few blokes have drowned just attending these courses but The Agency has world-class lifeguards and medics on hand at all times and has yet to permanently lose a student to water. The drowning side can actually help you. I almost drowned doing this course and nothing makes you more aware of the limits to which you can push your body. As long as you're able to pump your lungs before you're submerged, as long as you know to release it slowly, as long as you let your own natural buoyancy do as much of the work as you dare, as long as you don't panic and as long as you don't breathe the water, more times than not you'll live to climb onto dry land again.

I launched myself through the windscreen of the Earth Mover and was pulled clear by the current. I could see the African sun twinkling far above my head, sending golden rays through the dirty water to show me the way back to life, so I kicked off my boots, my jacket and my gun belt and motioned my arms and legs in gentle circles, clawing myself towards surface inch by murderous inch.

The current was mercilessly strong and for every three feet I rose, I sank another two until my lungs burned with impatience. I knew not to kick too frantically as that had been my undoing on The Agency course. You don't rise any quicker, you just use up your oxygen. Instead, I tried meditating my way to the surface. This sounds a bit gay, and I'll be the first to admit it, but it can actually save your life. By focussing inwardly and shutting down all extraneous activity, you conserve oxygen for your vital organs, granting you precious extra seconds to circle around in the swells as you float towards daylight. But it is an incredibly hard thing to do because you've basically got to fight against your instincts. I mean, when you're in thirty feet of water and gasping for breath, your panic stations will demand that you strike for the surface, but fighting against the water will only make you want to breathe all the more. What you actually have to do is take a moment to calm yourself, then relax as many muscles as you can (your back, neck, buttocks, stomach etc) and slowly and rhythmically waft yourself toward the light. Hopefully, if you've done it right, Saint Peter won't be standing there when you open your eyes to tell you you should have kicked, and you'll break the surface as gently as a sea turtle on its journeys around the oceans.

Of course, it's almost always those last few inches that actually kill you, tricking you into believing that you've made it when you haven't, and that's when you've got to be at your most disciplined and resist the urge to thrash for the finishing line.

Though this can be particularly hard when a semi-submerged tree branch stabs you in the face.

"Oh you... [cough]... fuckin'.... [retch]... cuntin'... fuck... [gag]... shi... [heave]... urghhh!"

I managed to somehow cling onto the branch and pulled myself the last few inches to the surface, though the pain that gouged my face almost knocked me back into the depths. I gulped down a bellyful of river and air, coughing and hacking with every breath until I was eventually able to keep some air down.

The river continued to pull at my feet but my arms were wrapped around the branch to keep me afloat.

I looked around to take stock of my situation but saw nothing out of the right eye but blood and shapes, and nothing at all out of my left. I felt my face and a shiver ran down my spine when I found a tangled mess of skin and bone where my left eye used to be.

"Oh shit!"

I splashed some water into my right eye to clear my vision, but I was still unable to see anything at all out of my left.

Blood started pouring down my face again, flavouring the water and banging the dinner gong for any nearby crocodiles, so I put my less immediate worries on hold for a moment and hauled myself along the branch until I reached the bank. The mud sucked at my hands and feet but a little more clambering saw me up the slope and away from the Zambezi's circling patrons.

I wanted to clean my face, push it back together and pick out any fragments of wood and dirt that were stuck in my eye, but my hands were caked with mud and my shirt was somehow filthier than the water it had just left.

I found some waxy vegetation nearby and did what I could to clean my hands up, and although I was still reluctant to put them into an open wound, what choice did I have?

A couple of bits of bark and one of the tastier splinters of wood fell from my face as I tried to flick it clean, along with one or two bits I think I was meant to keep. Only my hand was keeping my eyeball and eyebrow in place, so I untied my bandana from around my neck and did what I could to tie it around my head. My eye was gone, and a good proportion of my face too, but at least I was alive, which is more than a lot of people would be able to say come the end of this day.

I was stupidly just allowing myself to think that the worst of it was behind me when the same waxy vegetation that had served as my medicine cabinet began exploding all around me. I looked up and saw Captain Bolaji on the crest of the riverbank, emptying his pistol in my direction in a fit of ill-judged impatience. If he'd snuck up on me or had lain in wait, he would've had me for dead, but like so many inexperienced gunmen, he'd opened up on me from a distance, assuming I'd be as easy to hit at fifty yards as a paper target.

I was on my belly and scrambling before he'd got more than three or four shots off, and used the sloping bank as cover.

Captain Bolaji swore at me and told me to die, but I hadn't accommodated any of the hundred or so other piss poor shots who'd made similar demands in the past so I didn't see why I should make an exception for him.

If I'd still had my Colt and my 3D vision I might've stayed and taught Captain Bolaji how to shoot, but I was unarmed and hurt, so I scrambled through the undergrowth, keeping my head down and arse moving as I slithered for salvation. Thanks to the loss of my trousers my legs were soon scuffed to sirloin and together with all the blood that was pouring off my face I quickly realised a half-cut tracker with a hangover could've happily run me down, so I took the decision to lay up and wait for Captain Bolaji. If he was impatient enough to open up on me from fifty yards away, he was a good bet to run straight into a blade if I gave him the opportunity.

I rolled off the trail and pulled my combat knife from my ankle sheath. The Captain soon caught up with me, eyes to the dust as he chased down my blood trail, and I saw that he too had been hurt, presumably when his driver had taken a detour under my Earth Mover. This bolstered my confidence and I sunk back behind the tree and crouched with the blade poised to strike.

Sounds of twigs cracking heralded his arrival and I stabbed into a rush of movement but misjudged the distance thanks to my newly acquired 2D vision. Still, the shock knocked him off-kilter long enough for me to turn my attention to his gun and I slashed it from his hand, opening his tendons and veins as I did so.

Far from falling back as I would've expected, Captain Bolaji launched himself at me, seizing my knife hand and tumbling us both into a scrub-filled gully to crack our heads on the waiting rocks.

"Dog bitch!" Captain Bolaji screamed, trying to turn the knife on me.

"Fucking twat!" I screamed back, equally determined to be the one who did the stabbing around here.

Captain Bolaji smashed me on the side of the face with his free hand, rocking my head back and exposing my neck for a dangerous few moments.

However, I managed to use the momentum to bring my face straight back into his, head-butting him on the bridge of the nose with a sickening crunch. To be honest, I wasn't sure which of us had just done the crunching but neither of us seemed that happy about it and both reeled back with nausea.

"That wasn't good," I spluttered, and for one moment Captain Bolaji nodded in agreement.

Almost immediately though we were straight back to it, grappling and scratching at each other as we fought for possession of the blade.

My shock and blood loss must've begun to tell because Captain Bolaji started to get the upper hand. He rolled me onto my back and twisted the blade in my grip until my hand was almost at a right angle to itself. It was impossible to push the blade away when my wrist was at this angle, so I held him for as long as I could and settled for opening a second front on the bastard, whipping my knees up between his legs until I eventually won a coconut.

Captain Bolaji's strength slipped and I was able to push him off and turn the knife around. Captain Bolaji still had a hold of my wrist but the tide had turned and he knew it.

"No!" he gasped, as the tip of the blade began to pierce his neck.

I've killed a couple of people with a knife before and they always react the same way when the end comes. Pleading, desperation, pity and regret. Mr Fedorov, my late lamented Russian colleague, used to say that knife fights were like games of chess; each player started out on the attack with such intent, rushing their Queens and Rooks into the fray with only final victory on their minds until inevitably the issue was forced, and the losing King was left to run around in ever-decreasing circles until the final blow was struck.

Well, my knee-to-the-nuts had sapped Captain Bolaji of all his bishops, knights and rooks and only a few token pawns stood between him and checkmate. Captain Bolaji recognised this and did what everyone in his position usually did when their time came. He pleaded with me to "wait", used the last of his strength to delay the inevitable and prayed for a miracle to save him.

It arrived right on cue, just as I was about to deliver to killer blow.

11. THUNDERCLAP

A WHITE-HOT FLASH filled the sky behind me, searing my back and making me recoil in surprise. A supersonic blast of superheated air arrived right on its tail and me and Captain Bolaji scrambled away to escape its wrath, throwing ourselves behind a rocky overhang as bushes and trees spontaneously combusted all around us as far as the eye could see.

The nuke – I'd forgotten about it.

I could tell by the confusion on Captain Bolaji's face that he hadn't been part of His Most Excellent Majesty's strategy meetings either and was probably wondering if we'd stabbed each other and taken a tumble into hell as a consequence.

Because hell was exactly what we'd found.

Fire raged on all sides, sucking the oxygen from the air and choking us where we cowered. Having seen firestorms before I knew we'd suffocate if we stayed where we were. We had to get away, find air and a respite from the heat. The solution was no more than fifty yards away.

The Zambezi.

I shouted this at Captain Bolaji and he nodded to show that he understood, so we jumped to our feet and sprinted as one through the burning vista.

The heat was incredible, almost too much to bear, and it came in rolling waves as we careened in zigzags through the crackling vegetation, feeling the most bearable route down to the river. If we'd stumbled, we would have undoubtedly roasted where we'd dropped, but our movement prevented us from burning too deeply. Like hogs on a spit, we cooked all over, slowly but evenly until the river was suddenly there, broad and inviting, and we leapt into its cool waters without hesitation.

The relief was all-embracing and we bobbed in the swell as the current swept us downriver and away from the flames. But this was when our problems really started. See, we weren't the only ones who'd had the brilliant idea of hitting the water the moment the bomb went off. Every croc and hippo sunning itself on the water's edge had decided that was enough sun for one afternoon so that the Zambezi was now standing room only with all creatures great and small.

The first thing to have a lunge at me was a fifteen-foot crocodile with tan lines across his face. I managed to keep it at arm's length with a boot on the nose and a branch in its eye before I was helped out by a passing impala which floated straight into his outstretched mouth.

And the impala wasn't the only one who was having an off day. Lots of half-cooked antelopes and wildebeests clogged the waters in a desperate attempt to escape the flames, some were kicking and whinnying, some were not, but the crocodiles quickly recognised the bounty for what it was.

I decided to take my chances back onshore when a submerged hippo took exception to my proximity and I floundered and thrashed about in the rip until I fished up on a silt beach nearby.

I pulled myself clear of the water, but stayed close to the river for the air and finally allowed myself to actually put a little thought into my next move, rather than simply reacting to whatever was trying to shoot, roast or eat me.

After a little frantic splashing and a cry of "Oh, God please no", I had company in the form of Captain Bolaji, who hauled himself out of the water and who looked up at me warily. I barely had the energy to speak, let alone continue our game of chess, so I just shrugged to indicate that my bolt was shot and the Captain pulled himself up the beach and collapsed next to me.

Neither of us said anything at first. We just watched our surroundings burn and the sky turn black with smoke.

The radiation would follow, but as long as we didn't linger and as long as we didn't have a stiff wind on our backs all the way home we'd escape the worst of it. Well, maybe. We'd been about three miles from the blast when it had gone off and, judging from the fact that I was still alive to feel my wounds, I reckoned the bomb must have been a relatively small affair. Just a couple of kilotons or so. Plus it had been a surface detonation, maybe even a subterranean detonation if the late Admiral had driven the payload into the mine itself. All of these things had worked in our favour. We'd caught the bomb's flash and had felt its breath, but we'd been on the very fringes of the destruction zone and escaped with a couple of tanned necks and singed eyebrows. Much of the vegetation around us had burst into flames, but this was southern Africa, you only needed to turn on a flashlight around these parts to burn the place down. Oh yes, we'd been lucky all right. Or rather, Captain Bolaji had been lucky. I'd missed martyrdom by design rather than accident.

"What was that?" Captain Bolaji finally asked.

"His Most Excellent Majesty's secret weapon, I reckon," I told him.

Captain Bolaji looked at me in confusion.

"A nuclear bomb," I clarified.

"A nuclear bomb? You mean a nuclear bomb? Like an Atomic Bomb?"

"Yeah. Bloody things," I stewed, this not being my first run-in with one of Oppenheimer's firecrackers you see.

"The Europeans?" he immediately clicked.

"Yeah, probably," I confirmed.

"But why?"

"To destroy the mine," I reasoned.

"Destroy it? But why?"

"Well, we weren't going to steal it, were we?" I laughed.

Captain Bolaji still looked confused, and I could've explained that by detonating a nuke on the site of a mine, we'd just dirtied the ground – and any diamonds dug out of it – for the next thousand years, rendering them worthless. Not an altogether disagreeable turn of events if you happened to own a stockpile of diamonds that were rapidly depreciating in value following the opening of a mine in Caia, but which had now recovered their original worth (and then some) thanks to the Special Army's first and last heroic outing.

I could've explained this, but what would have been the point? I didn't know any of it for a fact and what's more, it didn't make a jot of difference to either of our bank accounts so who really cared?

"Don't ask me, mate," I eventually abridged, quoting the Affiliate's mantra. "I just work here."

But the Captain wasn't to be flannelled and asked me how I'd known about the bomb.

"I didn't. But I suspected," I told him.

"You suspected?"

"I had an idea."

"But you didn't tell anyone about it?"

"Tell anyone? Like who?"

"Like who? Like Mbandi? Kasanje? Jaga? The Colonel-General? They're all dead," he gesticulated.

I adjusted the bandana over my bad eye and retied the back to hold my face in place.

"Yes, they are," I confirmed when I was done. "But I didn't kill them."

Captain Bolaji's face fell, so I asked him what he would've done had I troubled him with my suspicions. Off the top of his head, Captain Bolaji reckoned he didn't know, but his reticence was clouded by hindsight, so I suggested he might've reported me to His Most Excellent Majesty at the very least, which would've seen me – and him – sporting matching blindfold up against a wall to prevent us from spoiling the surprise for everyone else.

"Either way, the Special Army would've still wiped itself out at Caia. Nothing and nobody was going to stop that," I said, though what I actually meant was nobody like me was going to stop it. Jack Tempest or Rip Dunbar might've had a crack at it had they been in my boots, but they'd clearly had more exciting missions on this week.

As much as it galled him, Captain Bolaji saw that I was right and tried to accept his sunny fortune with the good grace by which it had dropped in his lap. It still narked him something rotten that he was only alive by chance, but then again which of us wasn't?

"How did you suspect?" he finally plumped to ask.

It was a fair question and one to which he had a right to know so I asked him a question in turn.

"Have you ever read *The Fourth Protocol*?"

Captain Bolaji hadn't.

"Come on then, I'll tell you about it on the way to the airport."

12. THE SOLACE OF THANKS

AS YOU CAN IMAGINE, the towns and villages all around Caia were in a state of pandemonium. Buildings were on fire, people were running about screaming, and on the horizon, to everyone's horror, an enormous swirling mushroom cloud slowly rose towards the heavens. Me and Bolaji walked right out from underneath it and blended in.

We'd ditched what had remained of our Special Army uniforms and strolled into town wearing just our underpants and each other's blood. Nobody paid us any attention, nobody even noticed us as we washed our burns in the town's water pump, whipped a few clothes off a line and knocked out a local cop to take his jeep and weapons.

I urged Captain Bolaji to cut his losses and come with me to Harare, but the Captain was adamant about swinging by the compound to pay his final respects to His Most Excellent Majesty, so I agreed to go along for the ride.

Not that there'd be much point. I knew the plan, and I knew the tactics. I'd been here before.

As expected, there was nothing left of our old command headquarters but for a few burnt-out buildings and a scattering of bullet-riddled corpses surrounded by 9-mm shell casings. A Special Forces unit had dropped in for tea. All His Most Excellent Majesty's troops that had been left behind to guard the place had either been downed in position or marched out into the centre of the parade ground and dispatched there.

The adjutant had not escaped the clean-up operation either and lay dead in the grass fifty yards behind the main building looking none too happy about it. He still had his wallet (and his passport rather interestingly) so we spent a few minutes harvesting the rest of the bodies for petrol money and anything else we could find before Captain Bolaji found His Most Excellent Majesty's battered and bruised body curled up behind the Royal outhouse.

He called to me and for several seconds we stared down at our former Commander-in-Chief's swollen arse before Captain Bolaji planted a boot up the middle of it, causing His Most Excellent Majesty to suddenly wake with a start and begin wailing with fear.

"Why didn't they kill him too?" Captain Bolaji asked as we watched our magnificent leader cry his eyes out.

"I don't know, I guess it was just more fun to leave him alive," I said over the sounds of weeping.

"Brigadier Jones?" His Most Excellent Majesty finally saw through his tears. "Captain Bolaji? You came back?"

"Yes, didn't we just," Captain Bolaji scowled.

"Quick, get me some clothes," His Most Excellent Majesty ordered, spectacularly misjudging the mood of his men.

Captain Bolaji put a second boot up his arse to remind him of recent events and I cocked my gun theatrically to echo the point. His Most Excellent Majesty yelped in pain, then screwed up his face and began bawling his eyes out all over again.

It was hard to tell what he was saying, as so often is the case with crying children, but if I'd had to guess I would've said it sounded something like "please don't hurt me" and "I just want to go home. I want my mamma" etc.

Captain Bolaji looked at me and sucked his teeth. I'd already holstered my weapon and rage and was now just feeling like shit. Eventually, the Captain let out a sigh of frustration, then tugged a bloodstained jacket off a nearby sentry and threw it at His Most Excellent Majesty's feet.

"Put that on," he told him.

His Most Excellent Majesty studied the jacket and managed to stop crying long enough to pull it on, but his sleeves were too long for his arms and the breasts were riddled with bullet holes and this just seemed to set him off again.

"Stop crying Kimbo, or I'll give you something to cry about?" Captain Bolaji barked, comically dismissing His Most Excellent Majesty's recent run of luck as something less than a clip round the ear.

"Kimbo?" I asked.

"Kimbo Banja, it is his name," Captain Bolaji told me.

"Oh," I replied, relieved that I didn't have to keep on referring to this snivelling little kid as His Most Excellent Majesty any more, though it had helped with the word count over the last couple of chapters.

"Come on, let's go," Captain Bolaji said.

We gathered up a few final bits and pieces that we'd need for the journey then climbed into our jeep and bugged out. Kimbo didn't say much at first. I guess he had a few things on his little mind, but when he did it was clear he'd known less about the operation than we had. He'd been patronised and pandered to by the Euro boys, but when all the grown-ups had started to talk Sissiki had put him to bed. All he'd been told was that he was going to throw some crooked diamond miners out of his country and that when we were done, he'd be celebrated and revered, worshipped and rewarded, and big mates with David Beckham. He didn't have the first idea about the nuclear bomb and started crying his eyes out all over again when we told him about it.

The Europeans had been there with them, apparently to pop the cork on the Special Army's success, but the moment they got a radio call from their spotter on the ground, the mood had changed and their soldiers had started killing everyone. Nobody was spared, not even the wives of his senior officers, and Kimbo thought he was going to die too, but instead, all they did was parade him around in his birthday suit and tan his arse with their belts, before flying off into the sunset with laughs wobbling their bellies.

"Is everyone dead?" he swallowed in disbelief.

I looked over my shoulder from the passenger seat and nodded. Kimbo's eyes fell to his feet and he went quiet. Where once was a cock-sure, energetic young despot, all that remained was a fragile and scared little boy. All his authority was gone. All his confidence, his innocence and his pluck, all had been taken from him.

Would he ever fully understand what had happened? What his part in it had been? How he'd been used? Would he ever come to terms with this?

Maybe. Maybe not. But then again this was Africa. And bad things happened to little boys in Africa every day. What was one more traumatised toy soldier on a continent full of them?

After a few moments, Kimbo looked up and thanked us for coming back for him. I glanced over at Captain Bolaji, and he duly lifted an eyebrow, but left the home truths where they lay.

"I knew you would, Brigadier Jones," Kimbo continued. "Just like you said you would. Just like you saved your other commander, you saved me."

Kimbo leaned over the passenger seat and wrapped his arms around me in gratitude. His little body trembled against mine and soon he was in tears again. I let him cry it out for a few seconds before peeling his arms from my neck and putting him back in his seat. I fixed Kimbo with my remaining eye, gave him my steeliest look and then brought my hand smartly up to my brow to crack off the salute to end all salutes.

"It was my pleasure, Your Most Excellent Majesty," I told him, finally jogging a smile out of the nicest little super-villain it's ever been my privilege to serve.

*

Just outside Harare, there's an orphanage for children of war. It was set up by a nice old stick called Father Anthony who'd been working out in Africa since before Bob Geldof was in short trousers. The orphanage plays home to boys and girls who'd either lost everything through war or who'd been conscripted and put through the grinder themselves. Victims and former soldiers bedded and boarded together. They read, wrote, played, worked through their traumas and day-by-day, learned to become children again.

A new boy now resided there. To Father Anthony and the other pupils, he was simply Kimbo Banja. But I would always remember him as His Most Excellent Majesty, Supreme Ruler and Commander-in-Chief of the First – and hopefully last – Lumbala Special Army.

13. NONE BUT THINE EYE

"MR JONES, I've come to remove your bandages. Please sit up."

I recognised her sweet aroma before I recognised her sweet voice and smiled accordingly.

"Sarah Jessica Parker," I deduced.

"You remembered?"

"Of course, how could I forget?" I replied, moving to one side to make room for Nurse Parker as she perched on the bed beside me. "Lovely," I added.

Of course, this wasn't really Sarah Jessica Parker, but it's how I'd come to know and recognise her since I'd been here in the hospital so I saw no reason to stop with the sexy pseudonyms any time soon.

The sight in my left eye was gone. In fact, the whole of my left eye was gone, but worse still was the infection that had spread to the right, threatening to rob me of daylight completely. It had been a scary few days, but the doctors seemed confident that they'd caught it in time. Here and now we'd find out.

Nurse Parker began to unwind my bandages.

Sarah Jessica Parker was, and as far as I'm aware still is, an American actress, one of the girls in that show, *Sex and the City*. I'd never actually seen it myself, but I remembered who she was when I asked the nurse what perfume she was wearing and she told me, Sarah Jessica Parker, so this was how I came to imagine her throughout my time in bandages.

"Keep your eyes closed, Mr Jones."

Sarah Jessica Parker carried on unwinding the

bandages and daubed my eye with a crystal cold solution, wiping away the crust that had built up over the last two weeks in preparation for me seeing again.

Two weeks. That's how long I'd been here. Fourteen nights. That's how long my eyes had been bandaged.

Just over two weeks earlier, I'd arrived in Harare with Captain Bolaji after forty-eight hours on the road and practically fell out of the jeep. With no money, no passport and no strength, I'd been an unmarked grave waiting to be dug. Captain Bolaji had wanted to take me to the city's central hospital, but no offence to Harare, I would have stood a better chance doing the work myself. Plus, the authorities might've wanted to know where I'd picked up my injuries and why I was making their Geiger Counter sound like Flipper and his mates.

So I'd made the call. Or rather, I'd had Captain Bolaji do it on my behest, which had proved something of a revelation to him.

"An Agency looks after you?"

"Yes. It looks after all its people, which is more than I can say for half the bastards it rents us out to."

Captain Bolaji thought for a while. "How do I join?"

"You don't," I told him.

"Well, how did you join?"

"I didn't."

"You didn't? You just said you did."

"No, I didn't join. I was invited to join."

"Invited?"

"Yes. You don't choose to join The Agency. The

Agency chooses you."

Captain Bolaji thought some more on that. "Then how do I get invited?"

"That's easy, keep me alive until the plane arrives and they'll have a look at you," I told him before passing out on the grimy hotel bed.

The next few hours were a dreamy blur. I felt someone moving around the room and the swirl of the ceiling fan. I felt water on my lips and a cloth on my face, the ringing of a telephone, and eventually, the knock on the door. Voices, swabs and injections followed, along with a fast ride along a bumpy road, then a roar into the sky. More needles in my arm preceded stars in my mind but I no longer cared. I was too far gone. Too pumped full of drugs. Too pumped full of infection. Heat wrapped my body like a blanket and I finally succumbed again.

The next time I awoke, Sarah Jessica Parker was checking my blood pressure when a pair of shoes entered the room. Of course, it was an Agency interviewer, here to take down my story. "Plenty of time to rest later. Let's hear what happened first," he invited.

When only one man survives a job – in this case, Operation *Solaris* – the debriefing's much more intense because there's no one else to corroborate the facts with you. A polygraph is sometimes used, but not in this instance. My infections had messed with my system too much to render my readings useless, so instead, I just went over and over the story of what happened with The Agency interviewer, and all the whens, wheres, whos and hows that went with it. The

Agency isn't so much interested in the whys. That's their job to figure them out. They're the analysts, we're just the foot soldiers so they like us to stick to the facts, make our reports objectively and leave any interpretations to them.

For eight days the interviewer grilled me, at all times of the night and with increasing intensity as my recovery progressed. Eventually, after the eighth night, he told me he was satisfied with my story (which they always do to allay your fears) and got me to sign my statements — at least, I'm assuming they were my statements, but what with my eyes bandaged I could just as well have been signing half a dozen blank cheques for him. I doubted it though. Trust's very important at The Agency and it swings both ways.

"So, now let us turn to the matter of the raid on the Caia diamond mine," the interviewer had suggested, opening a new folder and scanning the chip in my arm to begin the process all over again.

As exhausting as this was, the debrief for the Caia job wasn't nearly as intense as it had been for the Soliman job because The Special Army hadn't hired through The Agency, so technically, they'd had nothing to do with it. But their fingerprints were still on the job. The appearance of my old friend Mr Smith, when the bomb had been delivered, told me as much, so I knew there were wheels within wheels here and played along accordingly.

At least, until the following question was put to me.

"And so what made you decide to abort the

operation when your driver Savimbi was killed?"

Now, at this point I should have told him the truth. I should have. But I didn't. Because Mr Smith had taken a chance for me. So weirdly, I felt honour-bound to do the same for him. Hmm, a few book club rules we hadn't discussed there.

Obviously, I told the interviewer that we'd encountered each other out in Africa and that we'd even talked. I told him that we'd said hello, that we'd previously been in a book club together and that we'd even discussed what we were currently reading. I'd had to tell him that much as The Agency's computers would match us as having worked together on Operation *Blowfish*. They'd also put us on overlapping jobs and they'd identify the fact that we'd both been in His Most Excellent Majesty's compound when the bomb had been delivered, so unless we'd been wearing balaclavas or some sort of kooky headgear (which were sometimes required) then we would have definitely clocked each other.

So I told the interviewer all of this. And I even told him the context of our conversation and the specific book titles we'd mentioned (*Perfume* and *The Fourth Protocol*).

I told him all of these things but I omitted the message behind the chat.

And this was a risk.

It was a calculated risk but a risk all the same. A very big risk.

See, if Mr Smith's job went off beam (as it inevitably would) and he lived to tell the tale, then at some point in the future he would have to tell this same tale to The Agency, with the same dates, the same locations and the same chance meetings.

If he didn't, if he held back, he'd be as good as inviting a bullet in the brain.

So he'd tell them he'd bumped into me. He'd tell them we'd talked books. And he'd tell them he'd recommended *The Fourth Protocol* to me. He'd have to. Because he'd know I would have already told The Agency during my debriefing. The only way to protect yourself during the debriefing is to tell the truth, the whole truth and nothing but the truth, so help you if you don't.

But would he tell them *why* he'd recommended *The Fourth Protocol*? Would I? That was the real quandary.

It was doubtful because he'd be dropping himself in it if he did. Losing his Agency Affiliation and all the protections and guarantees that came with it. I was in no such danger because technically, I'd done nothing wrong. After all, it was Mr Smith who'd voluntarily spoken out to save my life, not the other way around. He'd been the one who'd broken protocol. He'd been the one who'd taken a chance. He'd been the one who'd jeopardised an entire operation, not to mention his own life, to save a former colleague. No one could blame me for heeding his warning. I mean, who wouldn't in my shoes? So he'd only dropped himself in it.

If I'd wanted to, I could've told them all of this and relaxed safe in the knowledge that I'd done nothing wrong.

But Mr Smith had done this thing for me. And I wouldn't have been here now to tell this story if he hadn't. So I took a chance for him, and for the first time in my life told The Agency a lie.

"I sensed something like this double-cross was on the cards."

"You sensed?" the interviewer asked.

"Yes," I confirmed.

"How did you sense it? Are you psychic or something?"

"No. But I have been on dozens of jobs so I've come to know when something doesn't feel right. And when I saw the package the Russians brought with them and the accompanying scientists, alarm bells started ringing."

"Alarm bells?"

"Metaphorical alarm bells. Not actually alarm bells," I clarified – pedantic cunt.

"Metaphorical alarm bells. Yes, I see," he noted down. "So you decided to abscond from the Special Army when you saw the package?"

"Yes."

"Because you sensed that the Special Army was being used to take a nuclear weapon into the diamond mines of Caia? And that this weapon would be detonated, eliminating the Special Army along with the mine?"

"That is correct, if a little specific. My suspicions were more general than that."

"Nevertheless, your decision to abscond was based purely on these suspicions?" the interviewer pressed.

"I would say so."

"You would say so?"

"Yes."

"Then please do say so."

"What? Oh, yeah, my decision to abscond was based purely on my suspicions that there was trouble ahead for the Special Army and that we were being double-crossed."

"And these suspicions were entirely of your own making? That no outside influence had a hand in planting them there for you?"

"Only the actions of His Most Excellent Majesty, his Russian paymasters and fifteen or so years of experience planted those suspicions there. That is correct."

"Just so that we are clear about this," he pressed. "Nobody forewarned you about the bomb?"

"They didn't need to, I worked it out for myself."

"Whether they needed to or not is immaterial. All I want to know is if they did."

"No sir, they did not."

"Not even..." I heard the interviewer flipping through a few pages to refer to his notes. "... Mr Smith? He didn't warn you about the bomb?"

"No sir. We talked only about books."

The interviewer was silent for a few moments, then I heard some scribbling before he spoke again.

"I see. And what happened then?"

And there, with that single white lie, book club was forced underground. And the seeds of future events were sown.

"Okay, Mr Jones," Nurse Parker said a few days later. "Now open your eye."

14. DOCTOR PATCHWORK

NOW, I WASN'T QUITE so naïve as to believe that Nurse Parker actually looked like Sarah Jessica Parker, my suspicions first being aroused when she flattened my grapes and almost up-turned the bed when she perched next to me. But what I hadn't expected was her to be was black. I don't know why I shouldn't have thought this. I mean this was the Caribbean after all. The majority of nurses here were black. And most of them were old enough to be our mothers, even Jennifer Lopez who did the bed baths around here, which especially disappointed me.

But Nurse Parker didn't have a Caribbean accent. She was American, eastern seaboard unless I was mistaken, which had helped underline my Sarah Jessica Parker fantasies. But when the bandages came off and my vision as restored – albeit in only one eye – I lost them all to reality and a knowing wink from Nurse Parker.

Still, what the nursing staff around here may have lacked in catwalk poise, they more than made up for in medical abilities. They were the best – and I do mean the *BEST* – on the planet. This was The Agency's own private hospital and better medical and care facilities you'd not find anywhere else outside the 22nd Century. Doctors, nurses, physiotherapists and pharmacists: they had recovery and recuperation rates other military hospitals could only dream about. I guess it helped that there was an almost constant influx of trauma patients to deal with: gunshot wounds, shrapnel, burns, breakages and shark bites. Not too many patients were brought in here to have their wisdom teeth out. And such a workload only pooled experience and expertise until the hospital's staff led the field in patching up battlefield casualties.

Then again, for what they charged they should. My fees from Operation *Solaris* were covering my eye surgery and facial reconstruction. They had lain in The Agency's bank accounts awaiting my return to Britain but I hadn't made it – again. And so I'd called them in and used the money to save my own life. And patch myself together for next time.

"Now Mr Jones, we've removed what was left of your injured eye and replaced it with a plain silicone orb for now," Doctor Jacob told me from behind a heavy old cedar desk. Nurse Parker had wheeled me here for my morning consultation and left us at the doctor's request. The reason why was about to become apparent.

"If the orb feels comfortable, and you are happy with it, then we can have a cosmetic version made up for you that exactly matches your right eye so that no one would ever be able to tell you have a prosthetic eye. You won't be able to see out of it, of course, but cosmetically, you will look quite normal."

I glanced at my reflection in the mirror, at the six-inch gash that ran vertically down the left-hand-side of my face, across my eye socket and to my ear and breathed a sigh of relief.

"Thank God for that. My looks are all I've got."

The Doctor read between my laughter lines and assured me that they could lessen my scarring too.

"With skin grafting and laser treatment, we can reduce the visible injury to a few lines or slight discolouration if you want."

"If I want?"

"Certainly. But some Affiliates like to keep their battle scars. They find they get more contracts that way," he explained.

"Really?"

"Yes. Lots of gentlemen prefer to hire – how shall we say – more robust looking employees to action their duties. Such staff can often bring a certain pizzazz to proceedings," he said, nodding approvingly at my disfigurement.

I looked at the mirror again, screwed my face into a growl and warmed a little to the apparition who leered back.

"Yes, I suppose," I agreed, with a renewed appreciation. "Perhaps I'll leave it for the moment and see how things work out."

"Excellent," Doctor Jacob smiled, not so much as an eyelash out of place on his own face. "Your surgery credits will stay on your file for either five years, or until you sign your next contract, in which case any and all future medical work will come out of your fees from that job. Understand?"

I did.

"Good. Well, that's the small print out of the way," he said, rising from the desk and walking around to examine my eye at close quarters with a small penlight. "I must say it's a most excellent rebuilding job around the socket. Doctor Silverman, I believe it was."

"I'll send him a bunch of flowers," I said.

"Her. Doctor Silverman is a woman," Doctor Jacob replied.

"Then I imagine she'll like them even more."

"I expect so yes," he agreed, clicking his little light off and slipping it back into his pocket. "Of course, there are alternatives to simple replica eyes, you know. Look here."

The doctor wheeled me over to a medical cabinet at the back of the room and pulled opened a thin drawer. Inside, several hundred eyes stared back at me although they were like no eyes I'd ever seen before.

"You can choose pretty much any design. Your eye socket will support anything in here," the doctor told me.

There were plain white orbs, pupils as black as night, green, red, silver and gold. Some featured yellow smiley faces, skulls & crossbones, circular target designs, stars & stripes, musical notes, dollar signs and Oriental symbols. Others had silhouettes of naked ladies on them, lightning bolts, male and female symbols, bar codes, grinning devil faces and, most sinister of all, Disney characters.

"What's that one?" I asked, squinting at one in particular.

"That's a washing machine window. Look, there are little socks and knickers going around inside. See?"

I recognised the undergarments tumbling around amongst soap suds and bubbles and cooed accordingly.

"I don't like it."

"No, no one seems to. No one's ordered that one yet," the doctor agreed.

"Do a lot of people order eyes then?"

"Oh yes. Affiliates are always losing them," he told me, making me remember Victor Soliman and his glass eye.

"What's the most popular design?"

"The skull & crossbones," he told me, picking it out and handing it to me for a closer look. "It's a classic design and Affiliates don't seem to mind other Affiliates having it. Beautiful graphics," he smiled, studying the eye through a magnification glasses.

"I don't want something that someone else has got," I told him.

"No, and lots of Affiliates feel that way too, so when we prescribe them a design, they have the choice of being allocated the copyright, which is theirs to keep for life – however long that lasts."

It was then that I noticed little red stickers next to fifteen or so of the designs, a couple of which I'd had my remaining eye on.

"The stickers?"

"Unfortunately yes. All those designs are spoken for I'm afraid," the doctor confirmed, with an apologetic cluck of the cheek.

Amongst those already taken was the vintage sniper scope view, with the little crosshairs and yardage numbering that I was going to have. It was one of the best in the drawer and reflected the image I wanted to convey – deadly, but retro.

"No sorry, someone's already got that one," the doctor shrugged.

And that wasn't all. The biological hazard symbol, which would have been my second choice, had been taken too. And the nuclear symbol. And the dollar sign. And the hand grenade.

Even bloody Mickey Mouse had been taken.

"Oh. I don't know then," I frowned. "Can I try a few in?"

"Certainly, but why don't you take this catalogue away with you and have a think about it?" the doctor suggested, handing me a samples catalogue, then a life-sized picture of a man's face with several pieces either missing or on flaps so that you could fold them back to see what he looked like with no eyes, ears, teeth or chin. "To help you decide," he smiled.

"Oh," I replied suddenly feeling I'd gotten off quite lightly, all things considered.

"Now, another thing to consider is accessories," the doctor said.

"Accessories?"

"Yes. Because the eyes don't have to simply be cosmetic eyes, you understand. They can also be tailored to specific requirements, if that's what you'd prefer," the doctor then said.

"What do you mean?" I asked.

"Well, they can conceal tools, or weapons if you wish. Here, look here," he said, moving along to open a second drawer. In here were more eyes, only these had realistic pupils and looked like eyes, only with simple lettering inscribed on each to indicate their purpose – A through X.

"Now, this one here's a little camera," the doctor said, picking up A and showing it to me. "It can take over a thousand digital images, depending on what resolution you set it at. It has two gigabytes of storage, a ten times magnification lens, autofocus, infrared and it's completely water-proof." The doctor handed me the eye and I turned it over in my hand. There were a couple of little rubber buttons in the back of it and a portal for inserting a cable, but other than that, it looked just like an eye.

"How do you take the pictures?" I asked.

The doctor smirked, almost embarrassed. "You blink. Here look, when you want to start taking pictures, you just give the front of the eye a firm push to turn it on," the doctor said, doing just that to prompt a little click. "Then you just blink away until your heart's content and it takes one image per blink until you turn it off. Then you just pop it out and download the pictures onto a laptop. Rather neat don't you think?"

"Very nifty," I agreed. "And this one?" I said pointing to B.

"Oh, same thing, only it's also got a video unit on it so it's got a bit less space for photos."

The doctor proceeded to talk me through all the various eyes, giving me a little tutorial on each until I was baffled by the array of choice. Here's what was available:

A – digital camera
B – digital camera with DV camera
C – USB flash drive with 64 GB capacity
D – audio recorder/player
E – radio transmitter/receiver

F – radio traffic scrambler
G – GPS tracking device
H – fold-out blade
I – multi-headed screwdriver
J – torchlight with 24-hours of battery life
K – compressed O2 (approx 3mins breathing)
L – phosphorous flare
M – smoke flare
N – one-shot mini-pistol (.22 calibre)
O – iPod
P – laser-cutter
Q – plastique charge (with detonator)
R – incapacitating gas pellet
S – empty watertight compartment (for smuggling)
T – cyanide powder (for self-use or foul play)
V – eye scanning skeleton key
W – cigarette lighter
X – ballpoint pen (blue, black and red)

The doctor spent a few minutes demonstrating each, and they all worked flawlessly, all except the ballpoint pen of course, which the doctor gave up on after two minutes of futile scribbling against the back of his notepad.

To demonstrate the plastique charge, the doctor led me across the hallway to the test range and handed me a pair of ear protectors and an eye guard.

"It comes with a five-second fuse and should be enough to blow open most locks," he said, pushing the soft eye into the keyhole of a chunky padlock that was shielded by a couple of sandbags. The Doctor then pulling on a little red cord that hung out of the eye where the optical nerve should've been and ushered me clear. We ducked behind a wall of sandbags twenty yards back and were rewarded with a thunderous crack as the charge detonated. Doctor Jacob looked suitably amused and on scouring the room showed me what was left of the lock. Not much.

"It won't get you into a safe but it will get you out of a cell," he summed up.

The gas pellet was likewise as effective, filling the room with a noxious clear vapour that comatosed the doctor's canary in under five seconds.

"He'll be fine. He's been through it a few times," the Doctor assured me.

And besides all the weapons and designs, I also had the choice of a stationary eye or a magnetically responsive motorised eye that would match the movement of my right eye.

"It's a lot to think about," I confessed.

"Well, with the basic package we offer you five eyes. One, a purely cosmetic dress eye with watertight compartment and four others which feature whichever accessories you'd like, either of a design of your choice or replicas of your healthy eye."

"Oh, that's quite good," I said, no longer feeling quite so backed into a decision. "Well, I'll have a look through the brochure and get back to you. Thank you, doctor."

"You're welcome, my boy. And if that sniper scope view design becomes available again, I'll let you know," he replied.

"That would be great."

Nurse Parker re-entered after a quick fingering of the doctor's buzzer and invited me to retake my wheelchair for the ride back to my room.

"Remember Mr Jones," Doctor Jacob said, just before I reached the door. "Look after your new eyes and they'll look after you."

I nodded my appreciation and was swept from the room by Nurse Parker, already wondering if I shouldn't just throw it all in and upgrade my arms and legs while I was here.

15. A BLINDING NIGHT'S SKY

I LOOKED OUT across a crystal blue sea and watched the gulls circle and squawk above the crashing waves. I'd been recuperating here just short of six weeks and my strength and confidence had come back to me a little more each day. The surroundings had helped, naturally. It wasn't an accident that The Agency had one of its primary trauma hospitals in such an idyllic location. Your heart couldn't help but soar at the sun, the sea and the scenery. A little oasis of tropical paradise – that's what this was. Paradise. The guys in here had been to hell and back, seen and done things no man should be burdened with, and suffered injuries they had no right to survive. Yet here we all were, in heaven.

And hell's a little easier to forget when heaven's so beautiful.

I returned my healthy eye to the John Wyndham on my lap and soaked up a few more words. *The Day of the Triffids*. I'm not normally into science fiction – space ships, aliens, foreign worlds and "what is this thing you call kissing, Captain?" I find it all a bit of a yawn. Perhaps it's because I have trouble relating to it. Spaceships. Other worlds. Runaway robots. The situations and settings feel too artificial to me. But then again, I haven't read that much sci-fi in my time, especially "quality sci-fi", so maybe I wasn't giving the genre a fair shout. Perhaps I should take the plunge and get an Isaac Asimov or a Robert A. Heinlein as my next book? But then again why should I if I didn't enjoy sci-fi? There were thousands of books out there. Maybe millions even. I could read a book a day for the rest of my life and never have to worry about sci-fi.

If I'd still been with Linda, and if she'd been here with me today, she would've made me read an Isaac Asimov next. She wasn't into sci-fi either, she just liked making me do whatever I didn't want to do. It was the same with everything; food, clothing, movies or haircuts: if I hated it, didn't suit it or was allergic to it, she'd make me wear it, watch it or eat it. Naturally, she claimed she did these things to help me broaden my horizons, but really she just liked making me do the things I didn't want to do. And each time she got her own way she'd see it as a vindication of her own righteousness. And every time she didn't, she'd see it as a confirmation of my stubbornness and turn it into a fight about my drinking.

I looked out at the sea again and let a warm breeze carry these thoughts away before returning to my book.

As it happened I was quite enjoying *The Day of the Triffids*. It was the sort of sci-fi I could live with: fantastical and a bit of a stretch, but still within the realms of my imagination. Most of it was set in London or on the South Downs, where I lived, which was a big help. And the odd walking vegetable asides, there was nothing too implausible about the story. The circumstances were incredible I'll grant you, but the ways in which the characters analysed and reacted to their situations were always fair and believable.

Basically, this is what happens. Somewhere in the

future (and bearing in mind this book was published in 1951, so the future in question is the early 1960s) scientists develop an extraordinary plant whose oils are radically superior to anything on the market. This has global implications as far as world hunger, engineering, trade and peace are concerned, so you'd think everyone would be happy about it, wouldn't you? Unfortunately, there's a downside. The Triffids are deadly meat-eating plants that can walk around on their roots and kill people with a single flick of their stingers. But that's okay, because they are only plants, after all, not poisonous elephants, so they're kept in check, behind electric fences and farmed by experts for their oils. Then one evening, a spectacular meteor shower lights up the night's sky across the entire globe. Everyone rushes to watch it, only to wake up the next morning blind. Only a handful of people escape, our hero Bill Masen being one of them, because he'd been in hospital with his eyes bandaged up (like all good heroes have from time to time) so he missed the cosmic light show, which is lucky for him.

Things are naturally chaotic at first, with whole populations crying out for help in the darkness, and the sighted do what they can for the blind, but soon realise the situation's utterly hopeless. There are simply too many blind to look after, feed and care for, and too few sighted. They can't save everyone and disease and death are soon filling the cities, so the few sighted survivors take to the countryside and start afresh.

The Triffids don't actually come into it very much at first. Bill and his chums have a hundred and one other things to worry about in the early chapters, but as the book goes on, and the Triffids escape their captivity and start feeding like crazy on the bumbling blind.

Anyway, like I said, the situation's a bit contrived, but the characters are very plausible. Wyndham himself called his books "logical sci-fi" and usually made his central characters sensible men or women who used logic and reason to negotiate their way through extraordinary circumstances.

I liked this. And because Wyndham didn't feel the need to keep sending his characters out in the middle of the night in open-topped cars with empty fuel tanks simply because no one had been stung in a while, it made the whole story more palatable. I just wished half the blokes who hired us made some of the same decisions.

As a lifelong proponent of "common sense", I figured Bill might like this book too, so I made a mental note to recommend it to him when I got back to Sussex and dipped my eye into the next paragraph.

"Ah Mr Jones, here you are," a sweet American voice declared from across the lawn. Nurse Parker strode towards me with a little tray of drugs and handed me a cup of tablets.

"Margarita time already," I said, knocking them back and chasing them down with a paper cup of water. "Any chance of a beer?"

"Any chance of one-forty over eighty?" she replied, to the amusement of the assorted disabled villains lounging nearby.

"You're leaving us soon I hear."

"End of the week they say," I confirmed.

"Well, take care out there, Mr Jones. We do good work, but we don't do miracles."

"I will," I promised, which wasn't so much a lie, more an accepted response to such an undeliverable request.

Nurse Parker looked at the book in my lap. "You too, huh? Why is everyone reading that same book?"

"Everyone?" I said.

"Well, everyone here. Mr Collins and Mr Mihailov were reading it yesterday, or the day before," Nurse Parker reckoned. "And I saw Mr Hu with it last week."

"Well, you know how it is, one guy sees another reading a book and before you know it we're all reading it. We're a bunch of sheep really don't you know?"

"Clearly," Nurse Parker agreed, unsure what to make of the explanation and even less so the phenomenon. She shrugged the concern from her shoulders and made do with telling me that I shouldn't read for too long as I was putting a strain on my eye, so I switched my eye patch between eyes and asked her if that made her happier.

"Much," she replied with a giggle, then went about her drug peddling.

I returned the patch to its rightful eye and watched Nurse Parker go, before glancing over at Mr Collins relaxing in the shade of the palms. He seemed unfazed to have had his name mentioned by Nurse Parker and simply reached for his lemonade. The tall glass instantly shattered between his Tungsten fingers, once again making everyone laugh.

"Bollocks!" Mr Collins growled, his third such accident in as many days. "Fucking hand."

Well, we were all having trouble adjusting to our new accessories.

After another hour I came to the end of the book and slowed up my reading pace to soak in the last few words until the story finally gave way to blank paper. The last page of a book is like that for me. It's a curiously affecting experience, particularly if I've enjoyed the book, as I had with this one. I always made sure I read every single word to prolong the experience; the biography, the acknowledgements, the "also published by…" and even the legal guffins, probably because I didn't want it to be over. I didn't want to let go. For me, the end of a book is like the end of a journey, or like saying good-bye to an old friend whose company you'd particularly enjoyed. And when that final page was turned and you closed that book for the last time, all you were left with were the memories. And possibly a shit movie if they made one. Occasionally I'd turn back to the beginning and reread the first couple of pages, just to remind myself of where it had all begun, but it's ultimately a futile exercise because you can never retrace footsteps of discovery. You can only ever trample over them.

I closed the book, ran a grateful eye over the cover one last time, then slipped my feet into my slippers below the deck chair.

The sun was now dipping into the west, casting shadows across the lawn and freshening the breeze. Most of the guys had gone inside for dinner, or treatment, or for rest. Only Mr Gerber remained, his feet in his slippers, despite his slippers being nowhere near the rest of his body.

"Are you finished now, Mr Jones?" Mr Gerber asked, between breaths, as he back stroked lengths of the pool with his remaining limbs.

"Almost," I replied with a nod, setting the book down on the table at the end of the row from his, then heading off to the comm-link office. In the reflection of the glass door, I saw Mr Gerber look about then haul himself out of the water and walk on the flattened palms of his hands towards where I'd left *The Day of the Triffids*. Nurse Parker had been right when she'd said that she'd seen Mr Collins and Mr Mihailov reading it on previous days, and Mr Hu reading it last week. We'd only had one copy between us, so we'd been taking it in turns to read. It worked out cheaper that way.

It also made it easier to disguise the fact that we were part of a book club.

Surprisingly, no one who'd joined us so far had questioned the need to do things this way. I suppose we were all from covert backgrounds, so why shouldn't we? Secrecy was kind of habit-forming.

I watched Mr Gerber haul himself up into the deck chair next to where I'd made the drop and wipe his hair and body with his towel, before reaching for the book. I envied Mr Gerber for the journey he was about to take and the characters he was about to meet. Bill Masen, Josella Playton, Will Coker and of course, those terrible implacable Triffids, forever wandering the Sussex Downs and laying siege to the last few pockets of humanity. He was in for a real treat.

Still, I wasn't quite done with them yet and entered the ice-cold comm-link office through the tinted glass doors.

Mr Martin was on duty and turned to greet me when I entered.

"Email?" he asked.

"Internet," I replied.

He tapped a few keys on his keyboard while I filled out the access form and topped it off with an inky thumbprint.

"Let me see," he instructed once I'd cleaned my thumb. He studied it for a moment, pricking my thumb to draw blood to ensure I wasn't wearing a latex fingerprint, then asked me what machine I wanted. "Do you require privacy?"

"Will I get it?" I almost laughed.

"What I mean is, do you want a booth or are you okay with one of the table monitors?"

I looked around the empty comm-link office, then back at Mr Martin.

"Give me a booth."

Mr Martin managed to hide most of his smirk while he tapped a few more keys then told me to take the first booth on the left. I closed the door behind me and settled in front of the machine as it clicked and whirled to life.

I opened up the internet and searched a few sites: big boobs, girl-on-girl, anal sluts, that sort of thing, before selecting something suitably eye-popping for Mr Martin to get distracted by while he monitored my surfing from his own computer. It was rumoured that he had a penchant for interracial sex, particularly two or more big black gang-bangers ambushing a slender young white girl, which many of us thought was something of a cypher into Mr Martin's own desires seeing as he was neither big nor black.

I flipped my eye patch up, dug my fingers into my socket and popped my eye out into my hand. I gave it a quick wipe, then extended the jack and slotted it into the USB portal of the machine.

A little window opened up in the corner of my screen and piggybacked buttfuckers.org to our own website. This window didn't appear on Mr Martin's computer and what's more, no trace of it would remain once I'd pulled the scrambler. You could argue that these precautions were a tad OTT for a bunch of swotty book worms and you'd probably be right, but the fact remained that ours was an affiliation outside of the normal bounds of Affiliating and as such, it would be regarded with suspicion if The Agency or any of our employers were to find out about it.

Eight books had already been posted, with usernames and scores beside each. *The Day of the Triffids* had been read by sixteen guys so far, only seven of which were residents of this hospital. The others were Mr Smith over in Tajikistan (username: *Fail-Safe*), who'd given it a four, stating the fact that he thought it had drifted a little towards the end. Someone called *Cyber Guy*, also on the Tajikistan job, who'd given it a three; *Mr Mumbo* in Sri Lanka, who'd given it a four; *Captain Electric* in Belize, who'd given it a four; *Sergeant Ardent* also in Belize, who'd given it a five; *Snowman*, *Ice Man* and *Snow Flake*, all of whom were somewhere inside the Arctic Circle, who'd given it a four, a four and a five respectively, and *The Rt Honourable Baron Bean Boner* in Swindon, who'd given it a two. Who'd invited that guy to join?

This, together with my fellow patients' scores, gave *The Day of the Triffids* an overall score of 3.69 (rounded up to two decimal places). I thought this was a bit low so I logged on using my username (*Book Mark*) and gave it a five, bringing its average up to 3.76. If I'd been the first reader to score this book, I might well have given it a four myself, as a five is a big ask for any book, but the lads' harsher scoring of a book I'd really enjoyed had influenced my final decision causing me to weigh in with a maximum to correct the perceived wrong. I wondered if the others had been doing this too. And if so, what the book would have scored had we all voted with our conscience.

I made up my mind to have a word with Mr Alekseev after dinner. Mr Alekseev (username: *Tech Boy*) had designed and encrypted the site to my specifications from this very seat while recuperating from reconstructive facial surgery, so I figured I'd ask him if he knew of some way of fixing it so that each user couldn't see a book's overall score until they'd submitted their own. Then again, that would be a bit annoying, slogging your way through a pile of utter donkey shite just because it had been on our site, only to discover that everyone else had thought so too. It kind of undermined our powers of recommendation.

I wracked my brains a little longer as to the

problem before I was interrupted by a knock on the door.

"Mr Jones, the doctor would like to see you if you have a minute. We have the rest of your eyes for you to try."

It was Nurse Parker.

I pulled my eye from the back of the computer, erasing the book club window, then folded the USB jack into the orb and pushed it back into my eye socket.

"Does he want to see me right now?" I asked, opening the door and sheepishly fixing Nurse Parker with my good eye.

She glanced at the ongoing porn on my screen and framed her disapproval with a stare.

"If you're not too busy," she frowned.

I clicked the computer off then stood, remembering to theatrically retie my pyjama cord.

"Lead on," I invited.

"Like I say, Mr Jones, you only got one good eye left," Nurse Parker advised. "Go easy on it."

16. BETTER OFF DEAD

"FIRE!"

The first three opened up with their sub-machine guns, obliterating the targets to their cores. I let off a volley of automatic fire over their heads, warning them onto their bellies as Mr Herbert threw stun grenades into the mix.

"Move it!" I yelled. "Pick up the pace!"

They shuffled forward, splattered with dirt and peppered with that stinging dust that hits you when a flash-bang explodes nearby, but all of them made it to the wall.

"Get your arses moving, maggots!" I offered by way of encouragement.

I fired another burst of AK fire over their heads as they took to the ropes, then timed their splits on my stopwatch, stopping only when they fell out of my line of sight, and a whoosh from Mr Sato's flamethrower signalled he had them now.

"Next three!" I ordered, and three more cherries took to the target range and obliterated three fresh paper targets with their SMGs.

I'd been home only two weeks when I'd got the call. Was I available to help vet and train a new batch of recruits for The Agency? Well, blimey, I was so potless I would have gone on *Celebrity Big Brother* had I been asked to, so I jumped at the chance and a week later found myself in an enormous underground cavern on a private island just off the West Coast of Scotland, firing live rounds at The Agency's latest crop of temps.

"Get your arses moving!"

God this took me back. It only seemed like last week that I'd been here myself, face down in the mud, bullets whizzing past my head, methane filling my pants, wondering what the fuck I'd let myself in for. And those instructors! Just where the hell had they got them from? As a typical cocky twenty-something brain donor, I'd always thought of myself as Rambo's harder brother, but they'd scared the hell out of me. Particularly when they let that kid in my intake fall into the grinder instead of hitting the emergency stop button when it had become clear ropes weren't his strong suit.

"We won't be there to hit stop buttons when you're operational," our grizzled old veteran had growled at us afterwards, which had been a fair point, though one that hardly made it up to the pile of mince lying under the grinder who, just a few minutes earlier, had been worried about what they might say if we didn't finish the course in the allotted time.

And now I was one of them; seasoned, grizzled and decorated with the scars of a dozen different campaigns. I'd come full circle. Just as Bill had before me – which, of course, was where I'd met him. At least, it's where I'd got to know him. He'd been our instructor. Where I'd actually met him had been the same place the guys running around in front of me had met their various Agency recruiters – prison.

That's where The Agency does its recruiting. That's where it gets its guys from. Although it's not enough just to be a prisoner, you have to be a lifer –

and a lifer with a minimum tariff of at least twenty years. The Agency likes to know it can dump you right back in the hole it rescued you from should you ever think to question their terms.

It was the insurance we all had hanging over our heads. Me, Bill, Mr Sato, Mr Smith, all of us; we were all lifers, from far and wide.

Like most of the guys on the ticket, my sentence had been handed down for murder. And not just any ordinary murder either, but the murder of a policeman no less. Of course, it hadn't mattered that I hadn't known he was a policeman at the time. He'd been in plain clothes and hadn't identified himself properly, so I'd assumed he was one of John Broad's men come to rap my knuckles for ripping off his main supplier. I'd been wrong, although I hadn't known it until half a dozen uniforms piled in behind the unfortunate Sergeant Hopkirk, who by this time was sporting a rather fetching steak knife handle.

Well, neither his colleagues nor the judge felt in the mood to show me any leniency and after I got out of the hospital, I was bunged into a cell and left to rot for the next thirty years — at least.

And that's where I stayed, slowly doing my porridge, keeping myself fit so that I'd at least be able to have one last dance when they finally released me, and reading everything I could lay my hands on.

Then, after four years, a craggy old soak came to visit me. He'd introduced himself as Bill and asked me if I'd be interested in being reborn. He offered me a new life, a renewed hope and a way out of my confines. This was how he'd phrased it too, the big comedian, so naturally I'd assumed he'd been fixing to introduce me to his pal Jesus and sell me that whole Amway of hope.

But actually, as you know by now, he'd meant a proper new life. And proper renewed hope. And a proper way out of my actual confines.

My life as I knew it was forfeit. And there was nothing I, nor anyone else, could do about that. But there was a new life out there for me if I wanted it. It would be dangerous, merciless and in all likelihood short. But I'd see spectacular things. Be part of momentous events. And risk all for unimaginable rewards.

If I'd wanted it.

All I had to do was kill myself.

So that's what I did. Six weeks after Bill's visit, I knotted my bedsheets together and hanged myself from the window of my cell. The screws found me thirty minutes later and rushed me to the medical unit but it was too late, I was already dead. Asphyxiation caused by a ligature to the neck. That's what was written on my Death Certificate. And as I had no immediate family nor next of kin, my body was collected by a local undertaker twenty-four hours later where it was taken to an airfield just outside Durham and flown by Lynx AH.9 Battlefield helicopter to a very private hospital in the Scottish highlands and handed over to a team of specialists, who revived me, repaired the damage and handed me back my life.

Of course, I hadn't really been dead. I'd been in a deep deep all-but dead coma and shut down so completely that even an autopsy wouldn't have been able to ascertain if I'd still been alive – unlikely after an autopsy. But autopsies rarely looked into prison hangings. Bill had supplied the drugs. All I'd had to do was take them and hang myself. My coma would protect me for up to forty-eight hours until The Agency could get to me.

And if they didn't get to me on time?

"No problem," Bill had assured me. "There's a complaint procedure in case of such events but in all the time The Agency's been operating, it's never had a single action filed against it."

Like I said, he was a fucking comedian.

It took my body three months to recover but when it had, I was fed, drilled, trained and prepared, before being shipped off to East Timor to help Connaughtard Cottletrophff destroy the wheat crop of Australia, for somewhat megalomaniacal reason. That first signing on payment had settled my account with The Agency. It was also the first time I'd ever encountered Jack Tempest. And also the first time I'd ever seen someone drown in a vat of grain – poor old Connaughtard.

When I was extracted by The Agency, I was given a new identity – my current one as it happens – with all the accompanying documents; birth certificate, driving licence, passport, even a new National Insurance number. One job and I was a living, breathing free man all over again. My past had been erased. My time served. My debts repaid. No one was looking for me. And no one would. As long as I kept a low profile and avoided my old stamping grounds of course. That life was over for me. The Agency made that very clear. This was an entirely new life. And if I wanted to keep it, I had to let the old one go completely. That had been the deal. That was the price we all paid to be reborn.

So Bill took me in and put me up. We'd been in East Timor together and I'd thrown him on to the evac chopper after he'd been shot, so he'd taken me under his wing to repay me for saving his life, providing me with a sofa to sleep on and even introducing me to his family.

And Linda.

Oh well, that's enough disaster stories for one day. Back to shooting the new recruits.

"Son of a bitch!" Captain Bolaji swore as I blasted the masonry around the rope he was clambering, causing him to fall off again.

"Get up that rope you black bastard!" I shouted, fully aware that this sort of language didn't go down at all well in the workplace these days, but equally aware that while sticks and stones could break one's bones, grinders would also ruin your favourite shirt.

Captain Bolaji glared at me with contempt, then hurled himself at the rope and climbed hand over fist as I peppered the surrounding wall with the rest of my banana clip, chuckling to myself and grinning with satisfaction when he fell over the top and encountered Mr Sato's flamethrower.

"Priceless," I sighed.

Actually, not all new recruits had to be lifers. A few exceptions were made for former soldiers or time-served mercenaries with the right experience. Captain Bolaji had saved my life. So in return, The Agency door had been cracked open for him. A potentially dangerous situation for Captain Bolaji because there was no prison he could be returned to if things didn't work out; just the quandary of what to do with the lone African gunman who knew all about our secret organisation but who didn't want to be part of it any more.

Hmm, yeah, tricky one. No lawyers required I suspect.

"Last three," I shouted, and the last three recruits took to the range while I loaded a fresh magazine and reset my watch. "Move it!"

*

There were around thirty new recruits in all: four from Britain, six from the Continent, six from the States and thirteen from Asia. That left just Captain Bolaji sticking out like the sore thumb. Strangely, there weren't many Africans Affiliates. I'd only ever encountered one other in all my time at The Agency. I don't know why this should be. The Agency certainly wasn't prejudiced. After all, one man's money was just as good as another's. No, if I'd had to guess I would've said that most Africans didn't need to look that far afield for trouble. There were plenty of wars and local conflicts to interest its young men, so why travel?

Not that we were soldiers. Not really.

No, we were criminals, plain and simple. Straight down the line and no pretence at anything else. We were criminals, out to make a buck and feather our nests with all the gaudy trappings – ie: drink, drugs, women and leopard skin furniture.

And I think it was this, more than race or religion that was the hardest thing for Captain Bolaji to deal with when it came to fitting in. He didn't vocalise his doubts, that would've been silly, but I recognised the inner conflict that was raging away behind his eyes. See, when we'd been part of the Special Army, he'd been an ideological soldier. He'd genuinely believed in the cause and in particular His Most Excellent Majesty, which is why he'd been so easy to dupe. But now, here he was in amongst the dupers, or at least their kind, and it was a hard thing for him to reconcile.

I stared down at Captain Bolaji a couple of hours later in the boiler room and wondered if I'd been right to trust him. Then again, had I been right to trust anyone? There were two others with us; rock-solid recruits who'd stay the course and no doubt turn Affiliates if they survived their first operation. But would they be able to keep their mouths shut about the things that really mattered?

Who knew?

"The first rule about book club is you don't talk about book club," I told my three new recruits. "The second rule about book club is you don't talk about book club!" These were essentially the same rules, I'll admit, but I was having trouble making up the ten and Chuck Palahniuk had gotten away with it so I figured I could too.

Captain Bolaji crumpled his eyebrows and frowned.

"The third rule; no names – post usernames only when you're on-line. The fourth rule is no chit chat.

We're all copied into the same forum so no boring banter about West Ham's chances next season thinking we're all going to find it fascinating because we're not – book talk only. The fifth rule is no operational details. You can post your location, but not what you're doing there or who you're working for," I told them, pacing backwards and forwards in front of the boiler. "If you're really concerned about the safety of other book club members, you can, in extreme circumstances, recommend we avoid certain parts of the world in the coming months."

"Like what?" Mr Nikitin (username: *Smoker*) asked.

"Like, for example, you might post up something like; 'crikey, have you seen how much hotels charge in Washington these days? I wouldn't go there if I were you – especially not next April,' that sort of thing. You know, subtle."

Mr Nikitin nodded to demonstrate he understood. Captain Bolaji, who still hadn't chosen his username yet, just frowned some more.

"The sixth rule is no posting your own books. You are only allowed to read the books that are officially nominated. If you want to be a loose cannon, join a library. If you want to nominate a book, wait your turn and earn your credits. The seventh rule; you have to finish a book before you can comment on it. That's every single page. It doesn't matter if it's boring. If you want to give it a kicking, you have to finish it. The eighth rule is no giving away the endings. We're all reading the same books here, but not necessarily at the same time, so don't go spoiling the endings by boasting how you could see the big twist coming from a mile off or that they all did it, let us find that out for ourselves. The ninth rule is voting; if you read a book, you have to vote on it. No excuses. No abstaining. Marks out of five, one being the lowest, five the highest…"

"Well, obviously," Mr MacDonald (username: *Small Fry*) said. "I mean, who'd do it the other way around?"

"You'd be surprised," I replied. "And no favouritism. You're voting for the book, not your boyfriend's recommendation. There are no prizes for having nominated the most popular book."

"I'm not gay," Mr Nikitin objected, interrupting my flow.

"What?"

"I'm not gay."

"What's that got to do with anything?"

"You said we can't vote for our boyfriend's nomination. I don't have a boyfriend. I have girlfriends. But not at the moment," said Mr Nikitin, who The Agency had busted out of Yekaterinaburg Prison Camp a month earlier.

"I didn't mean literally. I take it you're not an actual maggot either, it was just a euphemism. You know, an insult?"

"Oh," he blinked. As time was of the essence and as Mr Nikitin didn't come across as someone who enjoyed the rough and tumble of blokey banter, I decided to skip straight to the end of the meeting.

"Tenth and final rule of book club is," I told the guys, pausing to make sure I had their total attention, "No chick-lit."

"What's chick-lick?" Mr Bolaji obviously wanted to know.

"Here are your scramblers," I said, handing out USB sticks disguised as .38 hollow tip specials. Most of the covert equipment Affiliates used on jobs was weaponry disguised as household objects, yet the equipment we used in book club was the exact opposite. I hoped the irony wasn't lost on them.

"Don't lose them. They're encrypted with your usernames and IDs, so you'll need them to post your scores or nominate your books," I told them.

"What happens if you put them in a gun and fire them?" Mr MacDonald asked.

"They produce an image of a computer screen that you'll be able to see if you look up the barrel. It's got pull-down menus and everything and you can scroll through them by pulling on the trigger repeatedly."

"Really?" Mr MacDonald cooed.

"No, not really. You'll just break the USB and probably blow your own head off, but do give it a go if you want because I might be wrong."

"I was only asking."

"Okay, so you all understand the rules and the need for complete secrecy?"

They did. Or at least, they said they did, which were two subtly different things, but indistinguishable from each other without the benefit of crocodile clips and a car battery.

"Alright then," I told them with a final nod of approval. "Welcome to book club."

17. THE GIRL WITH SPYDERCO HEELS

I DON'T KNOW what it is with right-hand men but for some reason, they love to fight everyone – even their own men. They're like small-town bar-room brawlers. They strut about the place, eyeballing anyone who looks at them and beating their chests at the merest inkling of disrespect – which again, just like small-town bar-room brawlers, they see everywhere.

Zillion Silverfish had a guy like that; five feet tall, six feet wide, fists like bazookas and the sense of humour of a hungover elephant. He used to have this stupid cowboy type boot-lace necktie too that he'd whip off and throw at people whenever it wasn't his birthday. If he got them right, which he did more often than not, it would wrap around their necks like mini boleadoras and choke them in seconds.

What was his name? Oh yes, that was it, Mr Karlssen.

"Mr Karlssen, show the gentleman out," Silverfish would say with a knowing smirk, then next thing you'd know – *whoosh*, the poor unsuspecting fella would be on the floor turning purple. Which would have been fair enough. I mean anything work-related, but Mr Karlssen couldn't keep it to himself and I personally had to rescue several of my colleagues from a stifling death just because they'd either let Jack Tempest get away or had eaten the last strawberry yoghurt in the canteen. Of course, Silverfish should've kept him in check but he never said a word, not even after Mr Karlssen killed that little Argentinean lad who'd made the mistake of wafting a hand in front of his nose when he'd tried entering the toilet just as Mr Karlssen was leaving. For five minutes he'd lain there before anyone had been allowed to go to him, but Mr Karlssen didn't get so much as a fiver docked from his pay packet.

Oh well, what goes around comes around, as they say, and while it's well documented how Silverfish met his maker handcuffed to that Patriot missile, it's less well known how his lapdog choked on his own particular bone. Obviously, it had been at the hands of his own tie – ironic deaths being harder to avoid in this game than the Child Support Agency. Jack Tempest had caught it with that hat stand that Mr Karlssen had bought for his Stetsons and twirled it around like a cheerleader's baton and thrown it straight back at him, scoring an unbelievable bull's-eye first time. It had been a hell of a shot. I personally couldn't believe it. I mean, of all the things to be good at! Tempest must've had one of those neckties himself (and presumably a similar make of hat stand) because I couldn't see how he could've possibly made a shot like that without months of practise. Still, that's Jack Tempest for you. And he wonders why everyone hates him.

Anyway, that had been the official version of Mr Karlssen's death although it hadn't actually been the end of him, because Tempest had ducked out to go after Silverfish while Mr Karlssen had still been struggling. Under normal circumstance one of us might have come to his aid but no one lifted a finger to save him. Oh we'd all been there, and close enough to untwine the boleadoras, but no one felt so inclined, not after all we'd endured at his hands, so we folded our arms, passed around the fags and watched him turn several shades of scarlet as he choked on this ultimate betrayal.

Mr Gonzales made sure with a bullet to the head – which is what Tempest should've done – then rejoined the battle. Personally, I decided to leave it when I saw all those airborne troops parachuting in and I got as far as Panama before The Agency had to pick me up once more.

So I'd had my fair share of run-ins with right-hand men but none, not even Mr Karlssen, compared with Sun Dju, who was the fruitiest bird I'd ever known – in every sense of the word.

I'd not crossed her path before but she'd come to the island just as we were completing the cherries' basic training. She'd been accompanying her boss, Xian Xe Xu, who liked to be called X^3 – which would've been okay had we been his Facebook friends but which created problems when we'd had to address him verbally. No one knew what to call him. X cubed? X to the power of three? Triple X? Nine X? I mean, seriously, what's your name mate? In the event, most of us had simply played it safe and called him "sir" to his face and "that X bloke" behind his back, which seemed to do the trick.

But I was talking about Sun Dju, wasn't I?

The first time I laid eyes on her was in the unarmed combat gymnasium. All the cherries were sat around a big crash mat while Mr Sato walked them through a few basic moves – knocking away a dagger, throwing someone over your shoulder, holding your hand in front of your face to stop someone poking you in both eyes with two fingers, that sort of thing. Easy enough and occasionally even useful, but hardly kung fu, which was when I noticed Sun Dju skulking around behind us in that painfully provocative way I'd seen too many times before.

X^3 was with her, smiling to himself because he knew what was coming, while I was desperately trying to avoid both of their eyes and keeping my fingers crossed that everyone else did the same.

Some hope. See, Sun Dju was one hell of a saucy bit of crumpet; six feet tall, as slender as a pack of Camels and peachy in all the best places. She also wore a red figure-hugging leather one-piece suit that was so tight you could make out what she had for breakfast. Yesterday.

I swapped my eye patch across from my bad eye to my good and carried on making out like I was monitoring the combat, hoping someone would give me a nudge when we broke for coffee. Big mistake. See, while I could no longer be tempted to gawp at her delicious candy wrappings, I could no longer look away either when she wandered past, then back again, stepping up in her six-inch stiletto heels to ask what I was staring at. "You wanna fuck or fight me?"

When nobody answered I peeled my eye patch back to see everyone in the gymnasium suddenly staring at me.

"You what?"

Sun Dju's face contorted into a deadly snarl and

before I had a chance to explain my negligence, her utility belt hit the floor and her long painted nails were beckoning me onto the crash mat.

Mr Sato and Mr Nikitin bowed at each other then quickly fled the square to make room and all too quickly I had no place left to go – except the mat. It didn't matter that I didn't want to fight or fuck Sun Dju – at least, not without the benefit of shin pads and a bottle of Rohypnol – I suddenly had no choice. As one of the combat instructors at the institution, I was expected to rise to any challenge. By the cherries, by my fellow instructor and by the Agency staff, who were now regarding me with raised eyebrows. See, X^3 was hiring. And it seriously wouldn't do to have members of the organisation they were hiring from chickening out and feigning back problems when challenged to a fight.

I slid the patch back across to my face, slipped my 'eye.Pod out' and dropped it into one of my shoes when I kicked them off at the edge of the mat.

Captain Bolaji looked up at me, as if to ask if I knew what I was doing, but unfortunately, I did. And it didn't make the slightest bit of difference. However, I did have one thing going in my favour. And that was that everyone to a man knew I was about to get the shit kicked out of me, including The Agency's senior staff (it's a done deal when one of these fruit-loops decides to prove themselves – you might as well kick your own head in and save them the trouble), so I didn't have the weight of expectation on my shoulders. Just the problem of getting in there, getting hit and going down as quickly and as believably as possible, before she could do any real damage.

She shaped up before me on the mat.

I was savvy enough to know not to bow and, sure enough, one of her boots missed my head by millimetres as she aimed a vicious spin-kick into my coconut.

"Fucking cheating bitch…" I spluttered falling back on my arse and scrambling away to the peels of evil Mandarin laughter. It was then that I also noticed she'd kept her heels on, only the sheaths of her stilettos were now missing, exposing two glistening six-inch blades to slice the crash mat to pieces.

Well now, I hummed, that hadn't been in the brochure.

She came at me fast, kicking and spinning furiously, throwing cartwheels and splits as she attempted to stab me with her ferocious footwear. I ran around in circles at first, backwards and forwards and from side to side trying to put as much distance between myself and Sun Dju's killer heels. But when I felt them rake the backs of my calves and spiral upwards into my vulnerable buttocks, I realised I was setting myself up to be sliced little and often, until the weight of my wounds slowed me down and allowed her to land the big one, so after several more seconds of scrambling, I finally turned to face her.

Sun Dju saw my pained and desperate expression and cackled accordingly.

The cherries and staff lapped it all in too, transfixed by the spectacle, but guarded enough not to display their excitement lest they be next. Captain

Bolaji gawked on with morbid disquiet, too fearful to look, too excited to blink. I was one karate kick from the mortuary.

Sun Dju finally dropped the laughter and came at me one last time, but far from fleeing, this time I darted straight at her, throwing myself between her whirling legs and engaging her at close-quarters. I made it with fractions of seconds to spare and planted a thrusting forehead into the epicentre of her surprise with as much force as I could muster. The resultant crunch almost made me sick, so appalling was the jarring thunk, and I staggered away with stars popping in my head and fell into the front row of cherries immediately behind me.

Still, if I think I'd caught it badly, this was nothing compared to Sun Dju, who was flat on her back and looking as if a grenade had just gone off in her face. Nose, mouth, teeth and eyes, they were all still in there somewhere, but now concealed beneath the geyser of blood.

"I think you got her there, Mr Jones," one of my cherries pointed out helpfully.

"What have you done? What have you done?" X^3 hollered, rushing to his comatosed lieutenant's aid and bundling her up in his arms. The Agency seniors were also looking at me in displeasure, somewhat stunned by such an unprecedented turn of events and wondering where this left their lucrative supply contract. Well, I might've proved myself but I'd also just undermined X^3 and Sun Dju's authority in front of a batch of potential recruits. Not a good thing if you're hoping to rule with an iron fist and a steel heel.

"What have you done?" X³ demanded again, but Captain Bolaji and a couple of the other cherries kept him at bay until I could wobble to my feet.

"She made me an offer," I eventually told him, X³'s face now just inches from mine. "Well, there's my reply. Though if you don't mind I think I'll forgo the fuck if you don't mind, I'm not really feeling up to it any more," I groaned, hobbling off towards the medical bay.

X³ continued to piss and moan in my wake, calling me an "ant" to his "Colossus", the usual stuff, but his protestations were now only falling on deaf ears when The Agency's senior staff reminded him where he was and who'd picked the fight in the first place. They eventually sent him packing in humiliation by asking the question that was dying to be asked; that was if he and his hard-boiled lieutenant couldn't even defeat a mere "ant" like me, what chance did they have against Jack Tempest of the British Secret Service?

18. LICENCE TO LITERATE

I WAS HAULED over the coals the next day for upsetting the applecart, but not too severely because nobody could really blame me for trying to stay in one piece, no matter how much it had let the team down. Still, I'd still cost The Agency a contract and could've potentially frightened away future business if word got around that they had some schizoid instructor who didn't know his place, so they returned my status to operational and sent me packing too.

It was a shame because I'd been enjoying my time on the island and, what's more, I'd been earning. Not a lot, but it had been a regular wage and the odd fighty bitch asides, the only serious danger I'd experienced was when I'd come perilously close to losing my nominating rights following some scandalously low scores for *The Kenneth Williams Diaries* which, while it had admittedly been overly-long and soul-sappingly tedious in large chunks, had thrown up a few interesting insights. It didn't matter though, a new rule was collectively voted for banning all books over five-hundred pages in length and anything even remotely *Carry-On* related.

I arrived back in Petworth later that night and wondered where I went from here.

*

I dropped by and saw Bill in Arundel after a couple of days, and was able to pay him back a couple of grand, which pleased Bill no end, but infuriated Marjorie beyond all volume control. I also took Bill for a pint and told him all about my recent adventures; my African excursions, my time in the West Indies, my stint as an instructor and even about book club.

Of all the things I talked about, the crocodiles, the nuclear blast, the run-in with Sun Dju, it was my book club that most unsettled Bill.

"They worry people they do," he said, sitting forward and leaning on his walking stick with both hands in a manner that reflected his discomfort at such a revelation.

"Book clubs?"

"No. Well, yes. Well more, organisations within organisations," Bill responded.

"We're only passing the time," I told him. "They're just books."

"Yeah, and Opus Dei is just teaching the way to spiritual enlightenment. But they still get to open fifty-million dollar headquarters in New York and phone up Presidents in the middle of the night with their political Christmas lists so don't go underestimating The Agency's reaction should they ever get wind of it."

"Well, I can see what books you've been reading lately," I deduced, reaching for my Guinness and knocking its head off it before setting it back down. "We're hardly Opus Dei. There's only two or three of us," I lied, apt to downplay the extent to which we'd spread in light of Bill's paranoia.

"Yeah, and so were Opus Dei when they first started out. What organisation's not? Two blokes having a chat and starting a club. But these things spread. They're fine if they spread independently in the outside world. That's fair enough and good luck to them, but you don't let a parasite lay its eggs in your brain just because they're only eggs, do you? Eggs hatch."

"And little Opus Deis are born," I finished for him.

"Exactly," Bill nodded, looking over his shoulder this way and that before figuring it was safe to take a sip of beer.

"So you don't want to join us then?" I put to him.

"What?" he double-took.

"You don't want to join our book club then?"

"Are you asking me?" Bill checked.

"Of course," I said.

"What seriously?"

"Yes, seriously,"

"Honestly?"

"For fuck's sake Bill, have a word with yourself."

"Straight up?"

I decided to stop knocking the ball back across the net as I figured this rally could go on for some time and eventually, Bill accepted that I was honesty, seriously, genuinely asking him to join. Straight up.

"Ah Mark, you're a star," Bill positively beamed, putting his stick to one side and shaking me by the hand as if I'd just announced I was having puppies.

"So you'll join?"

"Absolutely," he enthused.

"It's just a book club, Bill," I reminded him.

"Oh yeah, of course, no I understand," he brimmed anyway. "It's just nice to be asked," he grinned. "Nice to be a part of something again after all these years; part of something with the boys."

I gave him his USB stick, this one tailored to look like a Ladbrokes' pen, which is where Bill spent most of his retirement these days, and Bill (or *Pops* as he was to be known) savoured every word of it as I instructed him on how to use it.

Like I said before Bill missed the life. He'd been an Affiliate from the late-sixties to the early-noughties and had been involved in some of the biggest and most spectacular heists the world had ever seen. Or not, as the case may be. Forget The Great Train Robbery, that was handbag snatching compared to the stuff Bill had been a part of – the plot to blow the Hoover Dam, the hijacking of the Space Shuttle *Atlantis*, the underground germ warfare lab in Mount St Helens, the assassination of Henri Paul – Bill had led a life most men could only dream of. But it had all caught up with him in an abrupt fashion when a bullet in the back had finally ended his career in 2000. It had almost ended his life too, but I'd not given up on him. I'd worked on him non-stop until The Agency choppers had arrived, bundled him onboard of the first one out of there and got him to the hospital ship just in time. By the skin of my teeth, I'd saved his life – but Bill's fighting days were over. Despite being super-fit for his age, a partial paralysis to the right leg and the loss of a kidney meant Bill could never bear arms again. And a part of Bill died with his loss of operational status.

He'd kept his hand in by going back to the island as an instructor, but had lasted little more than a year after a new and painfully young Agency staffer was promoted to Overseer and did what all painfully young men do when they're promoted to senior positions – he got rid of all the old guard.

So Bill was unceremoniously thrown on the scrap heap. He had precious few mementoes to remind himself of his past glories either – well you didn't collect photos or visa stamps when one trawl of the family album could get you extradited to pretty much every country on Earth, did you? And unlike the veterans of legitimate armies, there were no days, no ceremonies, no medals and no obelisks to commemorate the campaigns we'd fought. Or the comrades we'd lost. Not when you were an Affiliate. No sir. When the fighting was over, we were expected to go away, keep a low profile and never speak of what we'd seen or done again. If we'd been lucky enough to see old age, of course. Which most Affiliates didn't because the lure of signing up again was always there. With all the unfinished business and unrealised riches that came with it.

So Bill missed much about his former life. He missed the action. He missed the huff and the puff. He missed the exotic locations. And he missed the camaraderie. But most of all, Bill just missed making a difference; even if that difference was invariably a terrifying plot that threatened to destabilise the entire free world. But like Bill said, it was just nice to be a part of something.

So a USB stick disguised as a bookie's biro and an invitation to join a reading circle might've seemed like a pretty poor proxy to most blokes, but Bill was made up with it all the same and couldn't shake the smile from his battle-scarred face. It was good to see.

"Thanks again, Mark. I really do appreciate it," he told me for the sixth or seventh time.

"It's okay, Bill, glad to have you on board. Welcome to book club," I said.

"And so, I just put this in the back of my computer do I?" he asked, popping the lid off his USB to examine it closely.

"Yeah, that's it. Just stick it in your USB port, log on with your username and password and off you go. Oh, there are some rules on it too, so you should probably have a look at them first before you do anything else," I remembered.

"And that's it?" he said.

"Pretty much," I replied. "Well, there is just one other thing."

"What's that?" Bill asked, his boyish enthusiasm exposing a vulnerable underbelly.

"The first book you have to read is by Russell Davies."

"Russell Davies," Bill noted. "Got it, no problem, what's it called?"

"*The Kenneth Williams Diaries*," I confirmed, figuring I might as well pay him back for letting that kid fall through the grinder at boot camp.

19. THE DYMETROZONE COUNTERSTROKE

THE WEEKS HANG heavy when I'm not working. It's not so much the inactivity that always gets to me, more the knowledge that my savings were plunging inexorably towards the red; and that when they were gone, they'd take my farmhouse and my comfortable life with them.

I can't live in a town. I can't live in a city. I'm a limbo man between lives. And as good as my documentation appeared to the naked eye, it wouldn't stand up to close scrutiny. It couldn't, because Mark Jones didn't really exist. And all it would take was one nosey neighbour or one inquisitive bank manager to get the Easter Egg hunt underway.

I had to stay in the sticks. I had to keep myself to myself. I had to stay solvent.

So I lived to work and I worked to live. Most Affiliates did.

Still, there was nothing I could do until a suitable contract came up. I'd put my name down on the short and middle term contracts lists, so all I had to do now was wait. Hopefully, something would come along before the year was out. I had enough money to get by until then – if I tightened my belt and stopped buying *Heinz* brand baked beans.

To pass the days in the meantime, I'd managed to get a part-time job in a little second-hand bookshop in Petworth. This contributed a few pennies to the coffers and allowed me to read all the books I wanted for free. Naturally, I didn't want to attract unnecessary attention or scare off customers, so I dispensed with the eye patch and wore my Sunday best cosmetic orb, though there was precious little I could do about the six-inch scar that ran across my face, so I stuck to the backroom whenever possible.

And it was while working here that the oddest things began to occur.

The boss of the place was an inoffensive old stick called Stewart, who was probably only about five years older than me, but who dressed more like my granddad's scoutmaster. Stewart was a remnant of the last century. He mistrusted anything that required batteries, refused to acknowledge more than four channels on his TV set and thought corned beef and pickled onion sandwiches were a pretty good thing. Not that Stewart spent much time watching his TV set mind. Books were his thing. They were his refuge, his passion and his livelihood. He bought them, sold them, traded them and consumed them. He even smelt like them and acquired great box-loads of paperbacks from house clearances and auctions and spent his afternoons going through them like lucky dips, occasionally cooing with delight when he'd find an early Graham Greene tucked in amongst several hundredweight of Mills & Boons.

Pretty much everyone around Petworth liked Stewart, despite his obvious eccentricities and musky odour. He was a character, but an amiable one, so it raised a few eyebrows when he was found unconscious at the wheel of his car, stinking of scotch and wrapped around a tree just outside of town. Stewart was arrested when he came to in the back of the ambulance but didn't have a clue how he could've got in such a state.

"I don't even like scotch," he protested afterwards. "Especially at eleven o'clock in the morning when I'm coming back from an auction, for goodness sake. I don't know what could've happened."

What indeed?

I didn't give Stewart's denials much credence because I had a few secrets myself, and fully intended blaming everything on a huge international Masonic conspiracy when my own skeletons finally caught up with me. But then a couple of nights later the bookshop was broken into – but nothing stolen.

I learned this when I strolled up to work on Thursday morning and found Stewart waiting outside his front door nervously smoking a cigarello.

"Hey, Johnny Walker, what's going on?" I'd been in the middle of greeting him, only to stop dead in my tracks when a uniformed police Sergeant stepped out of the shop doodling into his notepad.

"We've had a break-in, Mark. The whole place is a disaster area," Stewart said, rushing towards me as if a hug and a reach-around were on the cards. Fortunately, my stunned reaction was misinterpreted by all parties and I was able to regain my composure before the Sergeant focussed his pencil on me.

"And what might your name be, sir?" he asked.

What might your name be, sir? What a way to ask that! Why not simply, "What's your name?" instead of all the hyperbole? No wonder foreigners had such a hard time learning English with wordsmiths like him stalking our land, filling sentences with unnecessary prose. But then, his phrasing had been no accident. Those extra few words and inclination added rich layers of intrigue to the Sergeant's question and had me mentally feeling for the stubby throwing knife in my belt buckle.

"Mark Jones," I eventually replied when I remembered.

Stewart confirmed like a nodding dog. "Yes, this is Mark. Mark works for me."

The Sergeant lifted an eyebrow to join his tone. "I see," he mused. "New in town are you, sir?"

"No, I've lived around here for almost ten years," I replied, hosing down that particular line of inquiry to a fine steam.

"I've never seen you before. I'd think I'd remember you too," the Sergeant needled.

"The face is new. I'm not," I said, referring to my scar.

"Nasty," he whistled. "How d'you come by it?"

"At work."

The Sergeant looked back at the bookshop. "Paper cut was it?" he chuckled, all pleased with himself.

"My other work," I clarified.

"And what might that be, sir?" he asked, lining up his pencil in case it was breaking into bookshops at night.

"I'm an engineer," I told him.

"I see," he repeated, reminding me of the Agency interviewers. "And where exactly do you work, Mr Jones?"

"Abroad, the Far East mostly. Indonesia,

Mongolia, Malaysia. Bosco Drilling," I elaborated, which was an Agency front and employed half the battle-scarred engineers in Northern Europe. "Do you need their details?"

"No no, that's quite alright," he assured me. "Just an address will be fine."

"They're in Humberside somewhere. I'll have to look out their exact address."

"No," the Sergeant smiled. "I mean your address."

"Oh, it's Petherton Farm, Station Road, just past the river."

"Oh really, I know it. I've always wondered who lives there," the Sergeant perked up.

"Then the mystery is finally resolved," I told him.

"Yes, well quite," the Sergeant agreed then redirected his pencil at Stewart. "Well, like I was saying, it's probably just kids messing about but make a list of what's missing and drop it by the station as soon as you can and we'll keep our eyes peeled."

Stewart made as big a deal as he humanly could out of agreeing with the Sergeant, so the Sergeant suggested he allowed himself a nip of scotch. "For the shock. Just if you've got any with you," he added, raising an eyebrow my way before pedalling off with a chortle.

"Do you need a drink?" I double-checked.

"No, I don't," Stewart objected. "Why does everyone keep asking me that?" he fizzled.

We spent the best part of the day tidying and checking the stock and, sure enough, found nothing had been taken, not even the first edition John le Carré that Stewart kept in the window, the one he'd optimistically marked up £800 after someone had scrawled John le Carré on the title page, supposedly John le Carré, which could've been possible, but the love hearts and kisses looked an ill-advised afterthought on the part of the last trader.

The break-in had undoubtedly been kids. Stewart and the Sergeant both agreed on that and the file was closed with a claim to the insurance company, but I was less sure. Kids took souvenirs. Kids left fingerprints. Kids broke things for fun.

The shop had been trashed but it hadn't been joyously trashed. There was very little in the way of real damage. Books had been tossed out of the shelves. A window had been broken. A door yanked open. But the breakages looked somehow cosmetic. Like how you'd expect a bookshop to look had it been broken into by a bunch of naughty kids.

Something was up. Just what was Stewart into?

*

I was in my local in town a couple of nights later, having a quiet pint after work with the *Guardian* crossword when the pub rhubarb suddenly stopped. It took me a few moments to notice this, so entrenched was I to find a four-letter word that meant appendage, third letter M. I kept putting ARMS and scribbling it out when nothing else fitted, and it was only when I finally arrived at LIMB that I become acutely aware of the sudden silence.

I've experienced this before, not in my local, but in the jungle. A big cat will step into a clearing and all the tweeting and warbling will immediately stop. But it wasn't a big cat that had just stepped into The Star, but an astonishingly luscious piece of crumpet that would have the Ferraris piling into each other had she been waiting by the lights in Monte Carlo, let alone a few Rotarians choking on their real ale in Sussex.

She was a redhead, but a redhead of such dazzling richness that the second thought to cross my mind concerned her collars and cuffs. I almost didn't have to wonder either, for she was dressed in a figure-hugging mini-dress that revealed more than it covered and sporting an unbelievable set of pins, decked off with a dazzling pair of ruby heels that wouldn't have looked out of place sticking out from beneath a fallen house.

She ordered a Dubonnet Manhattan.

"Stirred, that's very important," she'd insisted, but had to rethink her whole order when a quick search of the optics (and the internet) by the landlord revealed they were all out of Rouge Vermouth, not to mention Maraschino cherries. Obviously, there had been a recent rush. After several more aborted orders, she finally had to make do with a vodka Red Bull and a bag of dry roasted before turning to face the gobsmacked pub.

Quick as a flash, the pub started staring at their pints again, including me, who'd inadvertently taken half a dozen digital photos of her arse while she'd been up at the bar. For the next few seconds, the redhead's eyes drifted across all the locals as her heels circled the pub, and eventually, her tumbler and packet of Planters parked themselves in front of me to indicate she'd made her choice.

"Osteology," she said when I looked up, taking a

careful little suck on her curly straw without breaking eye contact.

"What?" I replied.

"It's the study of bones," she elaborated, lifting an eyebrow to suggest she knew what she was talking about, even if I didn't.

"Is it?" was all I could think to say.

"Fourteen across."

"Huh?" it was then that I realised she was referring to my crossword. "Oh!" I finally twigged, and scribbled it in.

"Glory Days," she then said.

I checked the crossword to see where that one fitted, but she called my attention back.

"No, I'm Glory Days – *Gloria* Days," she said before adding, "*Doctor* Gloria Days."

"Oh, right," I acknowledged but left it at that. I didn't tell her my name. Not even my fictitious name as it was getting a little worn from all its recent use, so I just stared at her and waited for her next announcement.

Glory teased her straw a little longer before asking me if I'd ever seen charms like hers, dropping her eyes towards her chest to give me permission to check out her knockers. Clearly, she was referring to the weird geometrically-shaped pendant that decorated her cleavage, but I took it all in just out of courtesy.

"Ever seen anything quite like them?" she jiggled, a naughty smile dancing across her scarlet lips.

Now obviously, I'd seen tits before, even nice tits, and they're always a welcome distraction when I'm struggling to finish a crossword, but I was still stuck for what exactly it was she wanted.

"I'm sorry, but do I know you?"

"No," she replied. "But my father's Professor Days... or at least, was."

"Who's your dad now?" I asked.

"No, I mean, he's dead," Glory amended.

"Oh," I ohhed again, none of this meaning the slightest little thing to me. "Sorry."

"Sorry? What are you sorry for? You killed him after all!" she snapped, causing old Trevor to look up from his shepherd's pie in surprise.

"Me? Look, there's been some mistake, I've never even heard of your dad, let alone killed him. Are you sure you've got the right bloke?"

"Don't worry, he was an arsehole anyway. I'm not here for revenge," she reassured me, dispensing with her straw and staring over at old Trevor until he blinked and looked away. "But you should know one thing. I've got the Dymetrozone now," she whispered.

"Good for you," I said, still feeling my way around this conversation. "Can they do anything for it?"

"Tell your boss, if he wants it, he'll have to deal directly with me," Glory then instructed.

"And he'll know what this means? Because Stewart's not..."

"Remember, if he doesn't want it, I can always deal with the British," she warned me, before knocking back her Red Bull, ice cubes and all.

"I'll bear that in mind," I assured her, scribbling down Dymetrozone on the corner of my paper, tearing it off and folding it up.

"You have twenty-four hours to answer," she said,

crushing the ice cubes between her teeth without even flinching.

"That can't be good for you," I was just saying when she swept away, knocking over her chair and rushing headlong for the door without checking her stride or taking her peanuts with her.

Old Trevor looked up from his pie again. "Friend of yours is she, Mark?"

"I don't think so," I replied, thoroughly baffled by the whole exchange.

"Seems nice," he said, a piece of mash to his mouth as he thought to qualify his assessment. "I would."

*

I did as Glory asked and gave Stewart her message, but I might as well have given it to the cat for all the meaning it held.

"Like I said, if you don't want it, she'll deal with the British," I repeated for the umpteenth time.

"The British what?" Stewart asked.

"I don't know, she didn't say."

"But I'm British. Does she know that?" Stewart furrowed.

"I don't know," I simply shrugged. "I don't think it matters."

"What did she say she had again?"

"Dymetrozone," I said, reading the little corner of newspaper I'd torn off.

"Perhaps it's a book," he pondered, picking a random hardback off the shelf to look at its copyright page.

"It could be," I agreed, before heading off to the

backroom to sort through a box of Dick Francis that Stewart had picked up on his way to the shop this morning.

"Did she give you her number?" he called after me.

"No," I called back.

"Well, did she say how I should get in touch with her?"

"No."

"Is she going to the pub again tonight?"

"I don't know."

"Well, how am I meant to give her my answer if I don't know how to get in touch with her?" Stewart exclaimed.

"Beats me," I replied, unwilling to get drawn into Stewart's affairs too deeply.

I didn't know how much of his ignorance was genuine, because some odd things had been happening to him just lately so he was clearly up to something. I preferred not to know though. I liked this job. And I liked being around the books. I only worked here a few mornings a week so I could stay clear of whatever he was getting himself into, but if it was dealing hooky books (which was my guess) then he was odds-on to lose his shirt, socks and pants because he wasn't savvy enough to go head-to-head with some of the sharks that swam in that pond.

Oh, you might laugh, but there's a lot of money to be made from trading rare books. They were lightweight, practically untraceable and eminently forgeable. For every £1,000 of genuine sales, there's always a couple of hundred done away from the public gaze. And this money was easy to hijack if you were so inclined. And a little bit of cleavage and a suggestive look or two would certainly dazzle Stewart into parting with his life savings if that was Glory's plan. Or whoever had hired her.

I wondered if I should take Stewart for a beer and tell him about the facts of life but reasoned this could open up a whole horrible can of worms for me, so I kept my mouth shut, played deaf, dumb and blind, and continued filling our recycling bin out back with Katie Prices.

Stewart went to The Star that night. He had a shave, wore his best jumper and waited there until closing time, much to the concern of the landlord, who'd insisted on patting him down for his car keys at eleven but Glory Days never showed up. And she didn't show up the next night either. In fact, she left Stewart sitting there for three nights straight, drinking alone and vehemently denying he had a problem to whoever put an arm on his shoulder.

It was only on the fourth night, when Stewart had given up and I'd popped in for a cheeky half on my way home that she finally appeared again, decked out head-to-toe in a purple latex catsuit that was so tight, I realised why she'd not been able to leave the house for the last three nights.

"So, what's your answer?" she demanded without so much as a "how's it going?"

"Oh, for fuck's sake," I sighed at the sight of her camel's hoof.

"You think I'm bluffing, don't you?" she snapped in response.

"Listen, seriously, I don't care. Tell it to Stewart,

he's the bloke you want."

"Twenty per cent, that's my offer. If he can't come up with that then I *will* go to the British," she warned me.

"Then go, this has nothing to do with me."

Glory thought about this for a moment, then turned a chair around and sank down on it in a way that had old Trevor choking on his ploughman's.

"But it could," she purred, dispensing with the spikes and all but liquefying before me. "I don't have to sell it to your boss, you know. If you help me get a copy of the accelerant software, we can always go to the British together. And I know they'd pay more than twenty per cent too. I'd be personally extremely grateful."

She dipped a finger into my Guinness's head, let the creamy froth dribble down her digit, then sucked it clean with a murmur of indulgence.

"Are you alright Trevor?" I heard someone ask across the pub.

"That's an interesting offer," I admitted, momentarily wondering if I could con a quick handful out of her on account. "But I really think you should speak to Stewart. He's in the shop most days."

Glory's demeanour changed yet again. She refound the scowl she'd temporarily pocketed and snatched her more than generous offer back up off the table.

"Fine, if that's the way you want it," she hissed. "And there was me thinking you were someone I could talk to. Someone important."

"Nope, not me. Never," I promised her.

Before I could say another word, Glory was off

again, flying through the door in a hail of stiletto sparks and chairs.

I spent the next hour carefully reviewing my mental transcript of our last conversation and came to two conclusions; firstly, she probably wasn't selling books; and secondly, the boss in question probably wasn't Stewart.

As slow as I was to grasp this, when I finally did, it almost suffocated me like a blanket of nerve gas. My professional life had somehow caught up with me at home. But how? And who could be the boss Glory was referring to?

To the best of my knowledge, almost every boss I'd ever worked for had died, and died horribly at that (except for Stewart, although there was still time). Connaughtard Cottletrophff, Zillion Silverfish, Polonius Crump, Condoleezza Vice, Jed Choo, the Tamar twins, to name but a few. I wrote all their initials down the right-hand corner of my newspaper and saw that only Morris Merton, Hope Verity and Kimbo Banja had been alive when I'd left them, though Morris had just been taken into custody by the Turks, so I didn't fancy his chances of still being in large enough pieces to get anything going. Hope Verity, on the other hand, had shacked up with that hairy-arsed Italian secret service agent and blown the Nepal job just as we looked like pulling it off. A lot of boys had got roasted on that one, so there was a fair amount of ill-will floating about for her, not least of all from the Calcutta mob, who'd put up a ten-million-dollar contract on her the day after their outlay went up in smoke. Literally. But still, that had been seven years ago. And I've never known anyone to survive that long with a ten-million-dollar contract on their heads. Which left only Kimbo Banja. And the less said about him the better.

No, the more I thought about it, the more it worried me.

I stayed for another hour, chewing my fingernails off and worrying about unseen demons before leaving to go home.

And that's when things really got fucked up.

20. IT'S NEVER TOO LATE TO DILATE

THE NIGHT WAS quiet and the weather chilly. One or two cars were veering around the town's tight bends but there were precious few people about on the street itself. I pulled my collars up around my ears and lurched in the direction of home.

I was halfway along Station Road, just past the mini-roundabout, with the bright lights of Petworth on my back, when a black Transit van screeched to a halt beside me and flung open its doors. Two burly bruisers leapt out as I tried to flee, grabbing me by the lapels and repeatedly flapping a cosh against my head until they found the switch.

Lights out.

I've been knocked out a few times in my career so these days I'm able to judge just how long I've been unconscious by the size of the headache when I awake, and this one throbbed away like billy-o, telling me I'd only been under a matter of minutes.

My first sensations were rocking, as Bruiser-A threw the van around the twisting country lanes of Sussex, while Bruiser-B tore through my pockets. They were talking, discussing my fate as though I were a bag of compost, though I was barely able to make out the specifics because of the grinding split that ran down the middle of my senses. When I finally did manage to feel past it, I heard a third voice barking orders at the others and this one caught my attention; a female voice – harsh and authoritative, yet alluring and self-aware. I didn't even need to come around fully to know it was Glory Days.

"Give me his cell phone. And pull his wallet apart, he may have the key in the lining."

I groaned without meaning to, tipping them off that I'd just joined the conversation and Bruiser-B immediately reached into his pocket to sing me another lullaby, but Glory granted my brain a stay of execution.

"No, not yet. I want to hear what he's got to say first."

"Onnhh, my fucking head!" was the first information they got out of me, followed by an off-the-cuff observation about their heritage and what they could all go and do to each other.

Glory shoved Bruiser-B aside and laughed in my face.

"You'll talk, just see if you don't. Oh yes Mark Jones, you'll talk alright."

Bruiser-B leered at me as if his bonus depended on it, so I decided not to invite him to join book club and instead, told them I wasn't working for anyone at the moment. I propped myself up on my elbows and tried appealing to my brother Affiliates.

"You're probably both Agency boys," I implored, nausea all but clogging my throat. "Check the waiting lists with them, short and middle termers. I'm not signed up with anyone at the moment."

"Agency? The Agency? I don't hire through The Agency," Glory Days spat. "I want lions, not donkeys."

"We're RS," bruiser B informed me, meaning *Regenschirm Stellenvermittlung*, one of The Agency's ever-growing number of petty rivals, employing mostly ex-Stasi men.

As discouraging as it was not to be in the clutches of fellow Affiliates, it did offer me a chink of light, so I told Bruiser-B to give my respects to his disabled grandmother the next time the RS got together for Christmas and, sure enough, he clobbered me up the side of the head.

"Arhh, you fucker!" I gasped, curling up into a ball and clutching at my face with both hands.

Bruiser-B just laughed and made a few disparaging remarks about the manliness of Agency pansies, but like most great apes he didn't know what he was talking about. Agency Affiliates were the most professional, most loyal and most disciplined soldiers-of-fortune in the business. If anyone were lions it was us, not those fucking knuckle-draggers from the *RS* or *Executive Elites* or *los Hombres de Guerra*. It was just our misfortune that more often than not we were employed by donkeys; donkeys like Thalassocrat or Jed Choo or Hope Verity. Fucking narcissists who could take an audacious plan, a dedicated following and a winning position and throw it all away over the merest slight to their egos.

But then paradoxically, it was the loyalty of Agency Affiliates that more-often-than-not allowed them to do this. How's that for irony?

Still, that was by-the-by, and none of it was going to help me out of this van, but there was one other thing Bruiser-B failed to realise about us Agency boys. Besides being the most professional, most loyal and best-disciplined soldiers in the game, we were also the best equipped.

"There's more where that came from," Bruiser-B assured me, slapping my hands away from my face.

When I looked up, Glory Days recoiled in horror.

"Oh my God, you knocked his eye out?" she gasped, but had little chance to expand on her revulsion as a deafening crack suddenly blasted out the rear doors and sent Bruiser-B tumbling into the darkness.

The blast dumped Glory flat on top of me, so I headbutted her in the kisser, kneed her in her perfectly-formed clump and threw myself headlong into the night as Bruiser-A parked the careering van halfway up a Scots Pine. I hit the ground running and fled into the darkness, only to tumble straight over one of the larger bits of Bruiser-B.

Glory Days and Bruiser-A finally got their act together and came after me as I scrambled to my feet. The first whizz of hot lead told me the interrogation was over and that this was now about payback. See what I mean? So pointless.

More shots buzzed my ears, chasing me through the night like angry hornets and I ducked and dived this way and that, desperate to dodge that terrible sting of death for as long as I could, only to be suddenly blinded when a set of car headlights clicked on just ten feet in front of me.

I dropped to my knees and turned away as a whirling click thrust two mini-guns out above the wheel arches and they illuminated the blackness further still when they began spitting out three thousand rounds-per-minute.

To my on-going surprise, none of these rounds found their way into me, but Glory Days, Bruiser-A and that poor Scots Pine who'd never done anything to anyone all felt the full force and left this earth in a cloud of blood, sap and flames as the Transit's petrol tanks exploded to duly cremate all three of them.

The guns stopped firing and then trained on me with a whirl.

I braced myself for more pain than I'd ever known, but the guns stayed silent. Instead, the Jaguar XKR's passenger door simply swung open and a voice commanded me to get in.

"Unless you'd rather stay and explain to Gloria's friends what happened to her, of course," an unmistakable smugness snorted.

No! It couldn't be!

21. THE HOTDOGS OF WAR

JACK TEMPEST peered out of the open Jag door and beckoned me in.

"Aye-Aye, old chap," he chuckled, presumably to make me aware that he was spelling his Ayes like "Eyes" and that this was a pun about me missing an eye. "All aboard."

He trained a little Beretta Tomcat on me until I'd climbed in, then tucked it away into a door holster and thrust the Jag into first. The momentum of our acceleration slammed my door shut and we sped off into the night, dousing our headlights after half a mile. Tempest flicked a few switches on the control panel and suddenly we could see again as an infrared display was projected against the windscreen.

"I'd say her glory days were well and truly behind her, wouldn't you?" Tempest suggested.

At first, I thought he was referring to the gadgets on his car and simply grunted, "Huh?" forcing Tempest to elaborate.

"Doctor Days – her glory days are behind her," he repeated, raising an eyebrow to help with the translation but still not getting the laughs he was fishing for.

Have a bit of respect why don't you!

"Did you know her?" I asked in an attempt to head off any further quips.

"We'd met… on the job," he winked, turning my guts something rotten. "She was a brilliant scientist, but totally insane. Just like her father," he added.

"You knew her old man?"

"Knew him. Worked with him. And retired him."

"Retired him?"

"Permanently," Tempest glimmered.

"Oh," I finally got. Twat. "She accused me of that."

"Yes, she accused everyone. Even me. Like I said, she was insane," Tempest shrugged.

"But you actually did it," I pointed out.

"I had to. He gave me no choice after he went over to the Mexicans."

"Oh Jesus, look seriously, forget I asked," I told him in an attempt to head off any unnecessarily long storylines. "Just drop me anywhere, I'll walk from here." But Tempest wasn't done with me just yet.

"You were one of Thalassocrat's goons, weren't you?" he said, turning to look at me in the glow of his dashboard, his expression all-knowing. "The face is different and you're missing a few pieces but I never forget a goon."

"We don't say goon any more," I told him.

"No?"

"No. It's like calling your cleaner your skivvy or your PA your lackey. It's kind of derogatory."

"I see, sensitive souls, aren't you?" Tempest hammed, much amused with himself.

"Well yes, I'll admit it must sound strange to a civil servant like yourself," I accepted.

"I'm not a civil servant," Tempest corrected me, his amusement momentarily holstered.

"Well no, but technically you are," I told him, sensing a weak spot.

"No, I'm not," he continued to object.

"I'm only talking about strict classifications here."

"I'm not a civil servant!" he bristled.

"Well, what are you then?" I asked.

Tempest thought on this for a few sweeping turns of the black countryside. "I'm a tool," he concluded, and finally we agreed on something. "A surgical tool of Her Majesty's Government. I cut out society's cancers." Tempest fixed me with a steely glare. "With extreme prejudice."

"And that's what it says on your payslip does it?"

"Look, I'm not a fucking civil servant, all right, you fucking goon!" he snapped, glancing down at the passenger seat ejector button. "Now I don't care what you're calling yourself these days; tea boy, guard dog, wet nurse or thug, you were one of Thalassocrat's foot soldiers..."

"I don't mind foot soldier," I interrupted.

"I'm so pleased," he scowled. "So why don't you tell me who you're foot soldiering for at the moment, as if I didn't know?"

"I'm not foot soldiering for anyone," I told him.

"As if," he snorted.

"I'm not, and that's the truth."

Tempest's eyes narrowed. "So that's the way you want it, is it?"

"It's the way it is," I said.

"So be it," he snarled, pushing his foot down on the accelerator to send us hurtling through the night.

The hedgerows whipped by on either side and every now and again an alarm would sound on his dashboard advising us to take evasive action as traffic lights and other road users threatened to spoil the rest of our lives.

"You're going to get us both killed, you great fuckwit!" I cringed, hardly daring to look over at the speedometer.

"Danger's my middle name," Tempest breezed.

"I never said danger. I said killed," I pointed out. "And fuckwit."

We shot straight across a crossroads at over 100mph and the lane before us narrowed dramatically. A set of headlights appeared on the horizon and Tempest's eyes glimmered.

"I'm betting he'll swerve first," he quipped, gunning his accelerator to send the Jag's needle into uncharted territory.

"Oh bollocks," I braced, reaching for my seatbelt only to find it locked.

"Talk!" he demanded.

"I'm not working for anyone," I insisted, as the other car's horn grew louder and closer with every passing second.

"Talk!" he repeated, veering the Jag onto the right-hand side of the thin country lane when the other car tried to tuck in.

"I'm telling you the truth," I insisted.

"Talk!" Tempest simply snapped again, but it was academic by this point anyway. Even if I'd had anything to say, I'd run out of time to say it in.

"Look out…!" was all the confession I had time for as our headlight's blurred and our radiators met, but the terrible crunch I'd been expecting didn't happen. Instead, the other car simply shot straight over us and flew into a hedgerow in our wake. Tempest didn't blink. Not even when his control panel confirmed the car's "cowcatcher" had successfully deployed. A little LCD diagram of the Jag showed a thin wedge flashing just in front of his front bumper, turning the entire car into a huge speeding ramp.

"Now that's what I call getting off to a flyer," Tempest warbled.

"You great, stupid irresponsible twat. They could've been really hurt back there."

"Well, they certainly look bushed, I'll give you that," he chuckled.

"Will you stop doing that!" I pleaded.

"Then talk!" he demanded.

"Okay, I'll talk, I'll talk," I finally conceded, willing to promise anything just so long as XO-11 dispensed with the stand-up.

A little country pub presented itself right on cue, so Tempest asked me if I was in the mood to behave myself.

"Because we can always do this somewhere quieter if you'd prefer," he said, snatching up his Beretta Tomcat to underline the point.

"Look, just buy me a pint and I'll tell you everything," I promised.

"Are you armed?" Tempest asked.

"I'm not even armed with any money. Why do you think you're getting the beers in?" I told him.

As luck would have it, Tempest's car came with a First Aid kit that included an eye patch, so I made myself presentable before we headed in. Despite my assurances, Tempest insisted on wearing his gun and his air of shit-eating superiority into the pub and lorded them both over me with a constant display of eyebrow-raising semaphore. He also took his comedy routine on the road and bombarded the confused landlady with a succession of double-entendres that would have landed her a decent six-figure settlement and Tempest a restraining order had they worked together in The City.

"I prefer it hand-pulled myself!"

"Huh, you what?"

It was only after five minutes of painful over-familiarity that I finally managed to drag him away and we retired with a couple of drinks to the snug to get down to business.

"So tell me, who are you working for at the moment?" Tempest asked, sipping his gin and ginger.

I realised we'd just end up playing the same old game of pat-a-cake if I tried to simply answer his questions honestly, so I decided to take him around the houses first, as XO agents seemed to like that in a confession.

"I'm curious," I opened, taking my spiel from every pre-death gloat I'd ever heard to make Tempest feel more comfortable, "how did you get out of that turbine pipe on Thalassocrat's island?"

Tempest smiled to himself.

"Let's just say, I was rather stuck on the good Doctor," he quipped.

"No, let's not. Seriously, how did you get out of it?" I repeated.

"Hey, I'm the one asking the questions here, not

you, so tell me who you're working for before I forget my rules of conduct?"

"What makes you think I'm working for anyone?" I replied, trying to give him as good as I was getting.

The click of the Tomcat under the table caught my attention. "I thought you were going to behave?" Tempest pursed. "Now talk damn you!"

Despite the threat, I knew he wouldn't shoot me in the belly under the table of a country pub in Sussex, especially not one that had Michelin stars outside, that simply wasn't the done thing, so I felt safe enough to continue with a little interrogative chess just to get my point across.

"Just what is it you think you know, Tempest?" I toyed.

"Plenty," he replied. "Names, dates, targets and objectives. We have almost everything. It's just a few minor details that are missing."

"You might think you know plenty, but you don't really. Not *really*. You can't. Not the truth. Not what's really going on," I dangled. "You're too small to comprehend the scale of our operation."

Tempest duly batted.

"You under-estimate yourselves," he challenged.

"Then you know? You really do know?"

"Oh yes," he confirmed, then added, "Mark Jones," to show me he had one name at least.

"About Operation *Gozer*?"

"We have a man on the inside," he told me.

"Who is it? Venkmen? Spengler?" I said. Tempest just smiled. "Not Louis Tully?"

"Why don't you tell me what I already know? And

remember, if you lie, I'll spread you all over the wall, horse brasses or no horse brasses," he warned me.

I looked at the table, took a sip of my Guinness and frowned. "If you know about Tully, then you know we've got the proton packs working." Once again, Tempest confirmed that he knew everything about the proton packs so I told him; "We found the gateway a few weeks back. We've got Clortho and Zuul working on it and while they haven't managed to get it open yet, they will. Just as soon as they get the sign. And when that day comes, Gozer will rise again."

Tempest was frantically scribbling all of this down when a thought occurred to him.

"What the hell are you talking about?"

Some bloke on the next table who'd been scratching his head eventually answered for me.

"It sounds like the plot of *Ghostbusters*," he said and he was right. It had been on the box the night before.

"Are you playing with me?" Tempest demanded.

"Yes, because none of you will fucking listen to me. I am unemployed at the moment. I am between jobs. My last posting was base security for Victor Soliman," I told him, figuring it was best not to mention anything about Kimbo Banja, not least of all because I'd been party to a nuclear explosion, so I stuck to confessing my failures and left the Hague's prosecutors to bang the drum for my successes.

"Victor Soliman? The satellite refractoriser, wasn't it?" Tempest mulled, in an effort to show off his knowledge.

"I don't know, possibly, I was just the bloke guarding the vending machine," I told him. "But we were put out of business six months ago by Rip Dunbar of the SEO, which is where I got this," I lied, pointing at my face.

"Rip Dunbar?" Tempest grimaced. "That ape?"

"He speaks very highly of you," I told the big kettle, "but yes, that ape. Check with him if you like. Tell him I was the guy who shot his Nguni."

"Painful," Tempest quipped, "but that doesn't mean you're not working for anyone now, does it?"

"No, you're right, and in fact, I am," I corrected myself. "Petworth Editions. It's a second-hand book shop in town."

"I know, I've been in it," Tempest said.

I couldn't remember Tempest popping in any time while I was there, which meant he'd probably toured the place with a flashlight hanging from his gob.

"And what did you find?" I put to him.

"A lot of books," Tempest admitted

"Yeah, I bloody knew it wasn't kids," I said, referring to the break-in.

"Well, you would, wouldn't you?" Tempest accused.

"Presumably then, it was you who drugged Stewart and made it look like he'd crashed his car too? What were you doing, searching his load or planting a tracking STE?" I asked.

"Neither, that really was Stewart. He's got a secret drinking problem, didn't you know?" Tempest replied.

"Really?"

"Yes really, there's a load of bottles hidden behind

the Jilly Coopers if you look."

"Oh," I ohhed.

"I know a cover story when I see one," Tempest then said. "You're sleeping, aren't you?"

"If I am, I'm having a fucking nightmare," I told him. "You're tailing me, aren't you?"

"And lucky for you I was," he said, referring to this evening's earlier special guest stars.

"And that's another thing, where did she come from? Glory Days? Did you put her onto me?"

"The Admiral told me not to trust her. I knew she'd try to deal the Dymetrozone independently if she knew about you, and I was right," he congratulated himself.

I took an enormous sigh and rubbed my forehead. Unfortunately, I'd used up my only plastique organ, but I was of half a mind to pull out my real eye and throw it in his face just to get his attention.

"Look Jack, I'm an Affiliate for hire. I've worked for Thalassocrat. And I've worked for Soliman, just as I've worked for dozens of others in my time. You've got me banged to rights. But I ain't working for anyone at the moment," I tried to make him understand.

"You'd like me to believe that, wouldn't you?" he said.

"God preserve me," I gasped. "Just tell me this, how long have you been following me?"

Tempest considered the question before evading it. "Long enough."

"Five days? A week? Two weeks even?"

"Long enough," he simply repeated, though his

lustre had lost a little of its sheen by now.

"Then in all that time, have you seen me do anything other than stack books, nip into Waylett's for a pasty or struggle over the crossword in The Star?"

Tempest sipped his gin and ginger to buy time, before hitting me with the biggest revelation of the evening.

"What about Goodwood?" he levelled, then added, "And the man in the hat?"

"Goodwood?" I gawped, scarcely believing what I was hearing. "Goodwood was three months ago! You haven't been following me for three months, tell me you haven't!"

Tempest didn't know whether to look triumphant or embarrassed and settled for looking indignant.

"You've been following me for three months!" I pressed again.

"Gathering intelligence takes time," he defended.

"Obviously," I laughed. "Jesus Christ and you still haven't got a jot of it!"

"The man in the hat?" Tempest reminded me, showing me a black & white surveillance photograph of myself buying a hotdog off someone at Goodwood races a couple of months ago.

"Would you believe he sells hotdogs?" I suggested.

"And drives the very latest Lotus Exige?" he countered.

"Does he? Fuck me, maybe I should get into that game," I phewed. "Hang on a minute, you're following me because I bought a hotdog off some bloke who happens to own a flashy motor?"

"But you didn't just buy one hotdog, did you? You

bought three?"

"What are you, my personal trainer? So what? I had three hotdogs. I like hot dogs. Phone Weight Watchers why don't you?"

"You were Thalassocrat's goon. I recognised you from the island!" Tempest shouted.

"Thalassocrat is gone and so's my job," I shouted back.

"Never! You're working for someone, I know it," Tempest insisted, turning over the table and grabbing me by the lapels, but it was the act of a man who'd spent the best years of his life lining his pants with toilet paper only to shit his hat.

"Take it outside will you chaps," the bloke on the table next to us requested through a forkful of chips, so Tempest bundled me towards the doorway and threw me out into the road.

I tumbled over three times to put some distance between us, but I was too slow, Tempest was already on top of me, karate-chopping my back and scissor-kicking my legs out from underneath me to dump me on my face again.

"Will you stop fighting me and notice I'm not fighting back?" I shouted as Tempest spun about in the car park blocking shots that weren't coming.

Tempest eventually took a time out and asked me what was up.

"For fuck's sake," I growled, rubbing my shoulder. "What's the matter with you?"

"Some might say I don't like goons," he glared.

"While others might say you've just pissed away three months of the company's time following an unemployed hotdog enthusiast and you're having trouble coming to terms with it."

Tempest shaped into his fighting pose again, just as two old boys left the pub and walked past us to their Rovers.

"Night Ron."

"Yup, night Mick, mind how you go."

They barely afforded us a glance, Tempest hovering over me on one leg like the Karate Kid, me rubbing my elbows on the floor and the landlady wiping Shepherd's Pie off the blackboard behind us.

"Aren't you?" I demanded again when the old boys drove off.

The landlady turned, afforded us both a smile then also headed inside. Tempest's lethal hands flexed a little longer before they eventually melted into his trouser pockets.

"Fuck it," he spat. "The Admiral's gonna bite his pipe in half."

When Tempest didn't offer me a hand, I hauled myself up and dusted myself down.

"Are you really not working for anyone?" he asked for the umpteenth time.

"No. No one," I repeated, patting myself down.

"Then what are you doing around here?"

"I live around here," I told him.

"Really?"

"Yes really. What are you doing around here?" I asked in turn.

"I live around here too," he replied.

"Fucking nora!" I sighed for us both and we scratched our heads and wondered where we went from here.

"Fine, okay I believe you. You're not working for anyone at the moment, but I still get to run you in," Tempest said, pulling his Tomcat on me yet again.

"For what?"

"For what? You were one of Thalassocrat's men. One of Soliman's men. One of God knows who else's men. You've got crimes to stand trial for."

"Come off it, what happens on missions stays on missions," I said. "You know the score."

"You think you get to go home at the end of the day after doing what you do?" he almost laughed.

"Why not? You do," I replied.

"I'm one of Her Majesty's officially sanctioned Executive Officers. Licenced to…"

"… flip over other drivers while showing off your flashy Jag?" I finished for him.

Tempest spent some time with his finger in the air considering this one so I hit him with a few of the juicier rumours I'd heard about him, such as the time he'd sunk an American Coast Guard's Cutter by tearing underneath it in his mini-sub whilst being chased by a magnetised torpedo or the time he'd banged the Mayor of Bangkok's sister when the Mayor of Bangkok only had brothers. Then I spiced the pot further still.

"Besides, how's the Admiral going to take it that three months of costly surveillance work by one of his elite XO agents has produced nothing more than an unemployed goon and a hot dog vendor with an outstanding credit record?" I put to him. "I take it you do have people on him too?"

Tempest's silence said all that needed to be said.

"I could always just kill you," he said, jigging his gun up and down to remind me he still had options.

"Why? What's the point? I'm just a foot soldier. A goon. You said so yourself. Kill me when you see me next out in the field if you're that fired up about it," I suggested.

"There won't be a next time if I kill you now," Tempest pointed out.

"No, that's true, but there will be someone else. Someone you don't know. Someone you don't recognise. Would you rather that for a scenario?"

"It cuts both ways. I might not recognise them, but then again, they won't recognise me," he said, jabbing his gun in my ribs to underline the point.

"Oh, leave it out, will you, everyone knows what you look like. We've got pictures of you pasted up in every base and laugh our socks off whenever you wander into our places of business introducing yourself as Jack Stock of the *London Financial Times*. Fuck me, I don't know why you don't just go the whole hog and put on a white beard and a big red coat and come in as Father Christmas."

Tempest looked suitably insulted, which had been the intention, and told me he'd been highly decorated for his undercover work.

"Yeah well, perhaps you should try wearing your medals on the inside of your disguise next time you're trying to infiltrate us, Beau Jangles," I suggested.

"Now you look here…" Tempest snapped, less than happy to find himself the butt of a lowly goon's put-downs, but he should try being a fly-on-the-wall of The Agency works canteen for five minutes if he really wanted to know what defamation sounded like.

"Information," I said, catching him off-balance.

"What?" Tempest blinked.

"I said information. I can give you a juicy nugget of information to take back to the Admiral so you've got something to show for three months of overtime, and in return we'll forget we ever saw each other, right?"

Tempest eyed me with suspicion, not knowing what to make of my offer and reluctant to show too much enthusiasm for it until he was sure it had nothing to do with the Stay Puft Marshmellow Man.

Before we could get into it, more locals started spilling out of the pub, so Tempest holstered his Tomcat and bid them all good night, as drinkers have a want to do in rural Sussex at closing time, before finally biting.

"What's this information then?"

"It's a bit vague, but I can tell you who's hiring for a job just now," I said.

"Who?"

"Got a pen and a bit of paper?" I asked.

Tempest slipped a hand into his pockets and told me he could do better than that, pulling out a suped-up Palm Pilot with laser-lighting guidance beam, GPS tracking radar and go-faster stripes.

"That's no good, I can't do the little threes on it," I told him.

"It's got a three on it," he showed me.

"Not a little ones," I said, looking around for dust and a stick to write with before spotting something much better. "Look here," I said, leading him over to the pub's outside menu board and wiping it clean. I found a splinter of chalk just below it and wrote 'X^3'.

"X-cubed?" Tempest read.

"Your guess is as good as mine, Jack. His real name's Xian Xe Xu, but this is how he likes to refer to himself. Fucked if I know how to pronounce it, but he's recruiting for something big at the moment," I said, slapping my hands clean of chalk dust.

"And how do you know this?" Tempest asked.

"Because he passed through," I said, without wishing to divulge too much. "I was offered a contract but decided against because I didn't like the look of him."

"Fussy aren't you?"

"Not really, but some jobs you can tell are going to be trouble, particularly with that mad bitch he's got in tow."

"What mad bitch?"

"Sun Dju," I said.

"Ah, of the genus *Drosera*. A carnivorous plant that captures its prey by exuding a sticky honey from its shoots," Tempest lectured. "Beautiful, but deadly."

"God, it's no wonder you've got no mates," I told the boring pub quiz nerd. "Different spelling." I wrote Sun Dju's name out on the blackboard for him and watched XO-11 play with his Palm Pilot for a bit, trying to make a little ^{3} before giving up and simply taking a photo of the board.

"I guess it doesn't bother you that this information may lead to the deaths or arrest of whoever's signed up with Three-X," Tempest goaded. "Perhaps even friends of yours."

"Is that how you're going to say his name then? Three-X?"

"Just answer the question," Tempest pressed.

"He isn't taking on any of my mates, I know that for a fact," I assured him, safe in the knowledge X^3's labour force would be made up of *RS* or *EE* monkeys, not Agency Affiliates. And if a little corner of the world was to be threatened with annihilation by some Oedipus nutjob, I'd really rather it was stopped unless I was a part of it and on a generous completion bonus.

"Anything else?" Tempest asked.

"Yeah, just one thing, watch out for Sun Dju's shoes, she's got killer heels," I told him. Tempest clearly didn't understand what I meant but he nodded as if he did anyway, ever eager to play it suave.

"I love ladies with feet to die for," Tempest declared, starting his car and summoning it towards where we were both standing with a flick of his remote control key chain. The door sprang open and Tempest climbed in. "Fair exchange is no theft," he trilled. "I'll see you around then, Mark the Affiliate – either in Tesco's or Tora Bora."

"Oi!" I shouted after him.

"What?"

"How am I meant to get home? It must be bloody fifteen miles to Petworth."

"Shouldn't be a problem for you. I thought you said you were a foot soldier?" he guffawed, before thrashing his Jag through the circular gravel driveway and spinning it a hundred-and-eighty degrees to rejoin the road.

"Oi, Tempest!" I cried after him again when he passed and, to my surprise, he stopped and looked back.

"What?"

I knew he wouldn't give me a lift or lend me twenty quid for the cab home, so I asked him the one question he still hadn't answered.

"How did you get out of that turbine pipe on Thalassocrat's island?" but Tempest just revved his V8 engine and roared off into the night.

"Cock smoker!" I frowned.

The pub's lights suddenly dimmed behind me and the door clicked with the sound of a latch being flicked. Not that I'd had any money for another drink anyway, so I pulled up my collar, dug my hands into my pockets and began the long walk home all over again.

22. PROPERTY OF A GOVERNMENT

"TARGET APPROACHING. First strike operatives take your positions!" came the order as the twelve of us took to our chariots and clipped ourselves in. A rush of freezing air accompanied the bomb bay doors spreading beneath us and all at once, the deep blue vista of the Atlantic far far below took our collective recycled breaths away.

I wasn't altogether mad keen on this particular operation so I'd volunteered to be one of the first out of the plane, figuring I stood a better chance out there in the open skies than on-board our lumbering Tupolev once we'd broken radar cover. Now that I was strapped in, with nothing but 45,000ft and Flash Gordon's shopping trolley between me and a really bad day, I was suddenly regretting not volunteering to stay back and organise the lads' end of job party.

"Start chariots," a tinny American voice told my left ear, so I twisted the key in the centre of the dashboard and the instrument panel lit up accordingly.

That whole business with Jack Tempest had occurred a little over eight months ago and I'd spent five nights stewing on it and living in a camouflaged bivouac across from my farm to see if anyone else came for me. When nobody did I eventually accepted I was safe. Well, more or less. Tempest still knew where I lived and I didn't like that one little bit, but then again what could I do? Bolt? Of course, that would have been the sensible solution, but then most of my money was tied up in my property so I would've lost everything if I'd ran.

After a few sleepless nights, I eventually decided to put the whole lot on the market and up-sticks to East Sussex. Not exactly a monumental migration but the thought of a beachfront property and a boat suddenly appealed to me. Unfortunately, the housing market had taken such a tumble since I'd bought my farm that the pennies I was looking to make on it wouldn't have got me half an hour in a dinghy, let alone anywhere to live. The estate agent had been terribly apologetic about the whole situation, so much so that he almost moved into a one-bed shallow grave in my back garden for his smugness.

I was buggered.

I put together an escape bag and started dropping cash, documents and weapons in various luggage lockers and deposit boxes right along the south coast in case I had to leave in a hurry, but then salvation came along. A job. And this one was a compact little international hijacking with a very, very tasty payday. There was just one thing:

How did I feel about heights?

"First strike operators away!"

The brackets above our heads released and we plunged through the bomb bay doors and into the abyss in rows of three, two seconds apart.

The air was crystal clear around us and roared past our visors as we dead-dropped a thousand feet from the Tupolev before our engines automatically kicked in and blasted us forward. Tiny wings unfolded behind our knees and our chariots began to respond as we pulled on their sticks to climb once more.

We spread out to get our bearings before regrouping for our approach. A few more switches locked our guidance systems onto the C-17 Globemaster ten miles ahead and we accelerated as a unit on a count of three. Our chariots could travel just short of Mach 1 at this altitude, which closed the gap between us and the C-17 in no time at all, though we all had to remember to wear our thermals.

It was only when we fanned out into our attack formation that I noticed there were now only eleven of us. Someone's chariot hadn't started. I didn't know whose, but from the hastily redrafted orders that were now buzzing my left ear, I hazarded a guess that it had been someone in the third drop row, which meant either Mr Woo, Mr Hodgson or Mr Passey. Somewhat selfishly I hoped it was Mr Hodgson, as he'd voted against adding *The Hound of The Baskervilles* to our reading list.

Not that I had much time to think about it. We'd been spotted by the C-17 the moment our engines started because a starburst of decoys exploded in the skies right behind its tail and two of her three F-16 escorts peeled away to engage us.

"Break right!" Chariot Five told me and together we ripped through the blue and into the sun.

The nearest F-16 chased us, but we were too small and too fast for his plane's guidance computer to lock onto and without the time to reprogram it, he went route one and opened up with his 20-mm cannons.

A stream of white-hot lead filled the skies around us but the spread smacked of panic fire. We were so many in number and swarming all over him that he failed to pick out any single one of us.

After a few seconds of aerial mating, I swung around behind him and was rewarded with an urgent beeping in my left ear to tell me I now had missile lock. I wiggled my thumb to fire off four missiles and was momentarily blinded by their smoke trails as they raced for their target. The F-16 saw them as soon as they left my tubes and the pilot threw his plane in a desperate bank of rolls and turns as he fought to prolong his career in the US Air Force but it was to be in vain. More and more mini air-to-air missiles started homing in on him and when the first caught his wing, it knocked him into an unstoppable corkscrew that sent him spiralling towards the sea.

The pilot ejected a moment before the second, third and fourth missiles struck home, obliterating his place of work in a flash of light, to join Mr Woo in the drink.

The remaining missiles circled for a few seconds more, sniffing their own tails as they searched for another target before taking a shine to the poor unfortunate pilot himself. All at once, they darted in his direction with merciless intent and I could hardly look when all four self-destructed just a few hundred yards short as Mr Smith in Chariot One hit the kill override. He'd said he would do this if this happened. All we wanted were the F-16s out of the sky and now we'd achieved this, why kill for the sake of killing? It was bad karma. If truth were told, I wasn't that fussed one way or the other. The F-16 pilot was going to have his work cut out walking away from this day's work as it was, so a couple of hours dying inch-by-inch in the frozen north Atlantic would've probably had him cursing Mr Smith for his clemency anyway.

The other F-16 pilots didn't have the same quandaries as they'd not been as quick with their ejector seats, so after just another thirty seconds of aerial ballet the C-17 found itself flying on alone – unescorted, unprotected and open for business.

Phase one of Operation *Sky Flame* complete. Proceed with phase two.

When the Chariots regrouped, we found there were now only nine of us. Two more had gone the way of the crabs, but such losses had been factored into the planning of this skyjacking so we had more than enough men to see through our objectives.

We pushed our sticks in the direction of the C-17 and closed the distance in a little over two minutes. In all that time, we could hear the C-17's pilot sending out Maydays to whoever was listening, which would have been quite an audience, to be honest. Two carrier groups had straddled the Atlantic below us to underwrite this particular plane's transit across the pond and they were no doubt scrambling as many fighters as they could into the air this very minute. We had time, but not an inexhaustible supply of it.

"Flight KT-315, you are instructed to drop to twenty thousand feet and slow to two-hundred knots," Mr Smith told the C-17's pilot as we formed up around the plane.

The pilot ignored us and continued to send his Mayday.

"Flight KT-315, failure to comply will result in the

downing of this plane," Mr Smith warned him, but the pilot continued to do his own thing.

All at once, the C-17 banked violently, throwing its wings at our starboard formation. He was too slow and too ungainly to catch us though so instead, he took the C-17 into a steep dive to leave us in his jet-stream.

"Take him," came the order, so we dived after transport and fell some twenty thousand feet before levelling off at twenty-five. We descended on him immediately and despite another couple of abortive rolls, the C-17 knew he couldn't get away. All he could do was play for time.

Chariot Four was the first to try reigning him in, trailing the C-17's wing until they were like a shark and pilot fish swimming through an ocean of blue and white, but one particularly thick bank of cloud told for Mr Clarke as the C-17 flipped Chariot Four into the ocean with a flick of its portside fin.

Chariot Six was next to try, along with me riding Chariot Five. We closed in on a wing each and synchronised our flight paths until we were within touching distance. I knew I was one turn of the stick away from total disaster, but a little LED light started blinking on my instrument display, so I flicked the limpet-switch and was sucked hard onto the wing. And not a moment too soon either. The C-17 rolled once more, hoping to bat me into the blue, but the pilot would've had more luck simply strolling out onto the wing to tell me to "clear off" because I was now stuck fast and going nowhere.

Chariot Six had made it too and quickly got to

work overriding the plane's controls. Three minutes and a few magnetic cables later and the Globemaster's pilot was suddenly redundant. We now had the plane.

We took it down to the altitude and speed we wanted and the remaining Chariots formed up around it. Two of them rode up alongside the cockpit, while the remaining four dropped back to the plane's rear. As hard as the C-17 tried, they couldn't stop us from rolling open the rear doors by remote control.

A volley of small arms fire immediately erupted from the cargo hold to scatter the trailing Chariots.

"Flight KT-315, hold your fire. I repeat, hold your fire or we will retaliate," those on board were told, but the crew were determined to go out draped in flags and continued trying to repel us, leaving ourselves no option but to do things the hard way.

With Chariot Six flying the plane, I was surplus to requirements on the wings, so I deactivated my limpet and fell back a few hundred feet before my engine rebooted. I straightened up, stopped swirling and fired my boosters, clawing my way back through the sky until I came up beneath the plane where most of the other Chariots had clustered.

Some foolhardy USAF Rambos were hanging out over the tail ramp emptying M4 Carbines in our direction, but it would've taken a lucky shot to nail us from that distance, so we sailed in zig-zags to draw their fire as Chariots One and Three climbed up and around before dropping behind the tail to strafe them with 9-mm hollow points.

Several bodies fell out of the plane then Mr Smith put on a burst and took Chariot One right into the cargo hold.

"I'm in," came the staccato radio burst. With that as our cue, three more of us dropped around and accelerated into the back of the plane, crashing through crates and cargo netting before deploying grappling anchors to stop us from tumbling straight out again.

I slapped a button on the side of my helmet to turn my black visor clear and unclipped my harness to roll out of my Chariot.

Bullets were pinging all around me as the crew fired from deep within the belly of their aircraft, but their situation was only getting worse as their day wore on. Only ten minutes earlier they'd been a routine military flight, protected on three sides by the latest F-16 fighters and two carrier groups, now their escorts were gone, half their crew was dead, they'd lost control of their aircraft and armed raiders were on-board in numbers.

I shook off my thick thermal gloves, flexed my fingers a couple of times, then tore out my Model 61 Skorpion machine pistol and began picking off targets.

A square-jawed USAF Sergeant was crouching behind a tangle of netting and keeping Mr Smith's head down with clip after clip from his Colt .45.

I squeezed my trigger and ripped his foot clean off the end of his leg, before knocking his beret loose when he toppled into the picture. Now clear, Mr Smith jumped forward and took up position by a stack of netted crates.

"Bogeys spotted at nine hundred miles. What's

your status FSOs?" came the request from the Tupolev.

"We are moving forward. Bring down Mother," Mr Smith shouted into his mic as he peppered the galley with his own Skorpion.

"Roger," the Tupolev replied, and began its descent.

"Flight KT-315, you must give up or you will all be killed," Mr Smith tried one last time, but he was found no takers, so the four of us lobbed stun grenades forward, squeezed our eyes closed as they detonated.

We dispatched five airmen on our charge and a couple of Langley types who'd been overseeing the flight before securing the main cargo area. There were more airmen towards the bow, but they could stay where they were as far as we were concerned. We'd pushed into the aircraft as far as we needed to push. Now we got to work.

Mr Woo and Mr Vasiliev took up defensive positions while me and Mr Smith secured the prize – a CSMK radar jamming smart missile. It had just been developed by the US Air Force and featured the very latest in cutting edge technology, similar to a Cruise Missile, only with one very important difference; it was radar invisible. Completely. Very handy in a day and age dominated by early warning systems and counter-measures. If your target wanted to know what had happened, he'd have to ask Saint Peter when he saw him because he'd get no warning of any sort before the bomb hit. It was the ultimate tool of assassination. And those who held it were to be feared.

"Mother, this is FSO One, we have the tube. Bring forward the dentist," Mr Smith told the Tupolev, then muted his mic and looked at me. "Who comes up with these stupid names, that's what I want to know?"

I grinned through my visor then headed back to help with the winch. Chariot Twelve had joined us with two hundred yards of steel cable spooled around its rear. We anchored the Chariot, then threw the cable buoy out of the back and unspooled it until it reached the Tupolev.

At this point, the Tupolev's side door opened and the cable was attached and a rather reluctant scientist hooked on the end. A tiny motorised trolley whisked him over and we pulled him inside, unclipped him and pushed him in the direction of the missile. He scurried forward with his ratchets and screwdrivers and spent the next five minutes picking his way through the missile's nose cone before finding the circuit board he was looking for.

"Got it," he announced, departing once more to leave Mr Smith to plant a packet of C4. Mr Woo and Mr Vasiliev now fell back and we reattached the scientist to the cable and pushed him back out over the ocean.

"Mother, he has the chessboard," Mr Smith told the Tupolev, and we watched the scientist whizz back to the Tupolev and a cluster of arms drag him inside before the cable was cut free.

"Delivered," the Tupolev confirmed. "FSOs you are cleared to exit."

This wasn't exactly something we needed

prompting about. All five of us had spent the scientist's journey time hastily cutting our anchor wires and shoving our Chariots onto the exit ramp, and so we were all set to go the moment the order was given.

Unfortunately, as is so often the way with these things, we'd dropped our guard right at the death and a burst of automatic fire ripped into Mr Woo, throwing him backwards into Mr Smith and knocking them both off the tailboard.

Mr Vasiliev and Mr Jean immediately dropped and returned fire, but I'd already pushed my Chariot over the side and jumped out to follow it.

"Leader down! Leader down," I heard in my ear, along with a load of other garbled radio traffic as Chariots Three and Twelve fought to exit the plane. I was away and clear. I'd completed my mission and was now on to collect a very hefty pay packet. All I had to do was make it back to the Tupolev and dock.

There was just one thing stopping me from doing that.

"Leader down!"

My boosters roared to life after falling a thousand feet and I threw the stick forwards, plunging my Chariot nose-first towards the ocean.

Mr Smith was barely visible. A tiny black dot amongst an undulating backdrop of shadows and surf, but he quickly grew in form as I rocketed past him at four-hundred-miles-per-hour.

He didn't see me at first. I just cut past him in a blur, but then slowed and circled until I could get to within ten feet of him, but even then he still didn't react. I guess this was a difficult time for him and he was probably fixated on other things right now, so I steered as close as I dared and called out to him over the radio to "look left! Look left!" but he didn't respond.

I fired off my reserve missiles, emptied my mounted 9-mm machine gun and even beeped my horn to try to get Mr Smith's attention, but still he didn't look.

Barely five thousand feet below us now was the water and I knew we'd feel it on our ankles all too soon if I didn't fire my boosters, but I couldn't leave without Mr Smith. I wouldn't be alive and still borrowing books if it hadn't been for him. I'd be just a shadow on a charred corner of Africa without his warning. I owed it to him to try until the very last, but if he was determined to see what the Gulf Stream felt like, then I'm afraid he was on his own and good luck to him.

See, the trick to saving someone where they're falling is much like the trick to saving someone when they're drowning; you need them to know they're being saved so that they can co-operate with you. You can't just grab them without them knowing it, because chances are they're panicking and lashing out, and if they catch you a cropper in their death throes, then they're likely to knock you out, spelling problems for you both. So plucking someone from certain death has to be done delicately.

I continued to call Mr Smith's name as we plunged towards the Atlantic but all I got for my troubles were whirling arms and legs, and cries of unadulterated histrionics.

I took a deep breath, composed myself for one final go, turned my mic up full volume and spoke to him as calmly as I could.

"Okay, Mr Smith, you win, we'll read *It's Not About The Bike* next, if you just look left! Do it now! *Do it now!* Look left."

At last, this got through to him, probably because it was such a preposterously trifling concession to win in such horrifying circumstances, and Mr Smith's visor finally turned my way. I beckoned him towards me as the Atlantic did the same and Mr Smith kicked, threw and shaped himself until I felt his arms wrap around my waist.

I fired my boosters without waiting for him to get comfy and the kick almost dislodged us both, but we slowed our drop and circled above the waves at just a few hundred feet until our momentum once more took us up.

"Mother! Mother! This is Chariot Five. Sound off beckon. I repeat, sound off beckon, I have FSO leader," I radioed in, as we rocketed back towards where we'd just come from.

After a torturous wait to see if they'd respond, a homing signal finally lit up an LED light on my instrument panel, so I locked onto it and twisted back the throttle to singe Mr Smith's ankles.

"Be advised Chariot Five, bogeys at three hundred miles. You have four minutes to rendezvous. We can't give you more than that," the Tupolev told me.

"We'll be there," I confirmed, hoping against hope that I was right, because I seriously doubted I had enough fuel to make it back to Petworth.

We shot up into the sky crouching low on the Chariot to reduce the drag and eventually, saw the Tupolev way off in the distance above us. They'd risen to thirty thousand feet and increased their speed to four-hundred knots, so docking was going to require some care.

"Mother, we have you. Approaching from six o'clock. Make ready," I radioed in and, sure enough, a glint from their undercarriage told me the bomb bay doors were opening.

"Chariot Five, we have you. Nice and steady now, welcome home."

"Thank you," someone muttered in my ear and I realised to my surprise, that it had actually been me.

A vacant bracket descended from the bomb bay and willed us towards it. I took the Chariot up into position, almost to within touching distance, but then the machine shuddered beneath me. An electronic beeping laughed at us as my engines finally announced they were down to just fumes, and all at once, we began sinking again.

"For fuck's sake!" I cursed, but my Chariot had spent its load.

I had one chance to get on board, so I punched my buckle to unclip my harness and gunned what was left of the throttle, throwing us headfirst into the bracket.

"Jump!" I shouted as we crashed metal against metal.

We threw ourselves at the black steel and wrapped whatever we could around anything solid. Arms, legs and chins all clung onto the outstretch frame as my Chariot tumbled into a spin and fell away beneath us.

Our colleagues saw what was happening and immediately retracted the bracket, pulling me and Mr Smith up into the belly of the Tupolev, as the plane banked to turn north. Sirens and warning beacons flashed as the bomb bay doors crept closed in our wake and the light thinned to a narrow streak before eventually, it all went black.

"Repressurising," a metallic voice told my left ear.

After a few moments, I felt something on my arms and legs but I couldn't see what it was. I couldn't understand why I couldn't see at first, but then someone tapped the button on the side of my helmet and my visor tint cleared.

Mr Jean helped unwrap me from the bracket while Mr Vasiliev and Mr Kovács did what they could to prise Mr Smith away. Eventually, we trusted the floor enough to relinquish our grips, then shook off our helmets and followed the others forward to the FSO seats.

There were five spares.

"Bogeys closing at eighty miles," the captain announced. "It's going to be close."

My ears were popping and head swimming as the Tupolev climbed towards the stars. All at once, a proximity claxon filled the cabin, so we strapped ourselves in and braced ourselves for the worst, but this day had thrown all it had to throw at us. A sudden confirmation chime eased all our fears and won a well-earned round of applause from everyone on-board.

"Radar signal scrambled," the Captain told us over the intercom. "You can relax now gentlemen, the jets can't find us."

We continued our bearing north-by-north-west for a few more miles before tipping east to roll the sun around to the other side of the plane.

Mission accomplished. We were on our way home.

"Thanks for coming to get me," Mr Smith said, stretching a hand across the seat between us.

"No problem," I replied, taking and shaking it. "Thanks for Mozambique."

Mr Smith thought on that and a pensive expression spread across his face as he looked across at the other empty FSO seats. "You know, we *should* take care of each other," he said. "This job's dangerous enough as it is without giving up so easily on each other."

"You hear me arguing?" I replied.

"I'm serious," Mr Smith insisted.

And I could see he was. Nobody liked losing colleagues. It was never nice. Take today for example, we'd lost Mr Clarke, Mr Passey, Mr Hodgson, Mr Raj and Mr Lee. That's a lot for one morning. Some of them I knew. Some of them I didn't. But they were all good guys. At least they'd died on operation, and a successful one at that. This wasn't always the case. We'd all lost colleagues unnecessarily through either carelessness, neglect or sadism. Mr Smith himself had been lost, but I'd not given up on him and gone out on a limb to bring him back. This was unheard of in a business where the big picture was everything. Unless of course, you were the guy who'd laid it all on and employed us in the first place, then your own private quarters couldn't be packed with enough escape pods and parachutes to help you live to laugh another day. This morning's events had shaken something awake inside Mr Smith. He was a working man. A contract man. A professional. He took orders, followed orders and obeyed orders. I'd never known him to speak out of turn in all the times I'd worked with him, but Mr Smith wasn't a happy bunny today. And while it was true that he had just fallen twenty-odd-thousand feet to a certain terrible death only a few minutes earlier, there was still more to it than just that.

A determination.

Mr Smith had a determination in his normally automotive eyes.

The only time I'd ever seen anything like it in him before was when he talked about the books he loved.

And occasionally, the kids he loved too.

"Okay then," I quietly agreed, shaking his hand for a second time in as many minutes.

I wasn't altogether clear as to what we'd just agreed, but I knew we'd agreed to something. I just never knew the scale of it.

Or just how many lives it would eventually come to affect.

23. A LOYALTY FROM BETRAYAL

ODDLY, WHEN WE got back to Greenland, we found that not everyone was ecstatic about Mr Smith's miraculous escape.

Griffin Marvel sent the monorail for us the moment we touched down. Stupidly, we thought it was to congratulate us on a job well done so we all climbed in with buoyant smiles and rattled through the rabbit warren of caves until we reached the Command Centre.

"I ought to have you all killed this instant!" he screamed at the fifteen of us, prompting us to unbow our heads when we realised we weren't getting any medals today. "Every last Goddamn one of you!"

Captain Ackerman, the Tupolev's pilot, asked if there was a problem.

"A problem? A problem you say?" Marvel almost melted down. "Yes, there's a fucking problem," he confirmed. "I go to all this expense, all this risk and all this trouble to pull off one of the most audacious skyjackings of all time, only to have you cretins jeopardise everything by launching a fucking search and rescue operation in the middle of it!"

I saw where Marvel's fury was focussed and tightened my screws accordingly. Like the CSMK missile, I can make myself virtually invisible when need be and began wiggling my toes inside my boots to drift out of the firing line.

"But Mr Marvel," the Captain tried, "we succeeded in every respect. It was a triumph of ingenuity."

"There was nothing in my ingenuity about stopping to catch every careless fool who couldn't keep on his feet!" he roared, spurring my migration behind and around the back of Mr Vasiliev by a few more millimetres per second. I'd just got level with his ear-line when Mr Vasiliev noticed I was very, very slowly leaving the building and began to join me in my slide south.

"But Your Grace, it just shows what a spectacularly inspired plan it was then, that we achieved all our aims and still had time to save our fallen comrade," the Captain soft-soaped.

"Which comrade? You mean this comrade?" Marvel shouted, whipping a semi-automatic out from behind his back and shooting Mr Kovács between the eyes without so much as a second's thought. "You allowed the carrier groups' interceptors to close in on you for almost five precious minutes to save that fool, did you?"

No one felt the need to point out to Griffin Marvel that he'd just fired the wrong FSO, least of all Mr Smith, and we shrank as a group as Marvel's own personal body-guarding detachment poured in to the Command Centre from every door to surround us on all sides. Obviously, we'd been required to relinquish our guns before boarding the monorail and found ourselves staring down the barrel of Marvel's Omega Unit armed with nothing more than fluff and regrets.

"Dr Frengers, step away from them if you will," Marvel told our jet-hopping scientist who'd been cowering amongst us with miserable resignation. Dr Frengers seized the lifeline and excused himself from our party, only too pleased to distance himself from the tar bucket, but Marvel stopped him before he got more than a stride or two away and held out a hand.

"If you please, Dr Frengers?"

The Doctor dug into his zipper pocket and made a present of a little circuit board he'd extracted from the missile. Marvel looked it over with satisfaction, then shot Dr Frengers through the glasses to dump him across Mr Kovács.

That was when we knew we were all dead.

I'd been in situations like this before and what I've never understood is why nobody ever does anything about it. Marvel's Omega Unit stood around watching Dr Frengers hit the floor and none of them emptied their guns into Marvel despite there being the distinct possibility that they'd too end up cluttering up the place before this day was out. Because loyalty's a one-way street in this game, with often nothing more than broken promises, trap doors and piranha tanks waiting when it came time to paying the men who'd done the actual grafting.

Of course, this wasn't always the case, otherwise we'd have to be a right bunch of mugs to keep signing up, but every now and again we did encounter a rogue psychopath who got his kicks from firing his own staff. And every time this happened, almost everyone else stood idle. I include myself in this by the way. It always came as something of a surprise whenever it happened, I'll say that in my defence, but more than that, each time it happened, I somehow managed to convince myself that the person it happened to had somehow deserved it, because the implications of them not having deserved it were far too great for me to contemplate. So like a zebra on the Serengeti who'd survived yet another lion hunt, I would go about my business and continue nibbling the grass, simply thankful that it was someone other than me who was being picked over by the pack.

"But Mr Marvel," Captain Ackerman was pleading, "I implore you to…" but we never got to hear what Captain Ackerman wanted from Marvel. If it was to be shot in the head before he could put his side of the story across he got his wish.

"You were flying the plane. You were the one who turned off the scrambler," Marvel screamed at Ackerman's corpse, before waving his hands in disdain and holstering his gun. "Take the rest of them away. I'll deal with them later," he snapped. "And somebody clear up this mess!"

If there's one rule I've tried to live my life by it's never get taken away to be dealt with later. If you're going to get killed, try to get it done and dusted in the first few minutes because no good ever came of giving disgruntled sadists a few hours to ponder the problem at their leisure.

I made a grab for the nearest Omega monkey's weapon but I was hopelessly outnumbered and a shoulder-stock to the back of the neck put paid to my plans and ensured, come the entertainments, that Griffin Marvel took a special interest in the FSO with the eye patch and the disappointing attitude.

*

I felt the pain from the blow when I came to. It had sunk in through the back of my head to settle behind my eyes so I could tell I'd probably been out for about fifteen minutes or so.

I pushed myself up off the hard wooden bench and saw that we'd been put in one of the large detention suites. Eleven faces stared at me from around the room; the other FSOs, our three reservists / assistants, the Tupolev's co-pilot and navigator, and the Chariots' chief technician, who'd been with us on the Tupolev during the mission. It seemed like such a waste to be throwing away talent like this, particularly the technical lads, but Griffin Marvel no longer cared. He'd got what he wanted, the CSMK circuitry. We were merely the box it had come in.

Mr Smith looked down at me.

"Glad you came?" he asked.

A quick inspection of the cell revealed no air conditioning panels to slide off, no sewers to crawl through and no bars to hacksaw. There were no windows, full stop.

There was only one way in and one way out; a heavy steel door with a flap at the bottom for sliding food through – if so desired. They didn't. There was no handle on this side of the door either, just a flat plate to indicate where the mechanism was.

I wondered if my explosive eye would pack enough of a punch to blow it open. It contained about 50g of semtex, so I reasoned it might just. Which made it even more of a shame that I'd worn my GPS tracking eye then.

We spent a while discussing tactics, what we'd do when they came for us, and how we'd fight them off, but this was really just an exercise in keeping our spirits up and we all knew it. Well, all except for Lieutenant Copeland, the navigator, who fell for every word of it and came away with a level of confidence in our chances that our own mothers would've found hard to match. He was going to have the hardest of falls.

I prepared myself to meet my maker by picking over the bones of my life to see which particular mistakes had brought me here, while Mr Smith spent the time talking about his kids. It was clear he really loved them, four-year-old Ben and seven-year-old Kirsty, just as it became clear they were both sleeping beneath headstones. I finally figured this out when I realised that neither of them had aged in all the time I'd known him. It also explained his workaholic attitude to Affiliation.

"You didn't kill them, did you?" I tentatively asked, wondering if this was how he'd come to be in prison in the first place and how he'd come to the attention of The Agency.

"No," he told me, "but I killed the men who did."

After another four hours, the metal door finally cracked open and we braced ourselves for the worst. But to my continuing surprise, our time had still not come. Rather, another prisoner was pushed in to join us. I recognised him immediately and wondered if my problems could get any worse.

It was Rip Dunbar.

"Hhuuuurgh!" Rip grunted, as he was dumped on the cold hard tiles. His body was bloodied and his long hair greasy. "You fucking *sonsabitches*! Go fuck your mothers, you *mothers*!" he yelled at the guards, throwing himself at the door as it closed behind him. He collided with locked steel and pounded it with his tree-trunk arms for the next thirty seconds or so until we all got the general idea, then he flexed his pecks and turned his rippling intelligence on us.

"The same goes for all, you *mothers*. Who wants a piece of me?"

"I don't know if you've noticed this, but we're prisoners too," Mr Smith said, tapping the metaphorical blackboard.

Dunbar scowled at Mr Smith and told him to "Stay out of my way," before dumping himself off to one side to bench squat the evening away.

After thirty minutes of the noisiest exercise I've ever heard, Dunbar's top clung to him as if he'd won a Miss Wet T-shirt competition. The rest of us were faring little better with rivers of tears clogging our eyes in light of the stench now filling the cell.

Mr Vasiliev, who was the nearest to Dunbar, was the first to crack and pleaded with him to lay off for the love of God, but if anything Dunbar just punished his body even harder, all appeals falling on deaf ears.

That was until he laid eyes on me.

"You!"

"Oh crap."

Dunbar flew across the cell and chased me around in circles, over benches and scattering bodies until he was finally able to trap me in a corner. Ten fat, sweaty fingers wrapped themselves around my throat and a second later my back hit the wall.

"We've got a score to settle," he growled, his face

contorted in a mass of rage and unrequited man-love.

"What score?" I gasped.

"Jabulani, you killed him," Dunbar reminded me. "He was my friend."

"Well, so what? You killed plenty of mine that day too," I coughed, doing all I could to tear his fingers from my windpipe. "You don't hear me complaining about that though, do you?"

"Brother, your friends were scum," Dunbar sympathised.

"Yeah, and we're also all around you, *Einstein*," Mr Smith pointed out, as the rest of the cell rose to their feet and surrounded the SEO gorilla.

Dunbar lunged back to chop down Mr Smith with his leg, but Mr Smith had foreseen this and it was Lieutenant Copeland who copped a solar plexus full of combat boot instead. But Dunbar wasn't done; he twisted and kicked the unfortunate Lieutenant this way and that before booting him into touch against the far wall and swinging me around to use as a human shield.

"Get back, all of you, I mean it, I'll break his neck, you *mothers*!"

"Take a pill, *punchy*," Mr Smith suggested. "Are you so short of people to fight that you can't wait to go WWWF on everyone in here when our enemies are out there?" Mr Smith pointed at the steel door, staying Dunbar's hand. "We're all under sentence of death, so settling scores and comparing cocks with you is the least of our concerns."

"You're under sentence of death?"

"Yeah, even him," Mr Smith confirmed, pointing

at me.

"Why?"

"For disobeying orders," Mr Smith simplified.

Dunbar's arm continued to flex around my neck as this information rattled around between his ears before his grip finally eased. "Couldn't happen to a more deserving guy," he retorted, hurling me to the floor and taking my place on the bench.

I rolled over, rubbing my neck and chewing my lip as I picked myself up, and found a space between Mr Vasiliev and our Tech Chief. All the time Dunbar glared at me with menace dressing his face.

"What happened to your eye?" he snarled. "Did I do that?"

I told him he had, figuring he might deduct it from the bill if I looked miserable enough about it and, sure, enough Dunbar grinned at the thought.

"Good," he grunted.

"That's a point, what have you got in today?" Mr Smith asked me.

"Nothing useful."

"Nothing we can use?"

"I would have mentioned it before if I had," I told him.

"What's he talking about?" Dunbar asked.

There was no point lying at this stage so I told Dunbar about my false eye.

"You've got explosives in your eye?" Dunbar asked.

"No, not today," I repeated.

"Well, what have you got then?" he pressed.

"A GPS tracker. I thought I might need it if I went

down in the Atlantic," I explained.

Dunbar stood, reanimated after barely a minute of taking it easy. "You've got a GPS in your eye? Here? With you now?" he snapped.

"Jesus, what now!" someone asked, but Dunbar was already on top of me, slapping the back of my head to try to get it out.

"..kin' get off me!" I complained and was able to shove him away long enough to pull my own eye. "Here."

Dunbar snatched it from me without saying thanks and examined it closely. After a few moments, he asked if it could be reprogrammed to send a signal.

"A message? No, it's not got that capability."

"Not a message, an ID code. Can it be reprogrammed to send a six-lettered ID code?"

"Er..." I erred, but the Tech Chief was already on his feet and poking his nose in.

"It should be possible, theoretically," he speculated.

Dunbar shoved the eye in his hand and told him to make it. "SEO767. Send it out."

"Well, it's not as simple as that..." the Tech Chief tried, but Dunbar wasn't interested in what was possible and what was theory. The Tech Chief had stood up and got his hopes up and so that was good enough for Dunbar.

"Do it!"

But the Tech Chief told him he couldn't because he didn't have any tools, which was when Dunbar cut his fingers to pieces pulling a nail out of the wooden bench to equip the Chief with.

"No more talk, send the fucking signal!" Dunbar demanded.

The Tech Chief frowned and pursed his lips before getting to work levering the housing off my GPS eye.

"What are you sending? You're not calling in an airstrike, are you?" Mr Vasiliev wanted to know.

"And what if I am?" Dunbar shoved. "You think you're not expendable?"

"Hey, we're all expendable," Mr Smith said. "Just include us in on the conversation, yeah?"

"You'll see," Dunbar simply grunted, the merest hint of a smile teasing his eyes.

I wasn't sure we'd get the time though. The sound of boots marching and keys jangling echoed along the corridor to remind us that life was short and full of woe, and it was about to get a lot shorter and even more woe-filled, but then the Tech Chief looked up and smiled to tell us he'd done it.

Dunbar snatched my eye out of his hand and jammed it under the crack of the door, before banging on the locked steel to entice the guards.

"Come and get us, you *mothers*! Come suck my dick!"

He then grabbed Lieutenant Copeland, who was still curled up in a little ball and wheezing by the door, and dragged him clear, ducking down against the far wall, before inviting the rest of us to do the same.

"Everybody down!"

24. A BLACK HAWK PAYBACK

KEYS IN THE LOCK and barked commands just outside the door told me our presence was requested in the mortuary and I was really starting to hate Rip Dunbar when all of a sudden all hell broke loose. A blinding throb of heat and light filled the cell and threw us against the far wall, almost like a flashbang exploding in the room. Only there'd been no bang, just a flash. The back of my neck was savaged as if I'd sat under the midday Saharan sun for a full twelve hours and I discovered to my dismay that my clothes – and the clothes of those around me – were actually smoking.

Still, that was nothing compared to what had happened to the door itself – and those who'd been opening it at the time. It was no longer there. Nothing was; the doorframe, the ceiling, the floor below or the men who'd been stood on the other side. All were gone.

All that remained was a steaming, searing, crackling hole.

"What the fuck was that?" the Tech Chief asked.

"A little something from our buddies at NASA," Dunbar said, implying some sort of satellite had just targeted a photon pulse on our position. "Now come on!" Dunbar insisted, dashing out through the opening to look for things to karate-chop.

Mr Smith shrugged when I looked at him, as if I'd asked him a question, which I hadn't, then chased after Dunbar. I immediately followed, leaping across the steaming abyss and straight into a fire-fight. Dunbar, Mr Smith and a couple of the others managed to grab rifles off the smoking wounded outside and were now engaging the remainder of the Omega detachment as they poured in on us from both stairwells

"Heads up!" Dunbar grunted, and I turned just in time to catch an M16 straight in the face. As painful as this was, things could have been a lot worse as the space I'd just been occupying was suddenly filled with a whip of tracer fire.

I looked up the corridor to see half a dozen more Omega troopers squeezing their triggers in my direction and only just managed to avoid the fruits of the endeavours by squeezing into the adjacent doorway.

Alas, the hapless Lieutenant Copeland was not so fortunate and his crisp white shirt exploded with scarlet the moment he jumped out of the cell and across the line of fire.

Others too met with little forgiveness, as Mr Hasseen and our co-pilot were picked off as they tried to join the fight, but at least half a dozen of the guys did make it, with Mr Vasiliev and Mr Deveroux scuttling across the floor to peel M16s out of the crispy fingers of those who'd originally come for us.

Back near me, Dunbar was screaming as if he were cumming in his pants, emptying clip after clip into the Omega troops at the northern end of the cellblock corridor and doing his damnedest to get through his ammo as fast as possible. He'd also managed to lose his shirt in the last couple of minutes and was sweating as if his previous sweat had been a mere practise for this, the main stench.

"You *mothers*! You mother-*mothers*!!!" he was screaming, shooting from the hip on full automatic and painting the far end of the hallway with clouds of brick-dust and blood.

Mr Smith was right next to him, and pelted with a fine lick of sweat every time Dunbar spun around to engage a different part of the corridor. I half-thought about sending the pair of them over some more ammo and a packet of wet-wipes but never got the chance as shots were now zipping past my ears and peppering the walls around me as Omega troopers from the southern stairwell closed to within thirty feet.

I hung my M16 out into the corridor and took a bead on the trooper closest to me. His head bobbed in and out of cover as he shot in my direction, but I didn't fire. I only had one clip and needed to make every round count, so I waited for him to break cover and didn't have long. The Omega trooper lunged across the corridor, making for the cell doorway four doors along from mine, and I opened up with a measured burst, only to see him and the guy who'd followed flung back and turned into Swiss Cheese as Dunbar drilled twenty bullets into each of them, screaming; "Suck my dick! Suck my dick, you *mothers*!" before bounding off up the corridor to take the fight somewhere different.

"He's keen," I shouted over to Mr Smith.

"You can say that again," he replied, wringing his eyes and nose. "Keen as fucking Gorgonzola."

The base alarm was now blaring away over the crackle of gunfire, tipping off the residents that not all was well with the day. One of our lot, I don't know who it was, wasted a few bullets killing the speaker at the far end of the hallway, but it was a purely cosmetic gesture. Griffin Marvel would know from the Command Centre computer boards where the problem was coming from and he'd be directing all his resources our way soon.

A grenade went off next to Mr Egorov, ripping open his sides and splashing a considerable portion of him all over the far wall, but Mr Vasiliev was able to sling back the next two that dropped into our laps to give the Omega boys a taste of their own medicine.

I didn't feel bad about fighting the Omega lot. I had no friends amongst them and couldn't stand them as a unit. There's almost always a detachment on any job who think they're a cut above. They're invariably the boss's personal bodyguards or a special ops unit who've been given a Hollywood make-over and let it go their heads, but even by usual standards, the Omega detachment were still some of the biggest Wallace & Gromits I'd ever worked with. They wore red from head-to-toe, caps straight and laces tied in double-knots as if their mums had dressed them at the base gates. This wasn't the reason I hated them of course, because we were all at the mercy of whatever daft fashion sense our employers had, but it was the fact that they wore this get-up 24hrs a day. Even on their days off. Even when they exercised in the gym.

They never smiled either, which was always a bad sign. They had very little sense of humour, never laughed, barely chatted and ate their corn flakes each morning with military precision. But the thing I hated most about them was the fact that they were rude. Ask them a simple question: "Here mate, where's the washing powder kept? We've run out again," and they'd just look at you as if you were kicking over headstones in a pet cemetery. "Here mate, washing powder yeah?"

They weren't Agency hired either, which bodyguards often aren't, and as a result, their loyalties lay entirely with Griffin Marvel. They were his men, ergo an entire unit of boss's sons.

I finally managed to shoot one of my Omega persecutors, knocking him back into an electrical box to simultaneously fry him, and rather satisfyingly saw that it was the guy who'd dissed me over the washing powder, so it felt good to even the score.

As a result, the lights all along the corridor flickered, allowing us to break cover and close on the remaining Omega men, who were still lit up from the stairwell lights.

Mr Vasiliev, Mr Smith and myself cleared the southern end after a fierce assault, while Mr Deveraux, Mr Jean, the last surviving reservist Mr Capone, and the Tech Chief cleared the north.

For the moment we had the detention block to ourselves.

"How are we not dead yet?" the Tech Chief asked, but I was buggered if I knew. I just hoped it stayed that was for a little while longer.

"Where to now?" Mr Vasiliev then asked.

"The Command Centre, I gonna kill that arsewipe

Griffin Marvel," Mr Capone suggested, to universal dismay.

"Screw that, let's just go home," Mr Deveraux bettered, and this time we all agreed.

"Yeah, there's still more than a hundred men upstairs and they'll soon be in here on top of us if we hang about," Mr Smith pointed out. "Come on, to the monorail."

We gathered up what ammo and grenades we could off the fallen Omega men and took to the stairs. To our surprise, there were signs of a fight and bodies on every landing and that's when we remembered Dunbar.

"Should we tell him where we're going?" someone asked.

"Yeah, that's exactly what we should do," Mr Smith agreed, before adding; "Stupid ass."

We reached the middle level and found an unguarded monorail parked at this floor's embarkation point. After a quick look around we dashed towards the open carriages and jumped in. The Tech Chief hit the pedal and we moved off as one, rifles pointing out in all directions like a porcupine with attitude.

We rolled on through a long rock tunnel, dodging the lights and passing more bristling alarms, but we encountered no trouble along the way. Our luck didn't hold for long though and soon we emerged out onto an open concourse near the stores and into the line of sight of half a dozen Omega guys.

We opened up on them as one, riddling the small detachment with hot lead to knock them down like tin ducks. The Tech Chief didn't slow the monotrain for an instant and we continued gliding around the concourse before disappearing into another tunnel.

"Two more clicks to the helipad," Mr Smith told everyone, locking and loading his M16 as he slammed in a fresh clip.

The next cavern we emerged into was the snowmobile dock. This area was guarded by our own guys, guys we knew, not those Omega arseholes, so we lowered our weapons and waved a cautious greeting as we trundled on by.

One of them, Captain Collett, recognised us and flagged us down, prompting Mr Vasiliev to flip the safety off his Colt, but Mr Smith urged caution.

"Let me handle this," he whispered.

We slowed to a gradual halt and pulled up alongside the Captain and his men.

"Mr Smith, what's going on?" he asked.

"The base is under attack," Mr Smith told him. "A break-out from the detention centre."

"Who?"

"Us," he said, suddenly bringing his rifle to bear. Mr Vasiliev, Mr Jean, Mr Deveraux and the others all followed suit, getting the drop on the Captain and his men, but Mr Smith barked at everyone to hold their fire.

"Wait! Just wait a minute," he urged.

We knew Captain Collett to be a reasonable man (he'd given Joseph O'Conner's *Star of the Sea* a solid four out of five and you can't be much more reasonable than that) so we took a risk and explained the situation to him. The Captain was shocked to hear that we'd been locked up, sentenced to death and double-crossed. He'd had no idea, obviously – it wouldn't have been the sort of thing Griffin Marvel would've posted on the bulletin board – and as a result, he immediately threw his lot in with us.

"… because it'll be us next if we don't," he told his lads and to a man they agreed. I was so proud of them – book club members one and all. Except for Mr Lennox, who preferred his Game Boy – illiterate cunt.

"Okay, we'll secure the helipad and give you a call, then you come and join us," I told the Captain.

"Check," he agreed, sending his men away to take up defensive positions.

The Tech Chief hit the pedal and we glided away, around the snowmobile dock and into the next tunnel. I wondered if Captain Collett had come around to our side a little too easily. I mean, people do occasionally say things they don't mean when they've got half a dozen automatic rifles aimed at their chests, so I told the Tech Chief to take the long way around and approach the helipad from the rear, just in case the good Captain had phoned through to arrange a welcoming committee for us.

The next cavern was eerily empty. There should have been four or five white-coated technicians working here on the base's mainframe but the place was dead. I wondered if the technicians were too.

We circled south, taking a series of left-hand forks until we emerged into the enormous subterranean aircraft hanger. Here, there was plenty of activity – and gunfire. At some point in the last ten minutes or so, Rip Dunbar had traded his M16 for an M60, with a twenty-foot-long magazine belt and an under-hanging pump-action grenade launcher, and was taking on several complete units of Omega and general base security. This was a tricky situation because we knew some of the blokes from the base security unit, but there was no way of getting to them to explain the situation, so we did the only thing we could – we sunk out of sight inside the monotrain and continued on to the next tunnel.

Crash! Bang! Ratter-tat-tat! "Suck my dick!" were the sounds that echoed around the hanger as Dunbar waged war on anything in sight and blasted his way towards the Command Centre at the far end of the cavern. Griffin Marvel would be in there no doubt, frantically sending everyone else off to their deaths to forestall his own, but sadly I never got a chance to see how things panned out for him because we rounded the bend and disappeared into the next tunnel before riding the rail the last hundred yards or so to the helipad's southern elevators.

The Tech Chief stopped the monotrain and we all jumped out, taking up positions either side of the tunnel entrance, while Mr Vasiliev summoned the elevators.

The first appeared with a ping and the seven of us crammed ourselves in. Probably a bit stupid, to be honest, but like I said, when you're this close to the end of an action, it's so hard to stay focussed.

We glided up several hundred feet and emerged into a cold and blustery Greenland morning. The Omega Guards just outside the elevators went down with a short burst apiece and we fanned out across the helipad as their fellow Omega brothers ran to engage us.

It was winter in Greenland and the snow was piled high in dirty mounds at the edges of the helipad from where the dozer had scraped it back. Most of us were still in our white and black ops gear from the skyjacking and difficult to pick out as we dashed between the snow and rocks of the exposed mountain slopes, but unfortunately the Tech Chief still bought it as he moved on one of the Westlands. I saw him drop like a marionette who'd had his wires cut and he hit the cold hard tarmac probably not even realising he'd been killed.

As disheartening as this was, the Tech Chief was the only one of us they got, for despite being evenly matched in terms of numbers, we had one thing going for us that the Omega troops didn't.

Namely, we weren't wearing red against snow.

I hugged the black rocks on the Eastern side of the helipad and picked off colourful tunic after colourful tunic, painting the snow around them with short bursts until the entire Omega detachment were finally camouflaged – against their own blood.

"FSOs on me," Mr Smith shouted after the fight, so we drew back and took up defensive positions to watch over the elevators as Mr Deveraux checked out the Westlands.

"The birds are good; keys and full tanks in two of them. Enough to get us to Paamuit, maybe even Nuuk."

"That's it then, let's roll!" Mr Smith ordered,

covering me and the rest of the lads as we piled on to the nearest chopper before joining us himself.

It was only then that we discovered the flaw in our otherwise flawless plan.

"Er... does anyone know how to fly one of these things?" Mr Smith asked, when he saw that we'd all jumped in the back. "Mr Deveraux?"

"What?"

"Can't you fly a helicopter?"

"No."

"But you just checked them out?" Mr Vasiliev reminded him.

"No, I just looked to see if they had the keys and full tanks of gas. It doesn't take a pilot's licence to do that."

"Jesus!"

"But you all flew the Chariots," Mr Capone said, who'd been the FSOs' gofer on the Tupolev.

"That's different; different controls completely," I said.

"But if you can fly a Chariot, then presumably you can fly a helicopter too," Mr Capone insisted.

"That's right. And if you can program a washing machine then presumably you can hack the Pentagon's super-computer too," Mr Jean chipped in.

"I don't believe this," Mr Smith sighed.

"Well, what about Captain Collett?" Mr Vasiliev finally said, which wasn't a bad idea at all. He'd had almost a dozen men under his command when we'd rolled on through, so it was feasible that one of them might be able to fly a helicopter. It was worth a shot.

"Let's do it."

We tried him on the internal phone system, calling the snowmobile dock from the elevator phone, but no one picked up at the other end.

We whipped a digi-headset off one of the dead Omega troopers but still couldn't elicit a response from anyone at the snowmobile dock.

"Dunbar," Mr Smith said.

"Yeah," I remembered. He'd been fighting near the Command Centre and must have taken out the uplink equipment or the server lines.

"It's no good, one of us is going to have to go down there," Mr Smith said.

"One of us?" I said, not liking the sound of this.

"There's no point in all of us going. Some of us have to stay back to guard the chopper," he argued, which was a fair point but even so, I could feel the fates closing in around me.

"Okay, who goes?" I cautiously agreed.

The short answer was me, decided by a hastily convened game of rocks, scissors and paper that whittled us down until I was left despairingly trying to cut Mr Deveraux's fist in half with my fingers.

"Now if the comm-link is down, we won't be able to talk to you, so just bring them up here, okay?" Mr Smith said.

"And if none of them can fly helicopters?" I pointed out.

"Well…" Mr Smith pondered. "I guess we'll have to find another way out," he reckoned.

"Right, and I'll just sneak past a couple of wars, Griffin Marvel, Rip Dunbar, all those Omega wankers and come back and tell you about it then shall I?" I said, adding; "all the way back from the snowmobile dock?" to underline my alternatives.

Mr Smith accepted the unreasonableness of what he'd asked, so he sorted me out with a couple of distress flares and told me to fire one off if I left on a snowmobile.

At that moment the elevator phone rang so we picked it up and said hello.

"Help? Help us, anyone!" screamed a voice I didn't recognise. "Anyone, we're under…" the line went dead with a crackle.

Mr Smith looked at me.

"Don't be long," he suggested, pressing the button to take me back down into the mayhem.

25. A CRYSTALLINE KISS OF SLEEP

I FIRED OFF A burst of automatic fire as the elevator doors opened, just in case there'd been anyone waiting for me, but there hadn't. The place was quiet. Explosions and fire echoed from deep within the base but all human sounds had ceased. Smoke and the acrid smell of cordite hung in the air to indicate that this place had seen a fight, but those that had fought here were now silent.

The monorail train was also gone, so I hugged the wall and peered down the tunnel.

Nothing.

I really didn't fancy this but what choice did I have? We were in Greenland, a thousand miles from anywhere and fast approaching winter. We needed a ride out of this place. Anything less was suicide.

I said a quick prayer and moved off into the darkness.

Most of the lighting was down, just a few red emergency bulbs lit from the back-up generator pierced the blackness and after a hundred yards or so I looked out onto the main aircraft hanger.

Dunbar was gone too. As were the troops he'd been fighting.

Also the Command Centre. Nothing was left of it. A smoking mass of twisted metal burned at the end of the hanger where it had once stood and most of the planes around it were either on fire or soon to be. Thankfully the bay doors at the far end were open, so most of the heat and smoke was escaping out into the arctic but even so, it was still close to unbearable in the cavern, even from where I was sliding along the wall.

Very little could have survived this hell.

But I took care all the same.

I ran at a crouch, following the monorail track around the hanger until I was within a sprint of the next tunnel and made it with seconds to spare. Two hundred yards behind me, the Tupolev finally succumbed to its wounds and blew to smithereens with a blinding flash. I threw myself into the tunnel mouth as a thousand gallons of burning aviation fuel splashed the back of the hanger and ran blindly until I'd escaped the searing black smoke.

The next cavern was in much the same state. The mainframe computers were crackling in a way that suggested it was going to take more than a call to Apple to retrieve Marvel's emails for him. What's more, there were several charges attached to the housings I didn't like the look of so I quickly moved off, into the next monorail tunnel and towards the snowmobile dock.

On foot, the base was bigger than I'd realised and where I'd happily trundled around in comfort on the monorail before, I now inched and stumbled my way through the cramped tunnels in near-total blackness. Several times I caught my head on the bare rocks above, scraping my scalp and bloodying my hairline until all I could fantasise about were hard hats and TCP but finally I reached the end of the tunnel and peered out across the snowmobile dock.

The place was empty.

I pulled back and searched my brain for ideas, but none presented themselves, so I swore under my breath and stepped out into the open.

Once again I kept low, hugging the monorail track until I came to within thirty feet of a pyramid of crates. Only then did I take to my toes. I dashed the short open space between cover, wincing at the expectation of pain and winding myself when I slammed into the crates.

This was where I found Captain Collett.

I hadn't been able to see him from the monorail track but just around the corner, he was stood straight and true against another stack of crates, looking like one of those ramrod sentries you got outside Buckingham Palace who weren't allowed to move, smile or jangle their change.

Captain Collett didn't move, smile or jangle his change either, but that was because he was stone dead.

I approached him gingerly, half-expecting his shocked wide eyes to flicker in my direction, but the eight-inch engineering spike that had skewered him through the forehead had grabbed his whole attention.

All around his feet were spent .38 shell casings and the bodies of his men. I conducted a quick count and found they were all present and correct.

Damn.

I wasn't sure what had happened here; either Marvel's Omega troops had done this or Rip Dunbar had blundered through with his finger super-glued to the trigger. Not that it really mattered either way; the whos and what-the-fucks could wait for another day, but for now, my most pressing concern was getting the hell out of here before Dunbar called on his NASA buddies to delete this place off the map.

I grabbed a few essential supplies such as radio, GPS and winter survival kit then grabbed a cold-weather coat and threw myself at the nearest snowmobile.

The engine revved first time and I ploughed towards the dock doors, but the auto-door mechanism must've been shot out, because the doors stayed right where they were, so I slammed on the brakes, circled around in a big loop and approached them again. This time I popped the missile lock off the handle-grip and fired two mini rockets at the doors, obliterating them in a flash of steel so that I was able to jump through the hole and out into vast snow-covered wilderness beyond.

I held the throttle open until I'd put a good mile between myself and the base and only then did I slow to take a look over my shoulder.

Columns of smoke rose from dirty black scars in the mountainside, staining the crystal sky and advertising the base's whereabouts to anyone within fifty miles.

I looked towards the ridge but couldn't see the helipad from this distance. I couldn't even be sure the others were still up there, but I'd promised to signal if I wasn't coming back, so I shook off my gloves, pointed a flare at the sky and pulled the rip-cord. A halo of blinding red streaked across the morning's sky and fell away somewhere to the east, leaving a fluffy white smoke trail in its wake. This smoking trail might as well have had a big "You Are Here" arrow at my end because all at once, the snow around my feet started kicking in all directions as multiple machine guns opened up on my position.

"Holy shit!" I freaked, twisting the throttle to launch myself down the nearest slope and into the gully beyond.

Several rounds dinked my snowmobile and my own bodywork fared little better with a chunk knocked out my right calf to poleaxe me headfirst into a snowdrift. I rolled around in the snow, howling, hollering and clawing at my wound, but had precious time for little else as the six dots motoring towards me on the horizon compelled me to my feet. I hopped and stumbled thirty yards or so until I found my snowmobile overturned against a boulder and managed to haul it back onto its tracks with a little huffing and puffing.

I didn't know who the dots were or why they were shooting at me but after the sort of day I'd had why wouldn't they?

I got my snowmobile going once again and took off for the gully just as mini-rockets started obliterating my tracks. The dots formed up behind me like a pack of hungry wolves and I knew I'd have problems shaking them. Most of the weapons on this machine were front-facing, though I did have a couple of mines proved utterly useless. All six of my pursuers steered wide, suggesting they were probably using their snowmobiles' mine-sweeping radar to avoid my nasties.

They opened up on me with the fixed guns again so I slalomed around their hails, throwing my snowmobile down the slopes with almost suicidal abandon. It wouldn't be long before they hit me again, and when they did, I couldn't see my luck holding out for a second scratch next time.

I turned a crest and dumped my last two mines in their path, but every single one of them took the bend wide to avoid my explosives.

That was my last shot. I had nowhere left to go.

I ploughed on regardless, down the crisp white slopes and into the wilds below but my chips were cooked.

At least, they were until another chef entered the fray and this one wasn't as hygienic as the rest of us. An enormous explosion signalled rockets and mines meeting as one and from out of the fireball jumped a burning snowmobile to chase down the wolf pack.

It couldn't be!

One of the wolves blew to smithereens as rockets ripped his snowmobile to pieces while another was cut in half under a hail of cannon-fire. The remaining wolves scattered to meet this new threat but he already had the drop on them, strafing one into a bottomless crevice with his front-mounted guns while leaping over another to take his head clean off with his snow tracks. By the time the remaining wolves knew what was happening it was too late. Rip Dunbar was in amongst them and he was "pissed".

Seizing the lifeline I left them all to it and went all out to get myself off this mountain. I sped down a near-vertical slope, picking up speed and putting as much distance between myself and that mad Coloradan but all at once, he was the least of my problems. The sky shook as a squadron of Stealth bombers ripped through the blue and I barely had time to swear when they fired a volley of missiles that streaked above our heads and into the smoking remnants of our base.

They exploded like popcorn, blowing everything within a half-mile radius of the mountaintop to atoms and shaking several thousand tons of snow to tumble on after us.

"Oh shit!" I finally got around to swearing, twisting my throttle the last few millimetres to race for the safety of shallower slopes.

I had no chance.

A solid, fifty-foot tall wall of death roared after us, blotting out the horizon and shaking the ground beneath our tracks. Dunbar and the last remaining wolf put their differences aside and tried fleeing for themselves, but Mother Nature had lost all semblance of patience and was determined to show them who was boss. She raced down the mountainside faster than we could fall, deleting everything that dared stand up to her and roaring with indignation.

I had a few hundred yards on the others and got to preview my own death as the wolf's snowmobile was swamped in an instant, disappearing from view in less time than it took to blink.

Dunbar too was rapidly running out of mountainside but the instant before he was swallowed up, he leapt off his snowmobile and was encased by an enormous rubber balloon that suddenly wrapped around him from behind. It came out of nowhere, gobbling him up like Pac Man, and Dunbar rolled on in a big padded ball, shielded from death by injustice and the cheating miracle of American ingenuity.

"You bastard!" I shouted but this was lost against the thunderous crash of ice.

The whole weight of the avalanche was being funnelled directly after me by the contours of this gully, so I figured if I could make it across one of the ridges, I might just about be able to lose some of the snows on the crest. This meant steering straight across its path rather than simply trying to flee it, but I only had seconds to live either way, so I figured it was worth a shot.

I twisted my handlebars right, hanging over the left-hand side of the snowmobile as it cut a sweep through the snow, and gunned the engine one final time for the safety of higher ground.

If I'd had a moment to think I might've turned left instead of right because that was the side on which I had no vision, which would have spared the terrifying spectacle of that frozen tsunami closing in on me with merciless grace. I tried to ignore it but fifty thousand tons of snow has a way of distracting a man from his objectives and before long I was caught in two minds and swept off the face of the mountain.

I don't think I ever really knew what hit me. One minute I was hurtling around a snow-covered crag towards the crest of the rise, the next I was sideswiped out of my seat by a million frozen razor blades. I gulped down one last shocked breath, but was instantly smothered by an insurmountable swell of ice which turned me upside down, smashed me through a million more razor blades and turned my day into night.

I can't remember my last thought. I think it had something to do with Linda; how she'd react when she found out I'd died. How she'd remember me.

That was when I realised she wouldn't find out. No one would.

I was a thousand miles from nowhere, on the slopes of a deserted mountain in Greenland, and tumbling under thirty feet of snow – and snow that never thawed at that.

I was as lost as it was ever possible to be lost. Like one of those icemen that are uncovered from time to time in the Alps. Archaeologists would perhaps find me in a hundred thousand years time and wonder who I'd been. How I'd come to be here. And how I'd died.

They'd probably deduce I'd been a soldier, chased by an enemy, wounded in dozens of conflicts and finally buried under a winter's avalanche for posterity. But that wouldn't tell the whole story.

That wouldn't even tell a tenth of it.

All the events that had conspired to bring me to this point. All the people I'd met. All the operations I'd seen.

It's a shame because it was an amazing story, even if I do say so myself, so it would have been nice to tell it to someone.

But I couldn't. And there was nothing I could do about that anymore.

Because all at once, I was dead.

26. NEVER SAY DIE

I AWOKE IN HOSPITAL.

Bright lights. Urgent voices. Pain. Wooziness. Confusion.

I had tubes in my throat and needles in both arms. The moment I started to blink somebody shone a brilliant white light in my eye and reported I was dilating.

My memory was shot. I didn't know where I was or what was happening to me.

I was in so much pain.

I think somebody picked up on this because yet another needle skewered my arm and I was quickly stifled by a cold sensation that invaded me, creeping through my veins and into my body until I floated away, out of pain's way and deep, deep within myself.

*

More pain.

This time it was a duller pain: an ache of slumber, of distant injuries. Of recovery.

I've been under the knife enough times to recognise post-op pain when I wake up to it, although I was totally confused for a few minutes because I couldn't remember having gone in for surgery. I'd become separated from my own timeline and had to rewind my memories to a place I recognised before I could get my bearings.

The skyjacking.

The base.

The cells.

The firefight.

Captain Collett.

I played them through my mind, out of the snowmobile dock and down the gully until the avalanche rolled over me. But that was all I had. The tape was blank from that point onwards. How had I gotten out of there?

And where exactly was I?

A white-coated doctor entered and introduced himself as Captain Nekoroski of the United States Navy. I could address him as either Captain or Doctor, whichever I preferred. I tried them both but no words tumbled out.

"It may take you a few days to get your voice back, we've had a lot of tubes down there," the doctor informed me. "For the record, you are on-board the USS *John Wayne* in the IC unit and in the custody of the United States Navy."

"When...?" I somehow managed to mouth.

The doctor elaborated. "You've been with us for the last two weeks. You've been pretty badly bashed about, but nothing you can't take I'm sure. So we're gonna patch you up and send you on your way, first to Augusta and then to McCarthy – that's Fort McCarthy to you," he said in a way that set alarm bells off across my battered pain system. "So sit back, take it easy and let us know if we can do anything for you. Because this is as good as it gets. And it ain't gonna stay this good for much longer."

I have to say I wasn't a fan of the Doctor's bedside manner, but then again I guess he was part Doctor and part Naval officer and those were often two difficult hats to wear together. For the most part, he was perfectly civil, if a little officious, and I couldn't fault him on his standard of care because I was comfortable, pain-free and, most surprising of all, still alive.

But what was truly remarkable was how I'd come to be here in the first place. I mean, I simply couldn't fathom it, that the United States Navy had found me buried in a God-forsaken corner of nowhere under several thousand tons of snow and ice, thawed me out, resuscitated me and shipped me back to civilization. Or at least, as close to civilization as the USS *John Wayne* was ever likely to sail.

Actually, forget how they'd done this; I couldn't figure out *why* they'd done this.

Somewhere beyond my range of vision, a door opened and a pair of heavy combat boots entered the room.

The doctor looked up at the new arrival and saluted him before returning to the question of my blood pressure.

"How is he, Captain?"

"He's out of danger, sir. A few broken bones, torn ligaments and trauma injuries, but the ice protected him until we could get him to ICU. Residues of hypothermia, moderate concussion and a touch of shock but he'll recover, I'm sure," the doctor diagnosed.

"Good," my visitor replied. "Because I've got plans for him. I need him fit and healthy to play his part," he said now stepping into view so that I could see his miserable face.

Rip Dunbar.

"Thought you'd got away from me, didn't you, Cyclops?" Rip growled, his lips so taut they barely quivered. "Well, you don't get off that lightly!"

*

The Doctor was as good as his word. Over the next ten days, he and his staff nursed me away from the red readings and back to some semblance of health. Then when the tubes were finally pulled from my arms, I was strapped up all over again and shipped off to mainland USA. I couldn't tell you where exactly Fort McCarthy was, as I was required to wear a blindfold for the entire journey (presumably to prevent me from memorizing the air route) but I think it was up north somewhere. The cold winter's air that greeted me when we landed told me as much.

The place was quiet too. Almost unnervingly so. Over the sounds of Humvees tearing about the place and aircraft taxiing or winding down, there was almost nothing beyond the perimeter wire. No sounds of town. No distant freeways. Not even any birds twittering overhead, which meant no trees: just a lot of military hustle and bustle and a shrill wind to chill my soul.

I listened to a clipboard being signed, then a few cigarettes being exchanged, before I was loaded onto an armoured car and driven out across the plains. The road we travelled along was flat, straight and featureless. As far as I could tell we passed nothing and no one the whole time we were on the road. A brick on the accelerator and a broomstick to stop the steering wheel from spinning could have driven me out here, but bricks and broomsticks cost money so they had a Marine Corporal do it instead.

Then, after an hour of counting potholes and more cigarettes being smoked in the front, the armoured car slowed and we finally arrived at our destination.

We stopped and started three times in the space of half a mile or so, which told me we were passing through three lines of security, then we drove down a long sloping causeway until I heard the engine roaring back against itself to suggest we'd gone underground.

A few more twists and turns and we parked up to the sounds of an escort being formed up outside. The rear door was yanked open and a craggy gunnery Sergeant climbed on-board to push me out. A small squad of Delta Force soldiers was there to pick me up and finally my blindfold was removed, although my cuffs stayed where they were. I didn't know whether to feel flattered or sorry for the American taxpayer but I had time for neither because some three-star General with more ribbons than a maypole maker's daughter stepped forward to give me the welcome speech.

"I am Lieutenant-General Major of the Fourteenth Tactical Infantry Division and you are in the United States military penitentiary known as Fort McCarthy…"

"Never heard of it," I told him.

"Good. You are indicted to stand trial for crimes in direct violation of international law as well as those of the United States of America," which were obviously the ones he and his buddies were most upset about. "These charges are as follows," he said, looking down at his clipboard and rattling through them without pausing to see how they were being received. "Three counts international terrorism. Three counts international sabotage. Two counts crimes against humanity. One count international piracy. Thirty-eight counts of murder in the first-degree. Twenty-four counts of murder in the second-degree. Two counts conspiracy to commit acts of genocide. One count conspiracy to extort monies with terror…"

"Isn't that the same as terrorism?" I asked, but the General ignored me and carried on ploughing through my CV.

"… One count conspiracy to depose a democratically elected government. Two counts conspiracy to cause destruction of government property. Two counts international espionage against the United States of America. Four counts conspiracy to commit explosions. Three counts belonging to organisations banned under international law. And finally, one count of working to undermine the interests of the Congress of the United States of America and her allies, both at home and aboard. "

"Is that it?" I asked.

"As I say, you will be called to answer all these charges and face a military tribunal in due course. A lawyer will be appointed to act on your behalf and you will have the right of due process, though you are not permitted to make contact with anyone beyond these official channels. If you attempt to do so by any means, all rights and privileges will be revoked and you will face instant military justice under section twenty-seven of the special detainees' act. Do you understand everything that has been explained to you?"

"Am I allowed to choose my own lawyer?" I asked.

"Negative. A military lawyer will be appointed to work on your case but I repeat, you will not have access to anyone beyond these walls," the General reiterated.

"What about witnesses?"

"These are questions for your lawyer," he said with a snap of impatience, handing his clipboard to the Aid standing in attendance just behind him before completing his spiel.

"Welcome to Fort McCarthy."

27. YOU ONLY GET LIFE TWICE

CRIMES AGAINST HUMANITY? Conspiracy to commit genocide? Sixty-two counts of murder? They were having a laugh, weren't they? I'd spent most of the last dozen years guarding vending machines. Well, all right, so I'd been involved with a few unsavoury sorts and I had, admittedly, killed a few men in my time, but never anyone who hadn't tried to kill me first. How was that murder? Let alone genocide?

My military lawyer explained the finer points of the charges against me when he came to see me in McCarthy's infirmary a few days later. I still wasn't well enough to be moved to a proper cell yet so Captain Blakeney perched on the end of my bed, rested his file on my anti-biotics machine and went through the indictments one by one.

All of them related to my time in the employ of either Victor Soliman or Griffin Marvel, as Rip Dunbar's testimony put me at both scenes, so I was tarred with the conspiracy brush. ie. Victor Soliman had brought down a couple of satellites with his Star Ray, so that was international sabotage and destruction of government property. Griffin Marvel had threatened to blow up a big chunk of Finland with his CSMK guided missiles, so that was international terrorism and genocide. It didn't matter that it hadn't been me who'd pushed, or threatened to push, either button; all they had to do was slap the word "conspiracy" into the indictments and they could lay the same charges against me that they could lay against Soliman, Marvel or either of the blokes who used to fry the chips in the staff canteens (Anton in Mozambique, Eric in Greenland. Anton was useless – his chips really were a crime against humanity).

And the murders?

Thirty-eight military personnel and twenty-four civilians were recorded as having lost their lives as a direct result of action taken by either Soliman or Marvel (and one by Anton). American, British, Russian, French, Danish, Finnish, Canadian and Mozambiquean. I'd been part of each organisation at the time so I'd be called to answer for each death. Ironically, the authorities didn't realise I'd been part of the team that had skyjacked the USAF C-17 but I got charged with those murders all the same just by association.

In actual fact, there was only one murder charge on my entire rap sheet that was directly linked to me – that of Jabulani Mthunzi, that annoying little Nguni guide who'd so won Rip Dunbar's heart. That charge was laid out in meticulous, if slightly weighted, detail claiming I'd gunned him down while he'd been unarmed. Which I guess was technically correct but that told only half the story. I wondered if I'd get the chance to tell the other half.

"What am I looking at?"

Captain Blakeney followed my eye-line down to my manacles and blinked.

"No (literal cunt), I mean what sort of sentence can I expect to receive if I'm found guilty?" I spelt out, optimistically using the word "if" instead of "when".

Captain Blakeney sucked his teeth.

"Death," he shrugged.

"Death?"

"Yeah, for these charges, there isn't any other sentence."

"And what's the likelihood of me being found guilty?" I asked.

"Oh, it's a certainty," he replied without so much as a second's hesitation.

"Oh lovely," I scowled. "And so you're here for what? Just to keep me chuckling until it comes time to plug me into the mains?"

"I'm here to ensure due process and see that you get a fair trial," he said in all seriousness.

"Something tells me you don't get paid on results," I pointed out.

"Mr Jones, I don't see what else I can do. I mean you were there at the times stated. You were in the employment of both Victor Soliman and Griffin Marvel and took an active part in perpetrating these offences."

"How do you know I took an active part?" I demanded.

"You were employed in a combat role, namely installation security, therefore by definition you played a vital logistical role supporting the perpetration of these crimes. It's an open and shut case," he said, making no friends around here whatsoever.

"Then once again, what's the fucking point of you? Are you on the family payroll or something?" I fumed, rattling on my manacles as I sought to add a sixty-third count to my charge sheet.

"Mr Jones, there are more options available to us than just pleading guilty or not guilty," Captain Blakeney advised.

"Meaning?"

"Meaning, we could enter a plea. The indictments as they stand will get us fried, but if we can argue them down to a raft of lesser offences, we might be able to avoid the death penalty and receive a sentence of life imprisonment."

"Might we?" I said, fucking loving his use of the plural. "And why would they agree to that? If this is an open and shut case, as you say?"

Captain Blakeney cocked his head, as if to suggest I already knew the answer to my own question.

"Mr Jones, you are a small fish. But you've swum in a lot of ponds that will be of interest to the United States government. Now these charges only take into account activities relating to your terms with Victor Soliman and Griffin Marvel," he said, patting my file, "but don't for a moment imagine that we don't know you've worked for other organisations. So, give the SEO the facts; names, dates and places, outfits you've worked with, crimes you've witnessed. They'll have most of it anyway so you may not even have enough to save your life, but give them everything you've got and leave the rest to me," he smiled, laying a hand on my shoulder as a mark of his sincerity as I almost made it through the cuffs.

*

Given my options, I had no choice but to play ball. Or at least, some limited form of ball, because the one thing I had going in my favour was the sheer number of jobs I'd worked on in the last dozen years. Names, dates and places? I gave them more names, dates and places than they knew what to do with:

S.P.I.D.E.R (Special Political Infiltration Division for Economic Revolution), M.A.N.T.R.A (Millennium Anti-Nationalist Tactical Redeployment Association), D.E.A.T.H (Designated Elimination of Assets, Territories and Homesteads), K.I.S.S (Kingdom's International Secret Service). Operations *XY*, *Extreme*, *Blowfish*, *Sunburn*, *Chainsaw*. Zillion Silverfish, Morris Merton, Doctor Thalassocrat, Polonius Crump, Kris Kingdom.

I rattled through them and much more besides as SEO interrogated me over the next three months, first from my infirmary bed, then later in the interrogation block. They took down every detail, recorded my words and cross-referenced my testimony to verify my claims. Most of it was dead information about dead men and dead ideas anyway but they were interested, all the same, enough to make me comfortable, treat me right and feed me well. They even got me a new cosmetic eye just to make me feel like a person again. It had "PRISONER" stamped across the middle of it.

Amusingly, it wasn't just the stuff about the bad guys that interested my interrogators; they loved hearing the dirt on their so-called allies too. Jack Tempest of the British SIS. Jean Cabon of the French DGSE. Kim Hu of the Wind Brotherhood. Anything I had on these guys was lapped up like Ambrosia and cross-filed under military intelligence / Facebook gossip. But for the main, I just told them about the jobs:

Hong Kong, Siberia, Nanawambai Atoll, Geneva, East Timor, north Africa, southern Africa, western Africa, Cuba, Colombia and Kansas.

I'd clocked up some air miles in my time and was actually surprised at just how much I could remember. But then I guess when you've got nothing else to do for days and weeks it focuses the mind and you're able to dredge up all sorts of memories you thought you'd lost to time.

In the end, it was the sheer volume of information I gave them that allowed me to cover my more sensitive tracks. It was hard going at times, especially at the start of my questioning when they had me hooked up to a polygraph machine, because some of their questions were very searching indeed. But when you've got an endless supply of detailed intelligence to dazzle someone with, you can usually negotiate your way through even the stiffest of interrogations. So, like a holiday camp magician with a shiny cape and a tried and tested routine, I pulled an endless stream of colourful handkerchiefs out of my sleeves to distract my interrogators from the sleight of hand that brushed the more controversial questions aside.

Namely, questions concerning The Agency.

"And so, how did you get this job, Mr Jones? Who exactly employed you?"

"It was Polonius Crump's commander-in-chief, a guy called, Klive Andrevski, a former Colonel in the Stasi. He defected just before the wall came down with files on every agent known to the GDR and sold this information on, resulting in the assassination of some fourteen Western agents, including two of your own if I remember rightly. I think I can even remember their names if you want to double-check this?"

Which was true but it didn't actually answer the question. Not really. Not completely.

Of course, I couldn't dodge their questions indefinitely but The Agency had a time-served strategy in place for dealing with polygraph interrogations. For two days and two nights, they torture all new recruits mercilessly whilst we're plugged into polygraph machines. It's all part of basic training. It doesn't help us learn how to lie properly but it plants the memory of pain in our psyches so that any and all future polygraph interrogations sends our readings through the roof (bless 'em).

"He's lying."

"Cut the crap and tell us who hired you!"

And this is when you give them the other stuff.

See, besides ruining your happy memories of boot camp, The Agency also puts into place half a dozen cover stories so that if you're ever taken alive you have things to give your interrogators. Advertisements are placed in *Soldier of Fortune* magazine. Ghost offices are set up and closed down with phone records showing calls and correspondence sent to payphones and Post Office boxes near your home. Paper trails are laid. The Agency does this for every job, layering shadows on smoke until the truth's a half-lie, shrouded in uncertainty and buried beneath a mountain of more plausible alternatives. And then, when that's all in place they leave you with one final incentive – protect us, protect The Agency, and we will pick you up from any extraction point anywhere in the world within twelve hours of you making it over the wall.

Now I ask you, how can you rat out friends like that?

"Who else were you with? Who made it off the island too?"

"Eighteen of us; Mr Smith, Mr Petrov, Mr Kim, Mr Andreev, Captain Campbell, Mr…"

"Enough of this Mister crap! This isn't *Pride and* fucking *Prejudice*!" my interrogator barked, slamming the table between us. "We want names, asshole, otherwise we'll fry you on every fucking charge!"

"And I'm giving you names. At least, the only names I ever knew. We don't use our full names, not to each other, it's policy; we're just Mister or Missus. Or Captain or Sergeant or Lieutenant. We don't ask and we don't offer our full names for this very reason, in case we're ever questioned," I told him.

"Oh, you don't do you, well how very formal of you," he scoffed. "You know more than you're letting on, *dick wad*, so don't try to play games with us or we'll bring Major Dunbar back in here and let him question you personally."

"It wouldn't make any difference, I'm telling you all I know. I'm a mercenary, for fuck's sake, not a soldier of ideology. I'm not trying to protect anyone but myself. Which is why they put these safeguards in place, to stop soldiers in my position from selling everyone else down the river to save their own worthless hides."

The interrogator glared, flaring his nostrils as he snorted at me, then all at once, he sat back down and started asking me about my eye again.

That's the way it is with interrogations. They pump you with questions and hammer Formica surfaces as if their very lives depend on getting the answers, then hit you with a different line of inquiry while you're still up a tree over your first lot of denials. Linda used to do a similar thing; she would ask me about my day, then not give me a chance to reply as she scatter-gunned me with questions as I tried to get out my lies. Linda? It was funny how my thoughts kept returning to Linda. We'd only been married for two years but she'd cast such a shadow over the rest of my life that I sometimes wondered if she'd meant more to me than a simple marriage of convenience.

But that was a question for another day. For the moment I had other questions to worry about.

"Who patched you up? Where d'you get the GPS from, bozo?"

*

My time on the interrogation block blurs into a single overwhelming memory because there was no structure to it. They came for me day or night, sometimes for twelve hours at a time, sometimes for barely a few minutes. I got the occasional slap but on the whole, I was surprised by how little they physically abused me. Perhaps that was because I never tried holding back on them. Or at least, they never thought I was holding back on them. I'm sure if I'd mimed locking my lips and tossing an imaginary key over my shoulder I would've soon found my head in a bucket of piss but I didn't. I co-operated as best I could so that after three months of names, dates and places, picking mug shots out of family albums and drawing noughts and crosses on satellite photographs, my interrogators were gone and replaced by a ram-rod panel of military judges, called to McCarthy to decide how best to reward me for my co-operation.

"Mark Paul Jones," they said, "you have pleaded guilty to the following charges."

A military clerk stood up and read out what I'd won.

"One count of conspiracy to commit crimes against humanity. One count of conspiracy to destroy US government property. One count of murder in the second degree."

That bloody Nguni! My prosecutors dropped all the other murder charges and accepted that I couldn't be held responsible for killing so many whilst technically only responsible for guarding the Coke machine but Dunbar wouldn't have it. He simply wouldn't let them sully the memory of his matchstick mate with a grubby plea bargain so for the second time in as many lives I was convicted of killing a man who'd knocked on my door looking for a fight.

If only I could've killed him again.

"These are some of the gravest charges on record," the head-judge glowered. "Each a capital crime in its own right and in normal circumstances I should have no hesitation but to pass the appropriate sentence with immediate effect. However," he hammed, milking the moment for all it was worth, "in light of your recent co-operation with our investigators we have decided to treat you with leniency and it is, therefore, our judgement that you be sentenced to a term of ninety-nine years incarceration for each offence. Sentences to run concurrently."

"That'll help," I said.

"You will serve out the entirety of your sentence here at Fort McCarthy in the maximum-security wing of the special prisoners unit. As you are a British subject, your government will be informed of your presence here, though you will not be permitted to communicate with any persons beyond these penitentiary walls. That includes diplomatic staff, lawyers, journalists, friends or family."

"Can I at least call Raj's News and cancel my papers?" I asked. "I must be running up one hell of a bill."

The judge continued, unfazed. "Furthermore, any and all assets held by the convicted are hereby confiscated and turned over to become the legal property of the United States government," he said, his country suddenly one slightly run-down if heavily mortgaged farm in West Sussex the richer, before looking me straight in the eye to hammer the final nail into my coffin.

"Lastly, because of the nature of your plea and because of your full and unconditional acceptance of guilt, it is our judgement that you be denied the right of appeal for the entirety of your sentence. Mark Paul Jones, have you anything to say for the record?"

What was the point? It was over. I might as well

have been buried under all that snow in Greenland for all the weight my words would ever carry again.

I looked over my shoulder at a blazing Rip Dunbar, who'd made a special effort and actually put on a shirt for the occasion, before turning back to address the bench.

"Yes, I have," I told them. "I've been in US custody for four months now so will that go down as time served?"

28. IN THE LAND OF THE FREE

BELIEVE IT OR NOT, there were some actual benefits to being convicted and sentenced, the main one being that I was transferred from the detainees' unit to the special prisoners' block with immediate effect.

And wouldn't you know it, I was already acquainted with some of my fellow special prisoners.

"Mr Jones."

"By God, Mr Smith!"

We shook hands like old friends but stopped short of embracing and rolling around on the floor together. I guess that would come with time.

"I can't say I'm pleased to see you here," Mr Smith shrugged.

"Me neither," I agreed. "Still, it could be worse. I thought you were dead."

"Me? No," he shrugged. "We got the chopper moving after we saw your flare and got picked up in Tasiilaq before the extraction team could get us out."

"Who flew?" I asked as we were ushered through a huge set of doors and into a plain white tiled room with showers in the middle of the room.

"An Omega guy called Crow. Black hair, funny eyebrows; do you remember him?"

"Nope."

"Well anyway, he came up looking to bug out so we hitched a ride. He should be in here as well somewhere," he said, looking around at the other faces in our association batch as they began stripping us of our duds.

"So what did you get?" I asked. "What sentence did they give you?"

"Ninety-nine years, same as everyone else," Mr Smith confirmed. "It's what everyone gets, didn't you know?"

"No," I said, feeling suckered and somewhat less than special all at once. "Motherfuckers!"

"Ain't that a fact."

Of course, the authorities didn't just let us mingle at will. We were locked up two to a cell for twenty-two hours a day and allowed only one hour of association time a day. And even then, our association hours were staggered in such a way that barely twenty guys were ever allowed out at once. I guess the authorities didn't feel like taking the lid off a pot of snakes by giving four hundred professional mercenaries with nothing to lose the run of the place.

So we were shepherded out of our cells in batches, through the showers, through the dinner hall and finally up to the surface for a precious hour of daylight, before once again being led back to our cells. It wasn't much but that hour of daylight came to mean everything to us and the one and only bright spot in an endless succession of otherwise grim days. It also turned out to be the authorities' chief stranglehold over the prisoners and could be – and frequently was – withdrawn for any infraction of the rules. I guess that's why they gave it to us in the first place.

I'd find out all of this in the fullness of time but for the moment I was an old hand at settling into inhospitable climes and kept my head down until I'd learned the lie of the land.

I wasn't put in a cell with Mr Smith but someone else I knew, or at least knew of, Mr Rousseau, otherwise known as Cyber Guy to all at book club. He'd been picked up in Tajikistan by French Foreign Legion commandos following a visit from that tedious hair-transplantee, Jean Cabon. I was surprised to find him in American custody but like Mr Rousseau said of the French authorities; why build your own top-secret maximum-security prison when you can just pay the Americans to take your trash? Either way, he was a nice guy and I'm pleased to say we got on.

What's more, with Mr Rousseau, Mr Smith, Mr Woo, Mr Deveroux and half a dozen other guys in here already we were able to get book club up and running again within a matter of weeks.

Of course, we had to disguise it from the authorities as they came down hard on any sort of collusion but we'd been well versed at hiding it from The Agency so this didn't prove too problematic. Besides, there'd been a few reading collectives before we arrived so all it took was a little structuring and a mutual acceptance of the rules to put the basic infrastructure in place.

We didn't have access to computers, of course, so we logged our scores on the next best thing – the prison grapevine. This was a living computer in its own right and with consensus and accord and we were able to hold a record of everything we'd read and even update the scores as we went along. It's quite a testament to the human mind if you think about it, but at any given moment in time, any one of some eighty prisoners could've told you how Martin Amis's *Time's Arrow* was getting on.

Not too well as it turned out.

"It's just backwards, I don't see the point," Mr Deveraux said, as we walked around in closely monitored circles under the falling snows of early winter.

"That's exactly the point," I replied. "It's a whole life backwards, from death all the way through to birth."

"Yeah, I know that, I read it – in one evening I might add – but it just seemed like an exercise in seeing if he could write a book backwards. Big deal, he did it. Woo fucking hoo!"

"You don't think it was clever?"

"No, because I could see the end coming from page one, that he was going to disappear up his mum's chuff and then up his dad's dick at the end of the book."

I stopped to look out across the white plains, flat and as crisp as a new tablecloth under low hanging grey skies. Mr Deveraux stopped with me while I stooped to pick up a handful of fresh snow.

"I don't think it was meant to be a whodunit, Mr Deveraux. I think the message behind the book was that there's no set truth; everything takes on a different interpretation when you look at it from a different perspective." I opened my hand again to let a few dribbles of melted water drop to the ground.

"How profound!" he mugged.

"Well, you don't have to like everything on the list, just give it a shitty score if you didn't rate it."

"I did, I gave it a five."

"A five?"

"Oh sorry, I mean a one. Catching isn't it, this backwards business?"

"Hilarious. So that brings it down to…" I did a quick bit of mental arithmetic as we kicked our boots and got moving again. "Two-point-one? I'll double-check that with a pen and paper later but I think that's right."

"No, it's less than that now. Mr Hughes read it and he gave it a one, an' all," Mr Deveraux told me.

"When did he read it?"

"Last night, in the cell right after me. I told you, it only took me an evening to get through. It's really short."

"So all right then, hang on, that's now twelve scores logged; four *ones*, five *twos*, two *threes* and a *four* (mine)," I recalled, jotting them all up on my frozen fingers.

"It comes to exactly two," Mr Deveraux told me. "The average I mean. It's good when that happens, when we get an exact score like that, isn't it?"

"It certainly makes all this reading worthwhile," I agreed.

Of course, the real reason book club flourished in McCarthy was because it brought with it a sense of freedom to men who knew none. Our books were like windows out onto the world. Of course, they had been before we'd started book club, when they'd been read individually, but when you read books as a group, the worlds and stories that are held within their pages come to life even more because they become part of a collective consciousness. The experiences become richer and that window out onto the world opens just a little wider.

And in prison, the difference between hope and hopelessness is more often than not barely the width of a page.

So this was how we passed the time. We read. We shared our thoughts on what we read. And book by book we gradually rated the prison's somewhat limited library.

It's vital to have some sort of endeavour to throw yourself into because the enormity of a ninety-nine year sentence is almost enough to crush you. Naturally, it's easier for Affiliates to bear because we've been sentenced to life before but it's still a challenge to make it out of bed most mornings. The secret of survival is forgetting your former life, that's gone, you can't get it back, and mourning for it will do nothing but put knots in your bedsheets before the year's out.

It's hard. Of course, it's hard. It's meant to be hard. But when you sign on as an Affiliate, you're aware of the risks and prepared for the consequences. If not, then you've no business signing on as an Affiliate.

But the authorities didn't want us going off our chumps either, as that would do no one any favours, least of all them, so they did what they could to prevent the spread of despair. We liked reading? So they provided us with a few extra books. In addition, all the Affiliates that shared association hours were at similar stages of their sentences. Meaning, the first four hours of the day were given to Affiliates who'd served less than ten years. Once you got into the afternoons, the Affiliates who were let out then had been here for anything up to twenty years. And then, in the evenings, when the last lights were fading and the shadows stretched long across the prairie, the old-timers were given their hour of daylight. Most prisoners didn't make it to see their thirtieth year in truth but according to the grapevine, there were one or two in here that came out at night, that had long white beards and no idea Kennedy was dead.

Or even, that his son had become President.

This was our fate. This was what we were all heading for. Nothing could stop that and nobody could reprieve us, so why unsettle us by showing us our futures in the faces of our elders?

"Escape?"

"Well, that's the real reason, isn't it?" Mr Smith said.

"What?"

"If anyone knows how to get out of here or at least where the cracks are, it'll be the old-timers so they're not gonna let them anywhere near us, are they? Not with our fresh legs and unsullied spirits. Not that it would make much difference."

"Why not?"

"Well…"

Blinding spotlights suddenly cranked on all around us and loud hailers ordered to freeze.

Commotion and angry yelling followed as Delta

specialists poured in through the wire from all sides and ordered us onto our faces at gunpoint. Boots pressed into the backs of mine and Mr Smith's necks as plastic draw-straps were tightened around our wrists, then we were yanked to our feet and run across the exercise ground to the main prisoner elevators as our colleagues behind were subjected to ID and bar code scanning.

"Prisoners 2248 and 2251, you were recorded having a restricted conversation, therefore, you are both sentenced to a month in the hole with loss of privileges," Watch Commander Crockett told us. "Effective immediate. Take them down."

The Deltas bundled us in the elevators and we dropped like stones back into the underground facility, bi-passing our own level and carrying on straight down to the punishment block. When the doors opened two more Deltas took over from our escorts and we were run in different directions towards opposite ends of the wing. Before I was out of earshot I just managed to shout one last thing over my shoulder to Mr Smith.

"Well, what?"

"Well…" Mr Smith shouted back, "*this!*"

29. TIME'S DRIFTWOOD OF FORTUNE

THE ODD TRIP to the cellblock asides my first three years in McCarthy were pretty uneventful – as you'd expect. I didn't get gang-raped. I didn't challenge Mr Big for supremacy. I didn't make it over the wall or even try. And I didn't earn the wrath of Lieutenant-General Major despite continually referring to him as Lieutenant-Major General whenever I knew the long-range microphones were on me. I just survived. This was the minimum, maximum and only requirement at McCarthy.

I don't know why I chose to survive. There didn't seem to be much point. Some of the guys I'd come in with, Mr Deveraux for instance, opted for early release and went out in a wooden overcoat but I didn't. Not because I was scared or still hankered after a life outside the perimeter wire but because I was in no rush to go anywhere just yet. That's the best way I can think to describe where my head was. Death would eventually find me. And when it did it would last for a million billion trillion years, until the end of time in fact, if such an event even occurred, so what difference did my measly lifespan make? I wasn't suffering, I wasn't living in fear and I wasn't in pain. I didn't need my misery to end (it would've been nice but it wasn't a deal-breaker) and I didn't need to get back to any loved ones so I was perfectly resigned to my confined circumstances.

I think it also helped that I'd died under that avalanche in Greenland, or at least, thought I had, because as hopeless and as bleak as my situation now was it was still preferable to that. Being alive counted for something. Not much, but it counted for something all the same. And as long as I could feel the wind on my face for an hour a day, see the clouds in the sky or hold a thought in my head, it always would.

*

"Prisoner 2248. On your feet."

I swung my legs over the bunk and dropped to the floor, leaving Elizabeth Graver spread open on the bunk behind me – not literally, but I had been in prison a few years so I wouldn't have said no (maybe).

Mr Rousseau started getting to his feet as well but they told him, "Stand fast 2212 and stay on your bunk," flicking my trouble antenna in ways that got me grumbling.

"Against the wall," I was ordered, so I did as I was told and listened to sounds of my belongings being tossed, before being slapped into cuffs. Steel cuffs at that. Not plastic draw-straps.

Something was definitely up.

"Turn around!"

I turned to find Major-General Lieutenant, or whatever the fuck his name was, standing tall and regarding me with deep mistrust.

"2248?" he asked.

"That's my number, don't wear it out," I replied, figuring we could both stand a little levity right about now.

"Otherwise known as Jones? Mr Mark Paul Jones, formerly of Petworth, West Sussex, *Enger-lund*?"

"What's all this about? I haven't done anything," I said, before amending that statement. "Well, nothing I haven't already been sentenced to ninety-nine years for."

"Read a lot of books do you Mr Jones?" the General hinted, his eyes flickering towards Ms Graver on the bed then back to me.

"That's right," I told him. "I've gone right off snow-boarding just lately."

Despite the giggles, I was genuinely worried for myself. Like I said, the authorities in here came down hard on any sort of organising activities, even over something as innocent as reading. They liked to deal with four hundred individually broken spirits, not a single working resolve. That was dangerous. That was a challenge. That was absolutely positively not tolerated. It had taken them three years to find me but it seemed they'd finally located the mouldy old apple that was daring to corrupt the rest of their carefully harvested barrel. It didn't matter that our book club hadn't caused them any problems since its inception — all that mattered was it could.

"Bring him," was all the General said before about-turning and wheeling away up the landing.

I caught Mr Rousseau's eye and blinked three times to give him the order to shut up shop, but it was clear from his expression that he'd already swung the sign around.

I was frog-marched in the General's wake, through the special prisoners' wing, past a couple of hundred locked doors and towards the elevators, where two more heavily-armed Deltas were waiting for us. They snapped to a crisp salute at either the sight of me or the General then we all piled into the elevator and rode up two levels to the interrogation unit. Here, the door opened and yet two more Deltas joined the Conga, dancing me past a long line of cells and on to the main interrogation suite.

I remembered this place from my time under the desk lamp. It was an imposingly big room, even bigger than I remembered, probably thirty feet by a hundred, which looked vast to someone who'd spent the last thousand nights sharing an eight by ten. And it was dark. The edges of the room were lost to shadows while the centre was bright and stark. An empty table kept two plastic chairs apart and a chunky microphone hung from the ceiling like the Eden snake.

Two of our party dropped off to guard the door outside while four Deltas accompanied us inside to sink into the shadows of the four corners of the room. On his way past one of the Deltas relieved me of my cuffs so I rubbed my wrists and tried out one of the chairs for size.

"You will sit when you are told to sit," the General barked.

"When you start paying me you can start telling me what to do. Until that time blow it out of your fucking arse, Major," I suggested. Well, whatever they were going to do to me, they were going to do to me regardless, so I indulged myself and enjoyed the paradox freedom of the condemned.

That same Delta who'd freed me of my cuffs moments earlier was just about to slap them back on when a new different voice told them to stand down. The hairs on the back of my neck almost parted when I recognised the voice and turned to see the last person on Earth I'd expected to see in this God-forsaken place.

Jack Tempest.

If ever there was a face to make a man rethink suicide.

"I don't believe it!"

"Nice to see you too, Mark. You don't mind if I call you Mark, do you?"

"My friends call me 2248," I told him, prompting the General's features to chisel a few shaves.

Tempest looked around and raised an eyebrow, then asked the General to wait outside. "And take your men with you."

"Very well, but I'll leave one man here if you don't mind," the General replied, mistaking XO-11 for a man who liked to negotiate things as he went along.

"I do, take them all outside," Tempest clarified.

"This prisoner is a very dangerous individual, Commander. A professional mercenary with dozens of kills to his name," the General quibbled, overlooking the fact that the court had awarded me only one kill.

"Mr Jones and I are old acquaintances. He'll give me no trouble," Tempest assured him.

"That may be so but he is still a special prisoner of the United States government," the General pointed out. "And you, Commander Tempest, have no authority over either me or my men…"

"Take it outside, General. That's an order!" a new

voice barked off towards my left and my shoulders sank even further when these particular dulcet tones struck home.

"Major Dunbar," the General said, presumably to remind Rip of his rank.

"I have Presidential authority over this prisoner and I will bust you and your men down to privates and transfer you to the Iraqi army if you're still in my line of sight inside of five seconds! Are you clear, General?"

The Deltas certainly were and started making for the door before the General could flap his yap any more, and finally, the message sunk in: the cool kids were having a party and fatty wasn't invited.

"Yes… Major," the General mumbled, wondering for a moment whether or not to salute before deciding not and simply leaving.

"You remembered my birthday?" I said, jogging a grin out of Tempest and a glare out of Dunbar.

"That's right, Mark. We hoped you'd be pleased," Tempest replied, pulling up a chair while Dunbar paced restlessly behind him.

"Since when did you two start working together?" I asked.

"Since my dick fucked your mama in the ass, you *mother*," Dunbar shouted down my throat, slamming the table between us before resuming his pacing pattern over Tempest's shoulder. Tempest shifted somewhat uncomfortably in his seat and confirmed this was indeed a joint US and British operation.

"I see. Going well is it?" I deduced.

"What can you tell us about Operation *Candy*

Snatch?" Tempest asked.

"That depends," I told him. "What can you tell me about it?"

"We ask the questions, *dick wad*, so get talking!" Dunbar growled, balling up both fists to threaten the table again.

"I know a few things," I bluffed, wondering if I could con anything out of them with a few strategic fairy tales.

"Bullshit. He's lying!" Dunbar grunted.

"Why would I?"

"Garbage like you always lies. It's in your nature, *douche bag*," Dunbar replied. "This is a waste of time. I told you we shouldn't have come."

"I don't know if you got the memo, Rip, but I spilled my guts for three months when I first arrived. Ask away and I'll tell you what you want to know, for the right price of course," I invited, catching Tempest's eye.

Dunbar stopped circling and glared down at me. After a few seconds he shook off his tight black Special Op's jacket to show off his tight black Special Op's T-shirt. It had been three years since I'd seen him and it was clear his bookshelf had grown dustier in that time by the way his shirt now bulged like a bag of apples.

"Brother, I'm gonna ask you just one more time then you're gonna start hurting," he snarled. "Tell us about *Candy Snatch*."

I mulled this over, shrugged, then asked Tempest how he'd been keeping.

"Pretty fair," Tempest replied with a shrug.

Dunbar was obviously disappointed at how poorly his "bad cop" was going over but he resisted the temptation to insert any slap-stick into the act and let "good cop" take it for a bit.

"So what have you got for us Mark?" Tempest asked.

"What's on offer?"

"What do you want?"

"What do you think I want? A new wanking sock? I want out. I want to go home," I told him.

"That's a pretty tall order, Mark. I don't know if I could swing that for you, not after all you've done," Tempest said solemnly.

"Don't give me that, you can do anything you want, you've already said you've got Presidential authority. And you're obviously desperate for some sort of a lead otherwise you wouldn't be in here talking to the likes of me," I pointed out.

"Not freedom," Tempest said, shaking his head.

"Yeah, you're staying right where you are and rotting, you fucking *mother*!" Dunbar agreed, promoting me from brother again.

"Then what can you do for me?" I fished.

"Well, I can definitely get you that new wanking sock," Tempest conceded.

"Oh, you're hilarious you are," I glowered. "Thanks for looking me up, this so beats sitting in the hole for a month."

"If they die, you'll do more than a month in the hole, you one-eyed maggot. You'll do the whole of your fucking short-assed life down there," Dunbar snapped.

"If who…" I started to ask, before biting my tongue to claw back the words.

Tempest picked up on my lapse and raised an eyebrow. "You don't know, do you?"

"I know enough," I told him, frantically backpeddling to refill my spilt bluff basket.

"Of course," Tempest smirked. "So why don't you tell me about it?"

"I will, but first I want to know what's in it for me," I insisted.

"Mark, you've got nothing to trade and no knowledge of *Candy Snatch*. You couldn't possibly have. We knew that already," Tempest smarmed, opening a silver cigarette box and tapping a cigarette against the side of it before slipping it between his lips.

"Then what has all this been about?" I wanted to know. "Are you just following hot dog vendors again?"

Tempest lit his cigarette with a glow from his cufflink and puffed a long stream of blue-grey smoke towards the microphone.

"I wanted to see how amenable you were to doing a deal," he said. "After all, if you're willing to deal when you've got nothing to deal with, just imagine how amenable might you be if you found you actually did have something?"

"Is it Colonel Mustard with the candlestick in a fit of self-indulgence?" I guessed.

"That's it, asshole!" Dunbar roared, grabbing me by the neck and pushing me out of my chair.

Somewhere behind Dunbar's delts, Tempest was

shouting at him to desist and trying to wrestle the Major away, but Dunbar was conscious of the fact that he hadn't killed anyone in almost five minutes and that was a long time for him.

Eventually, Rip's fingers left my windpipe, though he'd choked me so hard it took me almost thirty seconds to realise this. Stars popped and floated in front of my eyes, which was interesting seeing as I only had one, but it was true and I saw with them both. I wondered why this should be and half thought about asking Dunbar to do it again, but suddenly I was being shoved into my chair again.

Tempest apologised for his colleague's behaviour and asked if I was okay.

"Don't apologise to that motherfucking killer, he murdered my buddy," Dunbar barked.

"Hmm, bad luck old chap," Tempest replied, although who he was saying this to, me or Rip, I couldn't tell.

When I'd finally caught my breath, Tempest warned Dunbar not to touch me again and fetched some water from the cooler by the door. I don't know why people did this. Being strangled doesn't make you any thirstier than normal. If anything, it actually makes it harder to drink than if you haven't been strangled but I took a sip all the same just to show my gratitude.

"I'd butt-fuck that fucking *mother* to within an inch of his life if it was up to me!" Dunbar was raging behind Tempest, finally pushing his partner over the edge.

"Enough Major. Enough!"

"Enough? Enough? You come in here and deal with this scum and you tell me enough, you *mother*!" Dunbar ad-libbed, straying off the page a beat or two.

"I wish I was your mother, Rip, because I'd wash your bloody mouth out with soap," Tempest replied.

"I'd like to see you try, you limey fuckwipe!" Dunbar invited, stepping up to the plate as Tempest took his turn in the firing line

"Fuckwipe?" Tempest grimaced in confusion. "What does that even mean?"

"It means my dick up your ass, you goddamn honeydew faggot, that's what!" Dunbar barked, making even less sense than usual. I wondered how Rip went down on first dates. In flames, I concluded.

Tempest looked around for subtitles. "It's just a nonsensical stream of Tourettes. Do you even know what you're saying yourself?"

"Goddamn right I do. You say enough, do you? Well, I say enough too. Enough talking!"

"Shall I come back later when you're both free?" I suggested, helping myself to another cup of water.

"Get your ass back in that chair, *eyeball*!" Dunbar demanded, aiming one of his fat, hairy fingers at my face.

I retook my seat and waited for Dunbar to slap the water out of my hand, but he was too busy laying into Tempest to concern himself with the basics.

"This is bullshit! I said from the start that this was bullshit and when it all blows up because you trusted this piece of garbage, I'll skull-fuck your fucking ass!" he insisted.

Tempest just stared at Dunbar for a moment, at a

loss to know where to even begin, before finally conceding the point.

"Fair enough, Rip. You can skull-fuck my bottom if it all goes wrong," he agreed, eventually retaking his seat and offering me a cigarette. "So Mark, why don't we talk about this book club of yours?"

30. OPERATION CANDY SNATCH

THREE WEEKS EARLIER, while I'd been away in Greenland partying with Rip, the British Secret Service had been running an operation of its own. Nothing unusual there, as the various intelligence services around the world are running dozens of operations at any given time. But what was so special about this particular operation was that the initial lead had come from me.

X^3.

That's right, that tenuously sketchy titbit I'd tossed Tempest outside the pub in Sussex had led him all the way to Marbella and back (nice work if you can get it) and right to the very centre of a plot to bury every sea port on the Mediterranean under twenty feet of sand by engineering a month-long artificial sandstorm in the Western Sahara. Don't ask me why. Perhaps X^3 had bought shares in Dyson or something. I didn't know but thirty dead scientists and one destroyed storm-maker later, the Med was once again safe thanks to XO-11 while Sun Dju ended up sinking into a bottomless Saharan dune in her somewhat unsuitable stilettos. Silly cow.

Hooray for Jack Tempest and British Secret Service. Martinis and medals all round!

There was only one problem "Triple X", as he'd decided to call him, had got away. And it was this lapse that would come back to haunt him three years later with the launch of Operation *Candy Snatch*.

The intention was total revenge. No payoff, no

prizes and no extortion. Just pure and simple satisfaction.

Okay, where to start?

The United Nations, that wondrously powerless organisation that was meant to foster peace and prosperity in the wake of World War Two, but in fact, oversaw one of the bloodiest half-centuries on record, came up with yet another "winning idea" when it charged the kiddy branch of its outfit, UNICEF, with the task of organising the PR stunt to end all PR stunts. The idea, obviously dreamed up over a bowl of cornflakes, was stunningly lame in its naivety; every world leader with a child under the age of eighteen was to send their offspring to represent them at the "United Nations Children's Summit", which was basically a weekend-long jolly with jelly, ice cream and six-thousand special forces bodyguards. I think the basic idea was that all the Kings and Presidents would see their little darlings playing happily alongside one another and go all Coca Cola on their neighbours, prompting a new dawn of unprecedented peace and reconciliation.

Yeah, my thoughts exactly.

Anyway, everyone got very excited about the idea, not least of all the kids when they found out there'd be X-Box, and astonishingly thirty-one world-leaders sent their little sweethearts along to the newly constructed UNICEF compound in Provence.

France, Italy, Spain, Ireland, the Czech Republic, Denmark, Norway, Taiwan, South Korea, Vietnam, Japan, Saudi Arabia, Pakistan, India, the United Arab Emirates, Egypt, Libya, Gabon, Niger, Mali, Zambia,

Argentina, Brazil, Peru, Mexico, Canada and New Zealand.

China.

Russia.

And of course, Britain and America.

Where elderly statesmen or women didn't have kids under the age of eighteen, they sent other relatives, or in the case of Ireland, a competition winner off the telly. The President of the United States sent his granddaughter, while the Presidents of both China and Russia sent their nephews. Britain, officially recognised as the most gullible country in the UN, sent the Prime Minister's youngest daughter, born just four weeks before the PM took office and at only six years old, the youngest of all the delegates. Naturally, her mother travelled with her, but she stayed out of camera shot with a dozen other proud mothers while their VIP cherubs put the world to rights and ganged up on Peru for his pocket money.

Well, everything went swimmingly that first day and proceedings were televised, if not watched, around the world. All the kids mingled, newspapers were filled with pictures and a small army of bodyguards got to enjoy the easiest assignment they'd ever known.

At least until the gas bombs went off.

For hidden amongst the fixtures and fittings of the UNICEF compound were dozens of canisters of a nerve agent that rendered everyone inside unconscious. Kids and ex-Spetsnaz minders dropped to the floor and slept like babes-in-arms, while those that were able to escape the suffocating clouds stumbled clear to raise the alarm.

Maybe a couple of hundred UNICEF and security personnel stationed around the perimeter avoided the trap, but with barely a hundred gas masks in the entire place and all of them held at fire stations within the compound, they were powerless to help the others.

That's when things began to stir within the clouds.

See, also hidden amongst the fixtures and fittings were several black figures, bedecked in breathing apparatus and cold suits, they'd avoided the extensive pre-summit security sweep with guile and technology. How long they'd been hibernating in their hidey-holes was anybody's guess but like snakes waking after a long cold winter, they slithered out of cracks in the furniture and began silently and meticulously gathering up the young.

Right at the centre of the compound, in an open-air courtyard between the buildings, stood a collection of life-sized plastic play vehicles: a fire engine, an aeroplane, a dumper truck and a helicopter. The most popular of these had been the brightly coloured helicopter, with its blue and yellow bodywork and bright red rotor blades. The kids had played on this all the previous day, pressing buttons and stirring the rotors. Now one of the black figures climbed aboard and inserted a missing chip underneath the yellow dashboard. The plastic helicopter suddenly roared to life, shaking off its garish red and yellow bodywork to reveal black steel beneath. The pilot huffed and puffed to throw out all the colourful plastic interiors while the others loaded the rear and soon a fully laden UH-60 Black Hawk helicopter warbled away in the centre of the playground.

"That's it, let's go," the pilot said when the final child had been loaded onboard and a moment later they took off.

Security personnel and UNICEF staff watched in dismay as this alien aircraft, with ugly crossed Tarantula legs liveried on its side, rose into a crimson sky. Several guards opened fire but were quickly wrestled to the ground by the others who realised what it was carrying.

The helicopter turned south, casually dipping its nose and moseying away to head out over the Mediterranean.

A few miles away, French and Italian Air Forces were scrambling birds into the sky to make after the Black Hawk and radar and spy satellites were following its every move, but the Black Hawk was in no rush. It didn't want to lose its pursuers or drop off the map. Quite the contrary in fact. It wanted to be followed. It wanted to be seen. It wanted the world to take notice of what was about to happen.

Ten miles out to sea, the door slid open and Habib Touré, the seventeen-year-old middle son of the President of Mali, was pushed out. He screamed as he fell, dropping a thousand feet to within touching distance of the waves, before a tiny parachute opened. It cushioned his fall as he crashed into the water and the life vest tied around his shoulders automatically inflated to take him back to the surface but the message was clear – get too close and the next one leaves the helicopter *au naturelle*.

The pursuing helicopters dutifully backed off and

after an hour's uninterrupted flight, the Black Hawk reached its final destination.

One hundred and fifty miles south of St-Tropez and seventy miles west of Corsica, a scragg of weathered rock jutted out of the sea. Unlike most Mediterranean islands, *Île de Roc* boasted no sandy beaches or raucous nightclubs, just a few old pillboxes and broken antennas left over from its time as an Italian observation post during World War Two. Abandoned in 1947, the tiny island had been forgotten by all but nesting gulls for almost sixty years until a lease had been taken out two years earlier. The paperwork said it was to become a marine research centre, but if this was the case it was to be the most heavily fortified marine research centre in the world.

The rocks parted as the Black Hawk settled on its plateau. The sides fell away and the basalt flat sank, sucking the helicopter into the island as the pilot killed the engine.

French and Italian pilots circled overhead reporting back all they saw until a cluster of sea-to-air missiles erupted from the water, chasing them through the skies and silencing them one-by-one.

And as the final few scraps of debris rained down, the rocks closed over the Black Hawk's blades, protecting the helicopter from reprisals and sealing the children inside, so that once again *Île de Roc* looked barren and lifeless.

"I see, yes, that's certainly a tricky one. Those poor kids," I agreed. "So what's in it for me?"

"You don't give up, do you, Jones?" Tempest snorted. "Here we are talking about the lives of thirty innocent children and all you're concerned about is what's in it for you."

"What's your point?" I double-checked.

"I told you, Tempest, he's scum. And scum like him only think of themselves," Dunbar growled from the wings.

"Hey, ladies, I'm here until I croak and it's a seller's market so let's talk windfalls," I said.

"You're not getting out of here," Tempest reiterated.

"Then neither are those kids," I reminded him, which wasn't a very nice thing to say but I refer you to my indictment sheet.

So why me? Why had Tempest and Dunbar come to see me? What did I have to do with this sorry mess?

The Italians had tried to assault the island. Twenty-four COMSUBIN frogmen had approached by submarine and swam the last mile under cover of darkness. They'd barely hauled themselves out of the water when the guns had opened up. In less than three minutes they'd been torn to pieces, partly due to the fact that there was no cover on *Île de Roc*, and partly due to the fact that the island's defenders had been planning for just such an assault for more than two years. Some of the guns were automated while others were manned but all were mercilessly effective. Only seven frogmen made it back into the water and only three of them back to the sub. The assault could not have proved more catastrophic. And not just for the military failure. But because now there was a penalty to pay. Though it wouldn't be the Italians who'd have to pay it.

At just eighteen-years-old, George Wilson was the eldest child to have attended the summit. The son of the New Zealand Prime Minister, he was intelligent and bright, popular and sporty; just how all good Kiwis should be. He was also wearing four pounds of high explosives in a vest around his waist. Again, just how all good Kiwis should be.

George was pushed out of a concealed steel entrance just below the helipad and the door slammed shut behind him. It soon became clear to the watching spy satellites that George was following orders, because he moved away from the entrance and climbed up onto the salty rocks until he was standing on a ridge just above the helipad. He unravelled a white banner along the rocks, on which was written a single word.

POENA

George then disappeared.

"What's poena?"

"It means penalty, or punishment, in Latin," Tempest told me. "It was a reprisal for the raid."

"Why not blow up the Italian kid?"

"This is more divisive. Half the nations are already at each other's throats so when the nephew of the Russian President can be publicly executed in retaliation for a botched American rescue mission, that's the sort of nightmare scenario that gets the rest of the world ducking under the table."

"Hey fuck you, Tempest!" Dunbar suddenly snapped. "If anyone's gonna botch a rescue mission it'll be you fucking tea-humping Limeys. We bailed you out of every war you've ever fought in so don't talk to me about botching rescue missions, *mother fucker*, because you're the fucking pussies."

"See what I mean?" Tempest said.

"Yes, I see. It's a dilemma," I agreed. "Which brings us back to a dilemma of my own, namely, what's in it for me?"

"*Motherfucker!*"

Actually, I think I misled you earlier when I said that X³ had made no demands, because he had. But it wasn't for riches or power or recognition or real estate, it was purely personal. In exchange for the safe return of the children, he asked for one thing and one thing only; that thirty of the most prominent intelligence agents currently operating be handed over to him for summary execution. This was punishment for the death of Sun Dju, who it turned out had been his fuck buddy as well as his personal bodyguard. They had thirty-six hours. Failure to comply would result in the pitter-patter of tiny shell casing every half hour until the island was messy with kids.

Now X³ wasn't just going to let the UN quickly groom a load of tramps for the exchange. He had a list of names all drawn up and this list was like a who's who of international super-spies; top-ranking XOs, undercover SEOs, expert computer hackers, deep cover moles. Basically, everyone who'd ever got in the way of a half-decent operation in the past.

So if the leaders of the remaining twenty-nine countries ever wanted to see their cherubs again, it was a case of asking (or if you were China, ordering) their best agents to do the honourable thing and offer themselves up for sacrifice.

Answers on a postcard if you can guess two of the names on this list? Winners will receive an all-expenses-paid trip to sunny *Île de Roc*.

"Oh," I finally got, fluffy tingles warming my innards in the most delightful way. "Awkward."

"Yes, isn't it," Tempest agreed.

"So when are you off?"

"We're not," Tempest replied.

"Why not?"

"Why not? Because Triple X would never live up to his end. He'd simply kill us and either make more demands or kill the children anyway. We'd be playing right into his hands," Tempest reckoned.

"But if you could get reassurances…"

"We've had plenty of reassurances but they're not worth the paper they're written on. The man's a maniac. There's no telling what he's capable of."

"But surely, if you could somehow arrange it so that you did the exchange one at a time, so that you could all take your turns as…"

"How about I stick my boots up your fucking ass one at a time?" Dunbar suggested, obviously not keen to explore the strategy further.

I allowed a smile to flash across my lips then asked for one of Tempest's cigarettes. He dillied up without a crack, telling me my stock had risen a few points, so I tried again with a question that was at the forefront of my mind.

"So, what's in it for me?"

Tempest pushed back in his chair and glared at me through a haze of cigarette smoke.

"Okay then, Jones, let's talk."

You know what, I still don't think I've explained my part in all of this yet, have I? What I was doing here? What did Tempest and Dunbar want with me? Well, it was a strange quirk of fate that dealt me a hand at this table. And one that surprised me as much as it had surprised Tempest and Dunbar.

It was book club.

For a couple of years now, various agencies around the world had been receiving intelligence that Affiliates were reading. Surveillance photographs, seized property, bugged conversations, etc. They were just tiny snippets of information, insignificant pieces of a greater puzzle, and for a long long time, most agencies didn't even realise there was a puzzle here to be completed. After all, it was only Affiliates reading. Big deal. So what? The nature of our work meant that most Affiliates spent long hours sitting around in trucks, guarding corridors or manning work stations before the inevitable balloon went up. This could be boring work at the best of times, so it was only natural that we should try to pass the time somehow. But, little by little, a pattern began to emerge from all of this unrealised intelligence that didn't add up; that many of the Affiliates were reading the same books. On different jobs. For different employers. On different continents? Time and time again the same titles would crop up. And they weren't always best sellers or Richard & Judy's must-reads either. Some odd and unexpected books were being carried through jungles and deserts of this big wide dangerous world of ours.

The Aristocrat by Ernst Weiss
A Short History of Tractors in Ukrainian by Marina Lewycka
Bodies by Jed Mercurio
The Book of Illusions by Paul Auster
Beloved by Toni Morrison
The Kraken Wakes by John Wyndham

Codebreakers began logging our reading lists to see if there were any sorts of signals to be found within the titles. After all, how was it possible that three different Affiliates, working on three different plans of global domination, in three different countries, could all be reading *Monty: His Part in My Victory* by Spike Milligan? It didn't make any sense.

Finally, some clever clog somewhere figured it out; that the Affiliates must be talking to each other. Back channels had to be open. Recommendations were being swapped. Gossip exchanged.

Even now, the various intelligence agencies didn't realise the full significance of what they'd stumbled upon because regardless of what the connotations might be, they were still only books, weren't they? But they listened in anyway, and began to ask questions about our book club when interrogating captured Affiliates, because as everyone knows, there are often juicy nuggets of information to be found amongst the back-channels, but what they actually found was more startling than they'd ever expected. This book club of ours had a rigid structure. There was a hierarchy to it. There were rules. And most extraordinary of all there was loyalty. Affiliates were saving each others' lives and tipping each other off when they became aware of double-dealings. Most staggering of all, this was often at the expense of our own employers and it was with shock and awe that the authorities discovered several plans had even come apart at the seams thanks directly to book club intervention.

The planned Wall Street gas attack had been one such job. Thirty guys in breathing apparatus and bio-suits had been set to walk canisters of a sleep agent into the New York Stock Exchange to obliterate all evidence of the insider deal of the century. Unfortunately, billionaire financier, Miles Hawthorne, who'd been the brains behind the operation, had made the mistake of ordering his equipment through Grevelink Systems, a black market supplier of stolen military hardware. So when an engineer at Grevelink was ordered to fill the canisters with the deadly nerve gas sarin and not the supposed sleep agent the Affiliates thought they'd be carrying – and more shockingly fix all but two of the bio-breathers to make sure they failed after five minutes – he logged onto his favourite website and shared this treachery with his friends. SEO and the CIA had always known Miles Hawthorne was dirty. They knew he was fraudulent. And they knew his greed knew no bounds. But what they could never figure out was why, two days before his company bought out one of oldest banks in America, he opened the doors of his private jet and jumped out along with his chief accountant.

The case had remained a mystery for almost a year until a dying Affiliate on a different job told a Spanish CNI officer the truth; that greed had caught up with the billionaire. And that a stowaway with a gas mask, a parachute and a pipette full of Hawthorne's own double-crossing medicine had taken that flight too.

Now this was a revelation, the CNI decided.

More had to be found out about this mysterious book club.

More had to be known.

Investigations started in earnest.

Lines were drawn.

Books were read.

Even *The Kenneth Williams Diaries*.

In the months that followed, a complex web of loyalties and links were sketched across Ops tables the world over. Usernames were discovered. Scoring trends charted. Lines of communication uncovered. This club was bigger than they'd ever imagined. And they'd only scratched the surface.

So they dug deeper. They eavesdropped on communications. They cross-referenced intel. And they co-operated with rival intelligence agencies until names began to emerge.

Snowman.

Tech Boy.

Page Turner.

Shotgun.

Big Cat.

The agencies learned the usernames and monitored communications. And the more they monitored, the more one username kept popping up over all others.

Book Mark.

This was the organisation's founding father. This was the person at the club's heart. If there was anyone with influence over all the others, it was he.

But where was he? He'd not been heard of in almost three years. He'd simply disappeared off the map.

"Mark Jones."

"What?"

"You're *Book Mark*," Tempest said. "*Book – Mark*."

"So what? Give yourself a bun if you like."

"It's not a very clever username, is it?" he pondered.

"I didn't realise it had to be," I said, before reaching into his silver case for another of his cigarettes.

"Er, not that one," Tempest said when I picked out the cigarette at the very end of the case. "It's got a thing in it… look, just not that one, okay?"

"So what I want to know is how you got out of that pipe," I said catching Tempest off-guard.

"What pipe?" Tempest pretended.

"Don't give me that. You know what pipe. Thalassocrat's pipe. How did you get out of it?"

"That would be telling," Tempest cheesed.

"Yes, it would. That's why I asked."

"Trade secret," he winked.

"Oh, but it's okay if I tell you all about my secret organisation and call in a load of favours to get you and Mighty Joe Young to slip ashore though, is it?"

Tempest thought about this then checked over his shoulder to see if Dunbar was within earshot. Better than that, he'd left the room to get a cup of coffee so I told Tempest to use the opportunity and make with the story.

"Magnetic belt," he simply said.

"What?"

"My belt buckle, it's magnetic," he repeated, standing up to show me his silver belt buckle. "It contains a powerful electromagnet that can be switched on and off at any time."

"So?"

"So when Thalassocrat put me in the pipe, I activated the magnet to clamp myself to the inside of the tube so that I didn't get sucked through the blades when he started the turbines," he said, demonstrating by clicking a switch and sucking himself onto the table.

"How did you breathe?" I asked.

"Now that really is a secret," he insisted, trying to sit down but finding himself stuck to the table.

"Just tell me, fuckwipe," I said, taking my inspiration from Rip, before doing an impression of a child who'd just been shot in the head. My twitching and pleading for mummy to take the pain away appalled Tempest, as it was meant to, but it had the desired effect.

"I've had an implant."

"An implant?"

"A tiny canister of compressed air, just above the windpipe. All XO officers have it done. It's about the size of a double-A battery, but it means we can stay submerged for up to eight minutes if we control our breathing," he said, wiggling the switch on his belt when he found he was still stuck to the table.

"Bullshit!"

"It's the truth."

"Then what about big tits? How did she breathe?" I said referring to the girl he'd come ashore with.

Tempest smiled. "She shared my air," he told me, before elaborating unnecessarily. "I kept her alive with my kiss."

"God, give me strength," I groaned, finally wishing I'd never asked.

Tempest chuckled when he saw my disdain then carried on trying to deactivate his magnetic belt. It was at this moment that Dunbar walked back in and clocked Tempest struggling to distance his trousers from the table.

"Holy shit!" he gawped. "I thought they were joking when they told me you'd fuck a table if you could."

When Jack was all done, the three of us sat down together and thrashed out the finer points of our deal.

"Twenty years, that's the best we can offer," Tempest insisted.

"For fuck's sake!"

"You still have crimes to pay for. And twenty years will see you out in your lifetime."

"That's easy for you to say," I snapped.

"Would you rather the ninety-six you've left to do?" Dunbar suggested.

"Ten," I tried.

"They won't wear it," Tempest said. "You have to do a serious stretch."

"What, and ten's not a serious stretch?"

"Not for murder and crimes against humanity," he reckoned.

"Have you even tried talking to them?"

"Hey, we don't negotiate with killers," Dunbar grunted, his forehead casting an even greater shadow than usual. "Take it or leave it."

"But I won't get out until I'm an old man!" I fumed.

"That's the idea," Tempest pointed out. "They won't release pros like you while you're still in your prime. Besides, sixty's not that old. Not these days."

"Time served."

"What?"

"If I agree to twenty, I want what I've already done down as time served," I said.

Tempest thought about this then looked at Dunbar.

"If we give you that, then you've still got seventeen to serve," he said.

"That's right."

He thought about it some more, while Dunbar simply glared in either contempt or confusion at the maths.

"Jabulani was worth ten of you," he grunted.

"Believe me, Major Dunbar, no one regrets Jabulani's death not like I don't," I assured him as solemnly as I could. "And if I could turn back the clock... well, that's all I've got to say about that."

While Dunbar mulled over those heartfelt sentiments, Tempest came to an executive decision without deferring to knuckles.

"Okay then Jones, have it your way; twenty years with time served. Now, get us onto *Île de Roc*."

31. THE BEST OF THE WORST

SOME FIFTEEN HOURS later I was on the well deck of the *USS Bataan* overlooking the hurriedly assembled assault team. I knew every one of them having served alongside them all in either field or can.

Mr Smith, Mr Woo, Mr Rousseau, Mr Jean, Mr Capone, Mr Petrov, Captain Campbell, Mr Son, Mr Kim and two-dozen other Affiliates. All Agency men. And all just a few years into their ninety-nines at McCarthy.

This had been a crucial part of the deal I'd struck; that we'd lead the assault ourselves and those who'd volunteered would get the same remission as me – twenty years minus time served.

The UN had been extremely reluctant but I told them to go ahead and think on it if they liked. Mull it over. Discuss it. Debate it. I had all the time in the world. I could wait. Could they?

After an hour of pointless stalling they finally came to their senses and all at once, my stock was such that I could've probably asked for a foot rub off the Russian President and got it.

I'd insisted on my guys carrying out the assault because our plan depended on our friendlies on the island helping us gain a foothold. If I'd simply called in a few favours to get Dunbar a free pass, then no one would've walked away from this thing alive. Not the enemy, not our guys and probably not the kids either.

I remembered only too well the fun he'd had in

Greenland. Rescue missions weren't really Rip's forte.

So we'd spearhead the assault. Dunbar and Tempest would tag along for the ride but they'd take their lead from us. We'd get them ashore. We'd breach the defences. And we'd rescue the kids. They'd be the ones who'd deal with X³ once we were in. It was a compromise everyone could live with, particularly the various Presidents and Prime Ministers around the UN table who could no longer hold each other responsible if things fell apart. We were independent. Therefore we could safely be blamed by everyone for everything.

Of course, the danger of mounting a full-scale assault on *Île de Roc* was the fact that X³ could just step up the timetable and start playing war with the kids the moment we stepped ashore. But this was where we'd really scored at the negotiations table. See, the beauty of having people on the inside meant that we could not only make it off the boats in one piece, but we had friends on hand to protect the kids from reprisals during the fighting.

This had been our ace in the hole and the one thing all the SEALs, SBS and COMSUBIN in the world couldn't ensure.

The only problem had been convincing our guys on X³'s payroll to change sides.

See, the promise of doing twenty years in a secret military prison wasn't likely to tempt anyone not already doing ninety-nine years in a secret military prison so the UN reluctantly agreed to grant them full immunity, plus pay them one million dollars apiece if they threw their lot in with us.

Payment dependent on results, of course.

Now, this was a very tempting offer because, like I think I've said before, most plans have a tendency to go socks-up more often than not, so a cast-iron assurance of cold hard cash from a legitimate government was one hell of an incentive. At least, that was the theory.

There was only one way to find out.

"I need a computer," I'd told them.

Surprisingly, the authorities still hadn't found our website yet, probably because we'd hidden it too well, so in order for me to log on, they first had to find me one of our encrypted keys. A search of the evidence stores at McCarthy turned up one of my hollow-point .38 USBs and I was able to log on.

The website had changed a lot since I'd last seen it. New pop-up windows appeared. Flashing icon, blogs and buttons had all been added. And *The Day of The Triffids* had taken one hell of a pounding, but I ignored the frills and got to work putting out feelers.

To my immense relief, I found we did indeed have three book club members currently plying their trade on *Île de Roc*. I'd had my doubts because of X³'s experiences up in Scotland, but he'd obviously had a change of heart about Agency Affiliates after his *RS-* or *EE*-manned plan had come apart in the Sahara. This meant that within a few emails I'd been able to make contact with some of his guys, identify myself as *Book Mark* and post five stars for John Grisham's *The Client*, which was far better than *The Chamber* in my opinion, but that's neither here nor there.

As you can expect, Tempest, Dunbar and most of

the UN insisted on eyeballing everything I sent but I'd still been able to stay on top of all the bullshit and structure the offer in such a way as to make it appealing to the boys. Basically, I'd told them that they weren't going anywhere following X^3's banner. Believe me, I knew. It was only going to end badly for them as it always did, but if they threw their lot in with us for once they'd reap the rewards. And not only that, they'd be helping out almost three dozen of their book club brethren who'd been swept under the world's rug.

"And saving the lives of twenty-nine children," Tempest reminded me.

"What?"

"I said, they'd also be saving the lives of the children as well remember? Which is the whole point of this exercise, surely."

I blinked at Tempest a couple of times and thought about this one.

"Whatever."

Our friends' response came back within the hour.

"0600 hours. We'll be expecting you."

My fellow McCarthy residents hadn't taken too much convincing either and one supersonic flight across the Atlantic later, we were refamiliarising ourselves with the tools of our trade on the *Bataan* under the contemptuous glare of a squad of SEALs.

"Fucking scum," one of them spat.

They were obviously scorned at having been overlooked for this mission in favour of a bunch of dirty cons, but I told them they didn't have to be that way.

"Lieutenant, if you'd like to go before us, please be my guest. There'll be less bullets to threaten us with and we can always use your dead bodies for cover."

"Hey, fuck you, dirtbag!" he replied, obviously a fellow of the Rip Dunbar school of deportment.

This jocular exchange would have probably escalated had someone not shouted "Officer on deck!" causing all the SEALs to snap to attention like toy soldiers as Dunbar and Tempest entered the fray.

"Make a hole!" Dunbar barked, sliding down a metal ladder and barging through the middle of the SEALs as Tempest followed closely behind apologising. "Excuse me. Sorry, can I just get through? Thanks…" etc.

"Hey Rip, how's it going?" Mr Woo beamed as he strode past.

"Don't talk to me," Dunbar hissed without breaking stride. Like us, Dunbar was togged up in his combats, but unlike us, he'd obviously spent the last three hours in the armoury filling every available pocket with bullets and bombs. One unexpected pat on the back and he could take the whole ship down with him.

Tempest, on the other hand, had opted for style over substance and was tarted up in Special Op blacks that fitted him so well he had to have had them especially tailored.

"Now listen up *dick wads* I'm gonna be watching all of you, so one step out of line and I'll blow your asses away!" Dunbar threatened, waving his Heckler & Koch under all our noses and simultaneously stepping in as many faces as he could.

"Really?" Mr Smith replied, locking and loading his own MP5 and pointing it at Dunbar. "Then I'm afraid, Major, I'm going to have to do this." Smith aimed the gun and pulled the trigger but nothing happened. He pulled it again, but the weapon just clicked. Dunbar flexed the muscles in his forehead as he glared at Mr Smith repeatedly clicking away on the trigger.

"You shouldn't play with guns, it's very dangerous," Tempest calmly advised, stepping in to take the gun from Mr Smith before pointing it out through the open well dock. He squeezed the MP5's trigger, but this time a burst of fire echoed around the deck as the submachine gun spat out 9mm rounds, ripping up the surf.

Dunbar continued to stare with homoerotic intensity but he did nothing. Mr Smith had just been larking around. Dunbar had been in no danger. See rather thoughtfully the US government had fixed the guns and vests with ID sensing microchips to prevent "blue-on-blue casualties" in the heat of battle. At least, that had been the official line. Really, they'd fixed them to stop us from shooting Tempest and Dunbar the first opportunity we got.

I didn't know about blue-on-blue but by the way Dunbar was staring at Mr Smith, we were in danger of suffering a few man-on-man casualties before this day was out.

"Try me," Dunbar finally invited.

Mr Smith just smiled and suggested they saved it for after the kids were safe. "After all, that's why we're all here, isn't it, hey guys?" he shouted.

On cue, everyone laughed raucously and agreed that "of course that was the reason we were here" much to Tempest's despair.

"The things I do for England," he sighed to himself.

*

We raced across the surf, flying towards *Île de Roc* at sixty knots on a quartet of Navy hovercrafts. It was three minutes to 0600 hours and the tiny island appeared on the horizon, black like a lump of coal against a blood-red dawn.

The execution party would be on its way to cash out the first kid. Time had run its course. For us. And for them.

There were ten of us on each craft, not counting the crew and SEALs manning the mounted guns. We'd planned to hit the southern and eastern slopes, taking our hovercrafts right up the rocky beaches to provide extra cover as we went in. This hadn't been an option the Italians had had because they'd been trying the stealth approach whereas we didn't care if X^3 knew we were coming. It wasn't important.

This was probably just as well because all of a sudden the skies above our heads ripped with a dozen F-16s. They hit the slopes with cluster bombs and cannon fire in an effort to knock out some of the defensive guns and I couldn't help but marvel in awe at the sight of *Île de Roc* flickering and flashing in the distance beneath all that death.

I wondered if any of the anxious parents could see what was happening. If so, they'd probably be having kittens at all the firepower dropping on *Île de Roc*. But this was necessary to soften her up, small explosions to take out the surface guns. It was doubtful we were even knocking any pot plants off the telly down in X^3's inner sanctum, so their little bundles of precociousness would be safe from our bombs.

In fact, hopefully even safer than they'd been two minutes earlier, because if all had gone to plan, the execution party would have been taken down by our friends on the inside and the kids shoved out of harm's way until the main force could reach them.

This was the optimum moment to hit *Île de Roc*. X^3's forces would be divided and his resolve fractured. But this window wouldn't stay open for long. Not once X^3 realised the moment had come to take off the gloves. We had to be quick.

"Thirty seconds," the hovercraft's pilot told us over the airwaves, a moment before the SEALs on either side of the ramp opened up with their .50 cals.

I wondered if it was possible for anything to survive all that we were throwing at it, but a curtain of tracer fire from the island assured me it was.

Just to my left, Jack Tempest was smiling serenely.

"Nervous, Jones?"

"Of what?" I asked, just as the steel ramp drawn up in front of us clattered with indents, courtesy of my peers on *Île de Roc*.

Tempest snorted.

"You know, you're a queer fish," he told me. "If we get through this thing, I might even buy you a drink."

"Why? Are you a queer fish as well?" I said. "Because I don't swim that way, mate, magnetic belt or not."

Tempest didn't have a chance to tell me he didn't mean it like that because all at once, we rose out of the sea and beached on solid rock. The ramp dropped in front of us and our moment had arrived.

After three long years of enforced retirement, I was finally in the game again.

32. OF CRADLES AND GRAVES

THE ROCKS WERE HOT, smoking even, from where the F-16s had been emptying their undercarriages but I canoodled the jagged basalt all the same as the sky above throbbed against tracer fire. I'd made it barely six yards before diving into an inviting blast hole to escape the hailstorm of flak. My feet cooked and my gloves started to smoke but at least I had a modicum of cover. And on this beach, that was going to attract a lot of towels this morning.

"*Book Mark, Book Mark, this is Big Cat, do you copy, over?*" my radio barked the moment our frequencies found each other.

"*Big Cat*, this is *Book Mark*. I read you," I told our man on the inside. "What's your situation, over?"

"*Puppies are safe and I have five guns with me, but…*" the transmission broke off with a crackle, although it wasn't a crackle of radio static but a crackle of gunfire.

"*Big Cat*, do you copy, over?" I asked before the response came back once more.

"*… I repeat, puppies are safe and five guns with me but we're being hit hard, over,*" *Big Cat* said, explosions and screams echoing over the airwaves to mirror the explosions and screams echoing all around me on the beach.

"*Big Cat! Big Cat*, can you hold out?" I had to ask several times before *Big Cat* responded.

"*Ten minutes but no longer.*" A raking hiss almost popped the earpiece from my ear as Big Cat roared at someone to *"Take that you bastard!"* before leaving me with a word of advice. *"Don't stop to read nothing, over."*

"Understood," I promised him, twisting the dial to dim the fighting in my ear just as the lip of our crater began exploding with ricochets.

At that moment, Mr Smith and Mr Capone tumbled in on top of me, knocking me against the sides of the smoking hole I was crouching in.

"Hey, how's it going?" Mr Smith asked, helping me to my feet again.

"Fantastic. You?"

"Pretty sweet," he agreed.

"Is this it?" Mr Capone wanted to know, rock chips spitting in our faces as the ridge of our crater was raked.

The three of us had been on the easternmost hovercraft to beach, maybe thirty yards from the next nearest craft, but we were pinned down by a suppressing force of fire from three separate gun positions. I had hoped more guns might have been knocked out by the time we came ashore. But then again, I had also hoped that Harry Potter might have been knocked out of book club by the time we came to commemorate our fifth anniversary but that didn't look like happening either.

I guess bad things sometimes happen to bad people.

"I see the guns are still firing?" Mr Smith pointed out as more splinters peppered our necks.

"Yeah, I thought this was going to be a cake-walk?" complained Mr Capone.

"When has anything we've been involved in ever

been a cake-walk?" I asked. "Fuck me, if we were to organise an actual cake-walk, to pick up cakes as we walked, we'd still lose three men along the way. You should know that by now."

"So how do you wanna play this?" Mr Smith asked. "We can't sit here all day."

"No, we can't," I agreed, mindful of the hell raging several storeys below us. "Let's see if some of this kit Dunbar gave us actually works," I said, slipping the backpack off my shoulder and pulling out one of my flying frags.

As you'd expect, the UN had kitted us out with some of the best weapons available. And then the US had taken us to one side and kitted us out with some of the best weapons not available. The flying frag had been one such under-the-counter item.

I pulled out the pin to arm the grenade and tossed it into the air just above our position. When the frag reached the peak of its throw, two tiny blades popped out of either side and began buzzing like bumblebee wings to hold it in mid-air.

Mr Smith pressed a couple of buttons on a tiny accompanying handset and a picture appeared on-screen of the landscape around our blast hole. Some hundred yards north we could see tracer fire pouring out of a gun slot only to explode around our hole a nanosecond later. Mr Smith used a joystick to steer the frag to the right, away from the stream of fire and across the terrain until he'd taken it to within a few yards of one of the guns. On the screen, we saw the faces of the two-man gun team, grim and determined as they unleashed a storm across our position.

Mr Smith inched the frag closer and closer, guiding it into the foot-wide gun hole until their expressions changed to one of disbelief.

"What the fu...!" I heard them shout just as Mr Smith pressed the fire button triggering a dull thud in the distance.

The firing around our hole immediately stopped.

"That worked," Mr Smith admitted as I tossed the next frag into the air. He read the pin I'd handed him and keyed the frag's "Pin Number" to take control of it, then began guiding it across the rocks to the next enemy position.

"If you happen to pass Rip on the way, do see if you can dock with his grenade belt," I suggested, much to Mr Smith and Mr Capone's amusement.

Pretty soon we weren't the only ones flying frags across the landscape and the gunners quickly cottoned onto the danger. But the frags were small, barely the size of King Edwards and coloured to match the terrain so that they were virtually impossible to spot, let alone shoot.

More thuds resonated along the ridge as the guns fell one-by-one and soon the only sounds of automatic fire were coming from us.

"That's it, move out!" came the inevitable shout, accompanied by a few gun-happy whoops from some of the loopier lads as we poured from our holes and out onto the slopes.

The rocks were dotted with dead, both ours and those of our Italian forebears, and I was sorry to see Mr Rousseau was amongst them. I'd shared a cell with him for three years and in all that time we'd only had one argument. Sure some of his habits had annoyed me, just as I'm sure some of mine had annoyed him, but I was still sorry to see him face-down on the shingle no matter how much the dirty bastard loved to pick his feet with my paperclip.

"*Big Cat*, we're coming!" I radioed without getting a reply.

Jack Tempest appeared alongside me as we ran for the ridge and afforded me a flash of his eyebrows.

"Still with us Jones?" he honked.

"For the moment, Jack," I replied, realising I was going to have trouble with this one before the day was out.

Just short of the ridge were a series of newly excavated trenches. We approached at a sprint but held off jumping in because we'd been advised they'd been booby-trapped. Unfortunately, Mr Capone couldn't have got the memo because that's exactly what he did, shredding himself to suet when he charged in like Braveheart, only to come flying out again like Rocket Man.

"What an obliging fellow!" Tempest quipped, jumping into the same trench once the smoke had cleared.

"I can't believe he just said that," Mr Smith gasped, hands on hips in outrage.

"Shocking isn't it," I agreed, equally disappointed with XO-11. Tempest had a lot to learn about respect. And more importantly, judging an audience. After all, Mr Capone might have been a professional bad guy but he was still a friend of ours. But more firing cut these sentiments short, along with Mr Williams a few feet from me, and once more we were diving for cover.

I looked over the lip of the trench and saw X^3's guys pouring out of the rocks a hundred yards north.

Our guys were taking them on, gun-for-gun, and making a fight of it, when all of a sudden a whirling blur came out of nowhere and ran right up the middle with the biggest gun I've ever seen.

It was Rip Dunbar.

He'd somehow torn one of the .50 cal machine guns off a hovercraft and was running riot. I had no idea how he was even staying on his feet, let alone aiming to fire it. I doubt whether I could've even lifted the enormous cannon or the ammo box that hung beneath it, but Rip seemed as happy as a lamb in spring as he scampered from gully to crevice, hosing X^3's men off the rocks with a continuous *chugga-chugga-chug*.

Tempest popped up beside me to watch the carnage for a moment or two. "Dumb gorilla," was his considered opinion before he sunk from view again.

A shaped-charge blew open the door at the far end of the trench before Tempest, Mr Smith and I slid down the rails of the steel staircase inside to catch those at the bottom with our sub-machine guns.

The time was 0605 hours. We'd used up a lot of minutes getting in. I just hoped we hadn't used up too many.

Base sirens were wailing and a sexy mechanical voice was informing the corridors around us that security had been breached in Sector Seven.

"We don't like gossips around here, sweetheart," Tempest said, shooting the speaker off the wall.

"That should fix the problem, I'm sure they only had the one speaker," Mr Smith said, but Tempest ignored the jibe.

"Come on."

Three more guards met with three more bursts of machine-gun fire as we sprinted through the sweeping corridors until we came to a crossroads. Branching three ways, signs pointed towards the Command Centre, Sector Six and the Submarine Dock. We opted to split up, with Mr Smith and Mr Petrov coming with me to Sector Six, while Mr Jean and the others headed for the Submarine Dock, leaving Tempest to pick his own path towards the Command Centre.

"You get the kids. I'll get Triple X," he said locking and loading a new clip into his MP5 with a theatrical flourish.

"Sure, if Major Dunbar doesn't get him first," I reminded him. Tempest didn't look too happy about that and dashed off without further consideration.

"How did we get lumbered with that bloke?" Mr Petrov wanted to know.

"*Big Cat, Big Cat*, this is *Book Mark*, do you copy, over?" I radioed.

A burst of static responded a few seconds later, sharp, crackly and violent and soon I realised it wasn't static at all – it was bedlam.

"*I read you,*" *Big Cat* finally came back. "*Where are you?*" he pleaded, his transmissions brief and to the point.

"Sector Seven," I replied. "Give us directions."

"We've fallen back to Sector Four, down as far as you can go. Stairs at Five... motherfuck....!"

"What's your situation, over?" I asked.

"Two dead. RPGs. Don't think we can hold..." a whoosh and a roar cut that transmission dead before Big Cat summarised the situation with a single word. *"Hurry!"*

"We're coming, over," I promised him, the heat turned up beneath my resolve.

We took off at a canter, gun-sights to the eyes, silencers to the fore and downed two more of X^3's boys along the way.

Sector Six was almost identical to Sector Seven as far as I could make out. Only the sector logos were painted in blue, rather than red. Here we met more resistance, though these guys played dirty, hiding behind doors in the corridor ahead as they waited for us to pass. Mr Smith, Mr Petrov and myself ran straight through the ambush, opening up on their doors as we ran past and reducing our would-be assassins to Swiss cheese before they could say "boo".

Normally we might not have stood a chance against such an ambush but thanks to the US military we had an advantage over the opposition. See, other than the guns, the frags, the body armour and hot knives they'd so generously kitted us out with, they'd also fitted me with a new eye. One that could see.

"We're clear," I said, scanning the corridor ahead for signs of movement but finding none.

Okay, it couldn't actually see, as in see – as in trees or horses or the faces of terrified children – but it could see all the same because I'd only lost my eyeball in Africa, not my optical nerve. The images were no more than colourful patterns, confusing and unintelligible at first, like those 3D picture books that never quite caught on in the eighties, but I'd soon got the hang of them and what they represented on the flight over. Ultra-violet, infrared, heat signatures, even sound, I could see all of them with a little tuning of the iris. It was just a question of fusing these images in my mind to create a decipherable picture.

And thirty seconds earlier, that picture had told me there were four guys with hot bodies and cold guns lying in wait for us in the corridor ahead.

I retook the point and we sprinted the last hundred yards until we came to a steel door that marked the start of Sector Five. There was movement behind the door's tiny window, lots of it, but Big Cat was continuing to die inch-by-inch in my ear so we had no choice but to proceed.

"*Anytime now would be good!*" Big Cat chided me, his voice barely audible over the never-ending sputter of machine-gun fire around him.

I smacked the green button on the door panel and me, Mr Smith and Mr Petrov ducked through and found cover before we were seen.

Sector Five was different still. It wasn't just a long series of corridors. It was an open hanger the size of a football pitch, with rocket tubes stretching all the way up to the concrete ceiling and scores of surface-to-air missiles lined up like terracotta warriors.

X^3's men were running backwards and forwards loading the tubes and firing off missiles, telling me either our air cover had just returned or that the UN fleet was now closing. Either way; the lads in Sector Five were busy, so the three of us tip-toed through as silently as we could and might have made it to the stairwell had some little drone in a white hard-hat not rounded the corner and blundered straight into us.

Mr Petrov dismissed him with a silenced muzzled burst but it was too late, we were clocked.

"There! There!" Sector Five's lieutenant screamed, pointing at us from his gantry position and winning a volley of 9mms for his troubles.

Several of the drones dropped their ordnance trolleys and started shooting, so we took cover and returned fire, until some little Chinese scientist in an orange boiler suit ran out into the fray and urged us all to stop shooting.

"You'll kill us all. You'll kill us…" were his last words before Mr Smith gave him something else to worry about.

It was only then, when a bullet missed my head by inches to ping off the white tube behind me that I realised what our little peacemaker had been so upset about – we were hiding amongst the missiles. The opposition seemed to twig this too because the shooting abruptly stopped and was replaced by gasps of exasperation.

"Jesus! What the hell! I forgot!" that sort of thing.

"Come out of there, you're surrounded," we were ordered.

"Make us," Mr Smith suggested, aiming his MP5 at the nearest missile.

"You'll kill the kids if you do that," he was told.

"And you'll kill them if we don't," Mr Smith replied.

A few of X^3's men started edging around to cut us off from the stairs. There must've been about eight or nine of them in total, six of whom were armed, so I slung my MP5 over my shoulder and pulled out my hot knife. Some enormous oily Krout a few feet from me smiled as he found his own blade and squared up for the fight.

"I'll have you for breakfast," he grunted, passing his knife from hand to hand and cackling with delight at the prospect. Knives were obviously this man's speciality. I would've stood no chance against him if this had been a fair fight.

But it wasn't.

I squeezed the rubber grip of my handle and whipped back the magnetic blade like a fishing rod, yanking the hulking murderer's knife from his hand as if pulled by an invisible cord. I caught it in my free hand and hurled it straight back before he knew what was happening, scoring a double-top as I skewered him between the eyes.

The others baulked in surprise, giving us the chance to disarm three more of them before the shooting started again. Mr Petrov let off a stream of lead at a couple of fleeing backs, cutting them down in their tracks and blowing a gas canister in the corner of the hanger. This got us all motoring and we dropped into the stairwell as fire extinguishers and screaming broke out behind us.

"Which way?"

Section Four stretched out in two different

directions and resounded with gunfire and explosions. It was difficult to tell which way the sounds were coming from, so I tuned in my eye and saw the sound waves pouring from the right-hand tunnel.

"This way."

We set off again, more cautious this close to the battle, and soon found men and mania to accompany the crash bang wallops.

Around a long sweeping bend, the corridor opened up and became a large provisions depot, with cupboards, shelves and crate after crate of Pot Noodles. About thirty men were here, running backwards and forwards between the crates as they tried to get to the kids. The far end of the store blazed with shrapnel and shards like the most spectacular indoor firework display ever and right there, in the very epicentre of all that hell, almost invisible against the sheer weight of fire being brought to bear on it, a lone gun fought back to keep at bay all the evil X^3 could throw at it.

It was *Big Cat*.

"*Big Cat, Big Cat*, we're here. Watch your fire and we'll push them into your path, over," I radioed.

"*Do it!*" Big Cat demanded, his voice now more determined than frantic.

We fought our way through the back-markers and into the stores along with Mr Woo and Mr Jean who'd secured the submarine dock and soon more Affiliates were joining us until X^3's men were the ones on the back foot, hemmed in on two fronts and suddenly fighting for their lives.

I don't think I killed anyone else over the course

of the battle. Not for the want of trying, you understand, but I used up most of my ammunition all the same covering the others as they thinned out X^3's men.

Mr Smith, in particular, fought like a man possessed, taking personal umbrage at those who sought to harm these kids and hacked away with his hot knife until he had to be dragged away.

"That's enough! They've given up!" I said, bundling Mr Smith away from the men on their knees before he could carve up any more of them. "Remember, it's just a job. For us and for them."

I held onto Mr Smith while he sucked in a few acrid lungfuls of smoke and eventually, he seemed to snap out of it.

"I'm all done," he announced, sheathing his knife and walking away.

Naturally, X^3 wasn't amongst our prisoners or the dead, which didn't surprise me in the slightest. I couldn't see him getting his hands dirty with this particular task, which meant he'd be in the Command Centre, either letting Jack Tempest out of tubes or having his eye sockets romanced by Rip Dunbar. Not that I cared. We'd done what we'd come to do. Everything else was above and beyond. And I didn't do above and beyond. I was a flat-rate kind of guy.

"Are we clear?" Mr Woo was calling.

"Clear."

"Clear!" we sounded off, kicking away the prisoners' guns and checking over the dead to make sure no one was faking.

When we were confident it was safe, we gave *Big*

Cat the okay and told him to come out. *Big Cat* was reluctant at first and I can't say I blamed him. Stacked up all around his hastily erected barricades were piles and piles of dead. Burnt, battered and mutilated; arms, legs and heads; it must've been a terrible fight but by the skin of his teeth *Big Cat* had somehow held out. I can't tell you how because I'd not been there fighting alongside him, but I knew him to be a survivor because we'd walked away from worse in the past – a nuclear blast and a tumble into the Zambezi being two such adventures – and finally, *Big Cat* rose from behind his makeshift battlements and shot me a broad, toothy grin.

"Good to see you again, Mr Jones."

"Good to see you again too, *Mr* Bolaji," I replied. "The kids?"

"They're shaken, but not too stirred," he said inviting us into his inner sanctum to see for ourselves.

I must say, with the limited materials at his disposal, Mr Bolaji had done well to protect them. He'd chosen a large, solid larder at the far end of the stores and worked to ring the entrance with crates. He'd stacked them up to form three lines of defence, forcing his former colleagues to funnel through a single point, then fallen back as each line had been breached, but only after making his attackers pay a heavy price.

The kids themselves were inside, huddled against the far wall and cowering under more bales and boxes. One of Mr Bolaji's colleagues, Mr Trent, was in there with them, covering the cell door with a mini-gun as their last line of defence. He and Mr Bolaji were all that remained. Well, almost.

Four dozen tear-streaked eyes turned to look up at me as I slung my gun over my shoulder and pulled an eye-patch over my falsie so as not to frighten them with the grinning devil's skull that stared out from my face – well, it is a classic design, you know.

"Come on then, children, let's go home, shall we?" I suggested, holding out my hand to a girl of six who was shivering uncontrollably nearby.

At first, she hesitated, flinching with fear and wobbling her lip, but Mr Bolaji reassured her I was a friend, helping her find the courage to climb into my arms.

"Okay then little darling, I want you to close your eyes, okay? No peeking," I insisted, speaking to her as softly as I could. The girl did as I said, burying her face into my neck for fear of what she might see outside, so I winked at Mr Bolaji – though when you've only got one eye, a wink can so easily be mistaken for a blink – and headed back to the surface.

33. A STING IN THE TALE

THE OTHERS FOLLOWED my lead, helping the kids to their feet and carrying the smaller ones out through all the carnage. With hands across faces and whispered reassurances, we did what we could to protect their minds as well as their bodies, at least until they were someone else's problem.

Even the lads on the other side wanted to lend a hand. We'd taken four prisoners at the end of the fighting and they were all keen to make amends for their recent paedocidal efforts. Well, when the shooting's over and the battle's won, there's no point in holding a grudge, that's for amateurs or the Rip *Dumbbells* of this world, so we let them come with us. Of course, we didn't let them anywhere near the kids, we weren't that silly, but instead, had them carry Mr Petrov out who'd lost a foot along the way.

Sector Five was deserted. Smouldering and bloodied corpses littered the floor, so I made sure the little girl's eyes were still closed before proceeding. They were. I wondered if she'd ever open them again.

If the rest of *Île de Roc* looked like this then we'd done all we'd needed to do, so I hijacked X^3's base frequencies and put out a call across the airwaves, telling the lads to finish what they were killing and make for the exits.

"Roger."
"Will do."
"Copy."
"Sector Three still hot. Avoid if possible."

"See you on the surface," came back their quick-fire responses.

All in all, we hadn't fared too badly today. Judging from the confirmations I received and the eight or nine men who were helping me move the kids, we'd probably only suffered some fifty per cent casualties, which is harsh by most standards, but not ours. Fifty per cent's actually pretty good for us.

It's mad when you think about it, but believe me when you're an ex-lifer on The Agency's books your life's not yours to worry about anyway. So we do what we're taken on to do and try to enjoy the ride. Because it eventually runs out for everyone you know, regardless of whether you drive a cab for a living or try to melt the North Pole. None of us can avoid it forever.

We'd made it as far as Sector Seven before running into more opposition. Two guys who'd not heard they'd been beaten were given a harsh heads-up by Mr Woo. He peppered them up against the walls with his MP5, startling both the guys and the kids we were carrying, filling the tunnels with their ear-splitting screams.

"It's all right, it's okay. Just a silly man being silly," I said, hugging the Prime Minister's daughter so tightly that I thought I might squash her. "Don't look darling. Keep your eyes closed."

I took a sneaky peek myself, and instantly wished I hadn't. Neither chap had any sort of face left, and in one case, the entire top half of his skull had come off too.

Mr Woo looked lip-smackingly pleased with

himself.

"Now that's what I call a splitting headache."

"Oi, do you mind?" I chided on my way past.

"Yeah, you pick up Jack Tempest's joke book or something?" Mr Smith echoed, looking equally disdainful.

"Fuck me guys I'm only trying to lighten the mood," Mr Woo protested.

"Language," Mr Jean reminded him, getting the little boy he was carrying to cover his ears as well as his eyes.

"You lot have changed, you know that?" Mr Woo moaned. "You used to be cool."

We hustled to the pipe interjunction at Sector Seven that led back up to the surface and found half a dozen Affiliates already there covering the stairs.

"We ready, Mr Choe?"

"All clear up top, Mr Jones," Mr Choe confirmed. "The fleet's ten minutes out."

"We got the signal?"

"He's right on time," he replied, a glimmer of excitement flickering across his eyes.

"Let's move it then," I suggested patting Mr Choe on the shoulder as I went.

We started taking to the stairs, men and children first, when all hell broke loose behind us. Machinegun fire, explosions and *laughter*, causing those of us caught in the open to scramble with our kids for cover.

Mr Choe and Mr Woo attempted to defend the rest of us as we scuttled away but were cut down by an unstoppable spray of lead within seconds.

We'd been hit so fast that it was impossible to tell what was going on. My main concern was for the PM's little girl (or more accurately, the years her continued breathing knocked off my sentence) so I bundled her out of harm's way under the stairs and unslung my MP5.

Coming out of the darkness of the southern corridor was a blinding flash of heavy machine-gun fire. I took a bead on its core and rattled off an entire clip, but the muzzle flashes didn't flinch. Not even a flicker. They simply turned on me and fired back, ripping up the pipes and the stairs around where I was crouching, causing me to dive on top of the PM's girl and hold my breath until the hailstorm had turned elsewhere.

What the hell was that?

Over the fighting, I could now hear the laughter more clearly. Evil, mirthless peels of cruel delight that grew and grew as the danger neared until it stopped opposite the main pipe bank.

"Come out, come out, wherever you are," the laughter challenged so I twiddled my false eye until I could see through the concrete I was sheltering behind. What I saw there when the stairs fell away I could scarcely believe. It was the outline of a man, only bulbous and unnaturally tall. It was clearly some kind of machine, like a robot, or even a protective suit, because it sparkled with flashes as scores of bullets ricocheted off it to no effect. Hot flashes shot from its arms, directing machine-gun fire to all corners and its legs trundled, rather than walked, suggesting it was on some kind of tank tracks.

A series of deafening blasts ripped through the stairwell, threatening to perforate my eardrums for a second time in as many minutes, when the lads hit it with their grenades but this only served to intensify the laughter.

"Is it my turn yet?" the booming voice asked.

The machine swung around to shoot mini-rockets to my left and I used the eye my mother had given me to take a sneaky peak around the stairs and saw that the beast was indeed some kind of suit. Like a deep-sea diving suit, the steel figure had two arms and two legs, while the head was a shiny smooth turret encasing a human face behind a thick polycarbonate dome.

It was X^3.

"Here's a bedtime story for you children!" he roared, machine-gunning every nook and cranny as he attempted to blast us from our hiding places. "No one destroys my plans. No one!"

This was a somewhat spurious claim to say the least because me and Jack Tempest had specialised in bunnying up his operations in recent years, hence all this revenge malarkey, but I decided not to quibble over semantics and instead, flew a frag around X^3's suit looking for the back door. The grenade detonated between his legs but it didn't even bring a tear to his eye. X^3 just turned my way and guffawed some more.

"Ha ha hah! Your feeble bombs are no match for my diamo-steel exo-skeleton," he boasted, cranking his wrist ninety-degrees to switch his weapons system from machine-gun to flame-thrower. A sheet of boiling napalm splashed across the stairs and pipes, forcing us to flee before his merciless jeers, and swarms of 7.62mm rounds followed us down the corridor to obliterate our surroundings.

I dived with my girl into a storage cupboard just off the main pipe interjunction, only to see the doorframe behind me disintegrate to matchwood a nanosecond later. The cupboard was just a couple of feet deep and offered us minimal protection, but we'd be toast the moment X^3 went past with his flame-thrower.

"Help me! Help me!" the little girl was crying, but I was in no position to help anyone – not even myself – and looked up to see the hulking mass of X^3's exo-skeleton lumbering into view. He turned to face me, a demented look plastered across polycarbonate dome, and I was just about to put a bullet the little girl's head to save her from the flames when Mr Smith appeared behind X^3…

… and threw his knife?

Well, I'm all for heroic gestures but Mr Smith's effort was not only feebler than knocking a shuttlecock at a Los Angeles Class submarine, it was also off-target – by almost ten feet.

X^3 saw the knife whizz past his dome and turned to look at Mr Smith, presumably out of sheer incredulity.

"Out of ammo already?" he laughed.

"You know what moved that rubber tree plant?" Mr Smith asked.

"No what?" X^3 replied, delighted to humour the biggest fool in the Mediterranean as a final request.

"Little old ants," Mr Smith replied, "with high

hopes."

Just then, Mr Jean stood up and threw his knife too, also missing X^3, and sticking it a few feet from where Mr Smith had stuck his. Mr Bolaji then followed, as did Mr Grey, Mr Kim, Mr Petrov and a dozen others.

X^3 couldn't have been more amused had they been throwing custard pies at each other but I finally understood what they were doing, pulled my hot knife from its sheath and twisted the handle. I ran at the door and hurled the knife at a cross-section of RSJ behind X^3 and ducked back out of sight again.

As amusing as these petty acts of defiance had been, X^3 wanted to get on with his rampage and turned to finish the job, but one-by-one the timers on the knife handles clicked to zero and X^3's diamo-steel exo-skeleton was suddenly swamped with powerful magnetic pulses.

He'd been swivelling to burn us out of our cupboard when he lost his balance and stumbled to his left. Here he ran straight into another pulse and was violently buffeted the other way.

"Let's go!" I told the girl, bundling her up and scuttling underneath the exo-skeleton's reeling arm as X^3 started panic-firing in all directions like the town drunk who'd been given a bottle of Malibu and a couple of Uzis for his birthday.

The others made a break for it too, keeping as low as they could to stay out X^3's range as he machine-gunned our polarised knives overhead, and soon we were taking to the stairs.

"No! No!! No!!!" X^3 screamed, alternating between

machine-gun and mini-rockets as he sought to kill us while he could.

We'd made it past him and to within a dozen steps of daylight when the inevitable happened and a stray pulse spun him around to face us. There was no time to do anything, we were caught in open ground, and the flames began spewing from a nozzle under his wrist – when a shape roared out of nowhere and smashed straight into X^3.

It was a forklift truck.

And it was driven by that whoop-crazy foul-mouth, Rip Dunbar.

"Eat this you *mother*!" he roared, naked from the waist up and as filthy as a Welshman six months from his birthday. Just what the hell had that bloke been up to?

He plunged X^3 into a knot of pipes against the far wall, diving from the forklift as it was engulfed in a whoosh of napalm, then rolled across the tiles, grabbing a discarded MP5 en-route and rattling bullets at X^3 as he spun away to cover.

The pipes behind X^3 erupted to drench him with steam but still he was able to fire his machine-guns, roaring with indignation as he fought to untangle himself from the steel.

It's a sad state of affairs when not even Rip Dunbar's best efforts can put a dent in your diamo-steel exo-skeleton, but all credit to X^3's machinists for producing such a quality piece of kit. Surely they were the real heroes…

… at least, until Jack Tempest stepped into view.

He appeared behind Dunbar with an MP5 and

shot up the pipework around X^3's head. A pall of sparks exploded as he cut through the main electrics cable, dropping it onto X^3's back to weld him to the spot and fry him alive inside.

"Don't look darling," I told the PM's daughter, pulling her face into my chest, but this was one death she was determined to see, fighting free to glare at X^3 as he exploded under his polycarbonate dome like an egg in a microwave.

"Okay, we can go now," the little girl said, taking me by the hand and leading me up the stairs and back to the surface.

Inevitably, Tempest had his own pithy take on X^3's passing.

"I don't know where he gets his energy from?" he quipped, looking about the stairwell for giggles but finding none, not even from the kids.

"Why did that man just say that?" the PM's little girl asked.

"I don't know, darling," I said. "But don't stare, it'll only encourage him."

34. LIVING FOR DAYLIGHT

WE MADE OUR WAY up top and did a revised headcount. We'd lost another five guys in the attack but luckily three of those guys had been X³'s own men. Less fortuitous had been the loss of both Mr Woo and Mr Choe. One had been North Korean while the other had been South Korean, though I'd never been able to remember which was which. I don't suppose it mattered now. It certainly hadn't to them. They'd both been wanted on both sides of the thirty-eighth parallel for multiple crimes against their respective states and neither of them had ever wished to return to either the peninsula so I guess they got their wishes in the end.

As we emerged into the glow of a new day, Dunbar and Tempest were arguing over who'd killed X³ but Dunbar broke off when he received a radio flash from fleet telling him an unidentified aircraft had just violated the exclusion zone and was heading straight for us.

"Kilo Two, Kilo Two, you are in restricted airspace and will be fired upon if you do not turn back," we could hear fleet's air controllers ordering. *"Kilo Two, do you copy, over?"* But Kilo Two ignored their warnings and continued racing for *Île de Roc*.

"What now?" Tempest sighed.

"Okay, everyone back inside. Move it!" Dunbar barked, snatching up the .50 cal he'd been playing with earlier and urging the kids back underground.

"It's okay Major, it's cool, they're with us," I

reassured him, pointing to the horizon to show him the broad-winged dot flying low out of the rising sun.

"What?" Dunbar said, but I didn't get the chance to explain fully because, at that moment, Mr Smith laid his fellow countryman out with a shoulder stock to the back of the neck. They might be hard to kill these gung-ho heroes but they're usually a piece of piss to knock out.

"Idiot," Mr Smith concluded.

Tempest saw this and snapped into action but he was surrounded on all sides and carrying a gun that was fitted with a blue-on-blue chip, whereas we'd ditched our MP5s in favour of the AKs and Bullpups we'd picked off X^3's dead.

"Careful Jack, we don't want to kill you but we will," I warned him, slowing Tempest as he twisted and turned in ever-decreasing circles before realising we had him cold. He threw down his gun and made a great show of it, putting up his hands and glaring at me as I radioed fleet.

"Fleet, this is mobile assault, stay your missiles, over. I repeat, stay your missiles."

"I knew we couldn't trust you, Jones," Tempest scowled.

"Relax," Mr Smith told him, pulling Tempest's hands off his head and urging him to chill. "You'll live longer."

"Mobile assault, who is this? Identify yourself, over," fleet responded.

"Fleet, this is Jones. Stay your missile. We have the situation under control. Over."

"Specialist Jones, we have Marines in transit. You are

ordered to take the puppies below and await their arrival, over?"

"Fleet, I'm not going to tell you again, stay your missiles, turn back your Marines, and do not attempt to impede Kilo Two in its flight or there will be consequences. Over," I warned them in no uncertain terms.

There was a short pause while they picked the bones out of that one before asking;

"Specialist Jones, what are your intentions, over?"

"Our intentions are to get off this island, over."

"Our intentions, Jones? Over."

"I have sixteen surviving Specialists with me, and we're all boarding that plane, over."

A new voice now came on the radio.

"Specialist Jones, this is Vice Admiral Buck Hendershot of the United States Sixth Fleet. We have a three-strong carrier battle group with a hundred and eighty planes, twelve destroyers and sixteen cruisers and we would strongly advise you to rethink your intentions. Over."

"And we have the kids," I reminded him. "Now stay your fucking missiles. I won't tell you again. This is Jones. Over and out."

Tempest grabbed my arm as I turned to head down to the beach.

"We had a deal."

"Oh yeah, and *I'm sure* you would've lived up to your end once we'd all been safely tucked up in McCarthy again," I hawed to show him what I thought of that, "but we decided to make our own arrangements, just in case there was any confusion over the small print."

"What sort of a man are you?" he demanded.

"A very tired one," I replied, nodding to my left.

Tempest looked over and saw Mr Bolaji parking all the children in a defensive trench before legging it down the beach to pile into one of the hovercraft landers along with the rest of the chaps.

"You're not taking the kids with you?" Tempest blinked.

"Hey, we're not even going to kill them," I said, causing one of the Affiliates who was passing to laugh. "Help yourself, they're all yours. Just do us a favour and don't tell the Admiral for fifteen minutes, okay?"

"This is a bluff?"

"Jack, we're not the bad guys. We just occasionally work for them," I explained.

Tempest's eyebrows twitched as he got a slight erection at the thought of being left alone to take all the glory, then nodded and told me to go.

"Before the fleet gets here. I'll give you a fifteen-minute head start. I won't try to stop you."

"Promise?"

"Scouts honour," Tempest said, saluting me Benny Hill-style with two fingers to his brow.

I smiled at that and held out a hand. Tempest shook it and wished me the best of luck.

"You too, Jack. Maybe I'll see you around," I told him.

"Somehow, I don't doubt it," he chuckled.

A big seaplane pitched past overhead at that point, banking just above the crashing waves to circle back for its final approach.

"Just one more thing, Jones?" Tempest said, stopping me as Mr Smith got the hovercraft engines roaring to life. "How did you do it? How did you arrange all of this?"

That was a good and fair question but I've been in this game long enough to know that you should never stand around giving good and fair explanations when you should be jumping on hovercrafts or flushing XO agents through turbines. Much better to leave them guessing.

"I'll drop you a postcard," I simply said, before jumping into the hovercraft as it spun around in the surf.

"Okay, let's go!" Mr Bolaji shouted when he'd pulled me on board, and a moment later we were falling into our seats as Mr Smith slammed down the accelerator to take us out to sea.

If Jack Tempest had ever read *The Client* by John Grisham, he might have known that one of the main characters (I won't say which in case you haven't read it) jumps on a plane at the end of the book and heads off to start a new life. This had been our *Fourth Protocol*, our pre-arranged signal to *Pops* back in Arundel to alert the extraction team to come and get us. The number of stars I'd awarded it and the comments I'd posted had simply explained the hows, wheres and whens.

A little forward planning, as Bill always said, goes a long way.

It paid to protect The Agency. If you kept your word to them, they'd keep their word to you and pick you up from pretty much any extraction point, anywhere in the world, within twelve hours of you placing the call. All you had to do was keep your mouth shut, send the signal and make it over the wall.

Tempest gave us one of his Sunday best salutes from the beach but I needed both hands to hang on as we ripped across the surf so I wasn't able to reply. Not that I'm sure I would've anyway. Saluting people you didn't need to salute is just one short step away from saluting flags. And the day I started doing that was the day I stopped trying to blow up large chunks of the world. Or at least, stopped guarding the corridors and vending machines of people who sought to do that sort of thing.

Not for me. No sir. I had bills to pay.

"Book Mark, Book Mark, this is Flying Tiger, do you copy, over?" the radio crackled in my ear.

"*Flying Tiger*, this is *Book Mark*, we read you loud and clear and we are ready for pick up, over," I radioed back.

"Copy Book Mark, coming in now. Keep that throttle open, over," Flying Tiger confirmed.

We were thundering across the waves at full pelt when the seaplane's shadow crept across us. It was barely thirty feet above our heads and slowing to descend in front of the hovercraft. The rear bay doors were open and two leggy stewardesses stood either side of the ramp to guide our approach.

A surge of spray soaked Mr Smith as the plane dipped its belly in the water but he just wiped his face and gunned the accelerator to take us up the ramp. Sunlight turned to darkness as we entered the plane, hitting the catchment net strung across the hold to stop us from crashing straight on through to the cockpit.

Mr Smith killed the engines as the girls retracted the ramp and all at once, we were tilting backwards as the plane left the water again. He'd barely skimmed the surface for fifteen seconds.

"Hold on boys, it's going to be a bumpy one," came a familiar voice over the speakers. The Agency had many pilots on its books but only one with such a killer-looking crew. "Don't think the Americans are buying your story," Captain Takahashi laughed.

A boom from the portside rocked the galley as something exploded just short of our wing but the Takahashi's stewardesses didn't look too concerned as they buckled themselves in. They were the human face of the good Captain's unshakable belief in his own abilities and he banked and rolled across the sky, dodging the flak and flying through a corridor of starbursting decoys to lose a swarm of angry *sidewinders*.

"Walk in the park," Captain Takahashi confidently declared. "There's merlot and sandwiches once we reach cruising altitude. And the film we will be showing today is *The Jane Austen Book Club*. Gentlemen, welcome back to The Agency."

We turned south for Algeria, for the nearest base, where we would no doubt spend the next four weeks debriefing the men in suits as to the events of the last three years. How we'd explain half of it was anybody's guess. I could hardly explain half of it to myself, let alone anyone else. How we'd been banged to rights, brushed under life's carpet and left to rot in the deepest, darkest hole in Christendom. And yet how an innocuous little reading group started a few years earlier had conspired to set in motion a chain of events that would eventually throw us the unlikeliest of lifelines?

Try telling that one with a straight face.

Whichever way it came out, one thing was clear, we'd been given the mother of all second chances and no mistake. Or was this my third chance by now? Or my fourth? Or fifth? I wasn't sure. I'd lost count after I'd ducked that nuke back in Mozambique. All I knew was that I was alive and free once again. Free – and not to be trifled with.

Our book club might've started out as just that, a book club, for reading, for passing the time, for fun, but it had become so much more than that now, snowballing to unimagined conclusions, beyond the sum of its parts.

We were no longer little old ants. We were one, beyond the law, beyond our employees and beyond even The Agency. We were unity. Strength in numbers.

Yet so many more of our numbers were still rotting away in McCarthy. And Yinchuan. And Severnaya Zemlya. And half a dozen other secret facilities dotted around the windier corners of the globe.

And that wouldn't do.

Oh no, that wouldn't do at all.

So we'd debrief The Agency. We'd put them in the picture and come clean about the vine that had crept through their organisation. We'd even offer them a pact. After all it's good to make alliances. If nothing else, the four hundred active members of book club had proved that. But when all was said and done, we'd be the ones calling the shots from now on. We were simply too powerful not to be.

And this was important because we had things to do.

And wrongs to right.

And nothing was going to stand in our way. Not even The Agency. Not any more.

Because I was Book Mark – the founding father and undisputed number one of book club.

And now I was out, there was going to be hell to pay.

ABOUT THE AUTHOR

Danny King was born in Slough in 1969 and later grew up in Hampshire. He has worked as a hod carrier, a supermarket shelf-stacker, a painter & decorator, a postman and a magazine editor and honestly can't recommend any of them. He lives in Chichester with wife, Jeannie, and four children and today writes books and screenplays.

Follow him on Facebook at 'Danny King books'.

If you enjoyed this book, please tell a friend or post a review as every mention helps. The superstar authors might have their publishing companies and their multi-million-pound advertising budgets but us little guys have you – our fellow foot-soldiers. *Thank you.*

BY THE SAME AUTHOR

BOOKS
The Burglar Diaries
The Bank Robber Diaries
The Hitman Diaries
The Pornographer Diaries
Milo's Marauders
Milo's Run
School for Scumbags
Blue Collar
More Burglar Diaries
The Henchmen's Book Club
The Monster Man of Horror House
Infidelity for Beginners
The Executioners
The No.1 Zombie Detective Agency
Eat Locals
Return of the Monster Man of Horror House

TELEVISION & FILM
Thieves Like Us (2007)
Wild Bill (2012)
Eat Locals (2017)
The Hitman Diaries (2010) – short
Run Run As Fast As You Can (2017) – short
Little Monsters (2018) – short
Seven Sharp (2017) – short
Romantic (2019) – short (Russia)

STAGE
The Pornographer Diaries: the play
Killera Dienasgramata (Latvia)

Printed in Great Britain
by Amazon